CAN'T BUY ME
LOVE

Praise for Georgia Beers

Aubrey McFadden Is Never Getting Married

"Georgia Beers has become a household name in the world of LGBTQ+ romance novels, and her latest work, *Aubrey McFadden Is Never Getting Married*, proves she is worthy of the attention. With its captivating characters, engaging plot, and impactful themes, this book is a pure delight to read. Its enemies-to-lovers narrative tugs at the heart, making one hope for resolution and forgiveness between its leading ladies. Aubrey and Monica's push-and-pull dynamic is complicated and knotty, but Beers keeps it fun with her quick wit and sense of humor. The crafty banter ensures that readers have a good time."—*Women Using Words*

Playing with Matches

"*Playing with Matches* is a delightful exploration of small town life, family drama, and true love…Liz and Cori are charming characters with undeniable chemistry, and their sweet and tender small town, 'fake-dating' love story is sure to capture the attention of readers. Their journey reminds readers of the importance of love, forgiveness, family, and community, making this feel-good romance a true triumph."—*Women Using Words*

Peaches and Cream

"*Peaches and Cream* is a fresh, new spin on the classic rom-com *You've Got Mail*—except it's even better because it's all about ice cream!…[A] delicious, melt-in-your-mouth scoop of goodness. Bursting with tasty characters in a scrumptious story world, *Peaches and Cream* is simply irresistible."—*Women Using Words*

On the Rocks

"This book made me so happy! And kept me awake way too late."—*Jude in the Stars*

Hopeless Romantic

"Thank you, Georgia Beers, for this unabashed paean to the pleasure of escaping into romantic comedies...If you want to have a big smile plastered on your face as you read a romance novel, do not hesitate to pick up this one!"—*The Rainbow Bookworm*

Flavor of the Month

"Beers whips up a sweet lesbian romance...brimming with mouthwatering descriptions of foodie indulgences...Both women are well-intentioned and endearing, and it's easy to root for their inevitable reconciliation. But once the couple rediscover their natural ease with one another, Beers throws a challenging emotional hurdle in their path, forcing them to fight through tragedy to earn their happy ending."—*Publishers Weekly*

Fear of Falling

"Enough tension and drama for us to wonder if this can work out—and enough heat to keep the pages turning. I will definitely recommend this to others—Georgia Beers continues to go from strength to strength."—*Evan Blood, Bookseller (Angus & Robertson, Australia)*

One Walk in Winter

"A sweet story to pair with the holidays. There are plenty of 'moment's in this book that make the heart soar. Just what I like in a romance. Situations where sparks fly, hearts fill, and tears fall. This book shined with cute fairy trails and swoon-worthy Christmas gifts…REALLY nice and cozy if read in between Thanksgiving and Christmas. Covered in blankets. By a fire."—*Bookvark*

The Do-Over

"You can count on Beers to give you a quality well-paced book each and every time."—*The Romantic Reader Blog*

"*The Do-Over* is a shining example of the brilliance of Georgia Beers as a contemporary romance author."—*Rainbow Reflections*

The Shape of You

The Shape of You "catches you right in the feels and does not let go. It is a must for every person out there who has struggled with self-esteem, questioned their judgment, and settled for a less than perfect but safe lover. If you've ever been convinced you have to trade passion for emotional safety, this book is for you."—*Writing While Distracted*

"I know I always say this about Georgia Beers's books, but there is no one that writes first kisses like her. They are hot, steamy and all too much!"—*Les Rêveur*

Calendar Girl

"A sweet, sweet romcom of a story…*Calendar Girl* is a nice read, which you may find yourself returning to when you want a hot-chocolate-and-warm-comfort-hug in your life."—*Best Lesbian Erotica*

Blend

"You know a book is good, first, when you don't want to put it down. Second, you know it's damn good when you're reading it and thinking, I'm totally going to read this one again. Great read and absolutely a 5-star romance."—*The Romantic Reader Blog*

"This is a lovely romantic story with relatable characters that have depth and chemistry. A charming easy story that kept me reading until the end. Very enjoyable."—*Kat Adams, Bookseller, QBD (Australia)*

Right Here, Right Now

"[A] successful and entertaining queer romance novel. The main characters are appealing, and the situations they deal with are realistic and well-managed. I would recommend this book to anyone who enjoys a good queer romance novel, and particularly one grounded in real world situations."—*Books at the End of the Alphabet*

"[A]n engaging odd-couple romance. Beers creates a romance of gentle humor that allows no-nonsense Lacey to relax and easygoing Alicia to find a trusting heart."—*RT Book Reviews*

Lambda Literary Award Winner *Fresh Tracks*

"[T]he focus switches each chapter to a different character, allowing for a measured pace and deep, sincere exploration of each protagonist's thoughts. Beers gives a welcome expansion to the romance genre with her clear, sympathetic writing." —*Curve magazine*

Lambda Literary Award Finalist *Finding Home*

"Georgia Beers has proven in her popular novels such as *Too Close to Touch* and *Fresh Tracks* that she has a special way of building romance with suspense that puts the reader on the edge of their seat. *Finding Home*, though more character driven than suspense, will equally keep the reader engaged at each page turn with its sweet romance."—*Lambda Literary Review*

Mine

"Beers does a fine job of capturing the essence of grief in an authentic way. *Mine* is touching, life-affirming, and sweet."
—*Lesbian News Book Review*

Too Close to Touch

"This is such a well-written book. The pacing is perfect, the romance is great, the character work strong, and damn, but is the sex writing ever fantastic."—*The Lesbian Review*

"In her third novel, Georgia Beers delivers an immensely satisfying story. Beers knows how to generate sexual tension so taut it could be cut with a knife…Beers weaves a tale of yearning, love, lust, and conflict resolution. She has constructed a believable plot, with strong characters in a charming setting."—*Just About Write*

By the Author

Romances

Turning the Page

Thy Neighbor's Wife

Too Close to Touch

Fresh Tracks

Mine

Finding Home

Starting from Scratch

96 Hours

Slices of Life

Snow Globe

Olive Oil & White Bread

Zero Visibility

A Little Bit of Spice

What Matters Most

Right Here, Right Now

Blend

The Shape of You

Calendar Girl

The Do-Over

Fear of Falling

One Walk in Winter

Flavor of the Month

Hopeless Romantic

16 Steps to Forever

The Secret Poet

Cherry on Top

Camp Lost and Found

Dance with Me

Peaches and Cream

Playing with Matches

Aubrey McFadden
Is Never Getting Married

Can't Buy Me Love

The Puppy Love Romances

Rescued Heart

Run to You

Dare to Stay

The Swizzle Stick Romances

Shaken or Stirred

On the Rocks

With a Twist

CAN'T BUY ME LOVE

by

Georgia Beers

2024

CREDITS
Editor: Ruth Sternglantz
Production Design: Stacia Seaman
Cover Design by Inkspiral Design

Acknowledgments

I am not a huge traveler. While I do travel a lot for work, attending conferences and retreats in different cities around the country, I really don't have an adventurous spirit. Maybe it's because I moved so many times as a kid, but adult me is a homebody and I'm my happiest in my own space with my animals, surrounded by my things. That being said, when I came up with the idea for this book, I knew I needed to send my main characters someplace very cool and very different, and after doing a lot of research, I landed on St. Kitts. And this non-adventurous spirit was not at all envious that London and Kayla got to hang out there as long as they did (read: yes, I was. Terribly, terribly.).

Writing about wealth was also new to me, but I've always been fascinated by the yawning valley between people who were born into money, who have never had to worry, and those who had to scrape and scrounge just to cover a mortgage or rent or food. I learned a lot from London and Kayla, and I also saw a lot of myself, my parents, my friends. It's always an interesting trip when you write characters that end up teaching you something.

I am so grateful for the people in my life that I love. I have the most amazing support group of friends, those who write and those who don't, and I truly don't know what I'd do without them. I'm literally writing these acknowledgments while on one of our writing retreats, and I'm so happy to be surrounded by their love and presence. I have a career I love, I have friends who understand that career, and I am super aware of how lucky that makes me.

The folks at Bold Strokes are some more who help this career run smoothly. Radclyffe, Sandy (thanks for the creative direction!), Cindy, Stacia, Ruth…all of them have a hand in keeping me on track and making me successful, and I am forever grateful. And thanks to Inkspiral Design for creating yet another very cool cover for me.

If you're holding this book in your hands (or reading it on your e-reader or listening to the audiobook), then you're a big part of why I'm here. The biggest, really. Thank you so much for all your support over the years. Keep sending those emails and messages, keep joining me on Patreon, keep watching the TikToks. You're the one who makes all of this possible, and I thank you from the very bottom of my incredibly grateful heart.

CAN'T BUY ME LOVE

CHAPTER ONE

"Bu t I'm not a guy. Or straight. Or a freaking war correspondent." London Granger flopped back against the couch with a huff. "If I was any of those things..."

"I mean, at least you're white," said Claire Lawrence, her roommate and best friend since she'd moved to the Big Apple several years ago. Claire flopped back next to her and heaved a huge sigh. "I'm the one who'd be screwed."

"Valid. Good thing you work at a big literary agency and not at a trendy magazine." She laughed softly and picked up her wineglass from the coffee table, thankful Claire was always able to find a little humor in situations that frustrated her. She took a sip of her wine, thinking cabernet wasn't her favorite, but this one wasn't bad. "I've been begging for an assignment that's real, you know? That makes people ask questions, think about the world we live in. And what juicy, super important article do they assign me in response? 'The Five Best Things About Dating in New York City.'" She groaned like she was in physical pain. "I mean, seriously? Could they give me something more frivolous and boring and overdone?" She shook her head, beyond frustrated with her editor at *The New and the Now*, or *TN Squared*, as most people called the magazine she worked for. "I left modeling to make a difference. To write about things that matter, not fluffy rom-com articles. Jesus."

Claire was unusually quiet, and when London turned her head against the back of the couch to look at her, Claire was tapping a finger against her lips, her nose scrunched up.

"What?" London asked. "I know that face. You make it just before you come up with a terrible idea."

"Hey! I resent that remark. I've had some great ideas."

"Oh, like the time you dragged me to that club, and it ended up being goth night? And I was wearing hot pink?"

"That was an honest mistake. I misread the schedule."

"Or how about last winter when you left the case of Diet Coke in your trunk because it would keep it colder than the fridge, and then it exploded all over your car?"

Claire grimaced, probably remembering the sticky mess they'd had to clean up in twenty-seven-degree weather. "Yeah, miscalculation on my part."

"And let's not forget signing me up on a dating app and forgetting to check that I was interested in *women*." London arched a brow at her.

"Hey, some of those guys were really nice. God, you're so picky." They laughed together for a moment before Claire said, "What if…?"

London inhaled a deep breath, then let it out slowly as she brought her wineglass to her lips. Claire's idea were often a bit out there, but she was fun and supportive, and London loved her. "What if what?"

Claire sat up, a spark suddenly appearing in her rich brown eyes. She set down her glass and turned so her knees were against London's thigh. She pointed at her as she spoke. "What if, instead of the dating article Silas wants you to write, you pitch a"—she tipped her head—"variation."

London squinted at her. "What kind of variation?"

"'What's It *Really* Like to Be a Billionaire?'" Claire spread her hands in the air as she spoke, an invisible banner above her head. She gave a firm nod, clearly sold on her own idea.

London snorted. "And how do you expect me to write that? Do you know a billionaire or two I could hang out with? Ask questions of? Observe in the wild?" She shook her head and returned her attention to her wine.

"No, but I bet Silas does. Or his boss does."

"I mean, I do like that your idea isn't about something as frivolous as *dating*." She made the air quotes. "But how do I get him to go for it? I don't know. Silas is a tough nut to crack, especially when I question his ideas." She shook her head. It would never work.

Claire's grin grew slowly. "Because you can slide some very astute commentary in amongst the fluff…things about the socioeconomic divide, how it's getting worse, the rich get richer, the poor get poorer, etcetera, etcetera. Something that might reel people in under the guise of a puff piece and ends up being a real human-interest story."

London blinked at her roommate, thinking *Wait, is she actually making sense? How is that possible?* Claire's harebrained ideas were usually easy to yank apart. But this one…this one actually might have some legs.

As if she could hear the wheels turning in London's head, Claire went on. "And then…" She waited for London to meet her gaze. "Bam! Book deal."

London blinked at her in surprise.

"Parlay, baby! You parlay the article into a book deal where you explore the subject more deeply. Yeah? I mean, you already live with an agent." Claire sat back again, still grinning, clearly pleased with herself. Normally, this was where London would dismantle—kindly—the entire idea and then they'd laugh at how silly but creative Claire was, and then they'd turn on *90 Day Fiancé* or something and that would be that.

But it wasn't that.

Not this time.

She stared at Claire until her friend turned to look at her. They stared at each other for a moment before Claire's eyes went wide with understanding. "Oh my God, you're actually thinking about it, aren't you?" She sat back up again, her excitement manifesting as a huge smile that showed off her high cheekbones. "Tell me you're thinking about it."

London poked the inside of her cheek with her tongue and waited a second or two before saying quietly, "I'm thinking about it."

"Yes!" Claire jumped to her feet, pumping an arm as she held the *S* sound long enough to be mistaken for a snake. She did a little dance around the coffee table that made London laugh, but when she sat back down, her expression took on an element of seriousness. "Listen to me, UK." London smiled at the nickname Claire had given her when they'd first met, despite the fact that she was actually from Connecticut. "You are always telling me to have more faith in myself, that I sell myself short, that I underestimate my own abilities. Well, I have one thing to say to you. Right. Back. Atcha."

"That's three things." But London nodded, because she knew it was true. She was an excellent cheerleader for her friends. She talked them up. She gave them pep talks. She reminded them of the amazing women they were.

She was much harder on herself.

"It can't hurt to give it a shot, right?" Claire's eyebrows rose in expectation. "And if it doesn't work, it doesn't work." She shrugged and took a sip of her wine. "If Silas shoots it down, at least you can say you tried, rather than wonder what might have happened if you had. Right?"

She wasn't wrong. "I mean, chances are, he *will* shoot it down. But…" She let it dangle because Silas could be a giant pain in the ass, but he knew a good story when it was presented to him. She'd need to spend a little time fashioning just the right pitch. She would need help with the aspect of the story that had to do with a billionaire, but he knew a ton of people, and again, if she pitched it just right, and if he liked the idea enough, she was pretty sure he'd help. She knew him well enough to know that. What he wanted more than anything was to publish good work—fluff included because it was necessary. "Let me roll it around," she said to Claire, leaving it at that.

Claire gave one nod, obviously accepting London's end to the conversation without argument. Slightly unusual, but maybe Claire understood that she'd started the train of thought rolling, and now she needed to leave it alone to see if it would pick up speed on its own.

London didn't tell her that not only had that train picked up speed, but London was in the first car, wearing an engineer's cap and blowing the train whistle.

❖

Silas York was the first person London had ever met that made her understand describing somebody as a *fireplug*. It was a word her grandmother had used on occasion, and she never quite got it. Until she'd met Silas.

He was a sixty-year-old man who looked more like seventy-five. Short, but built like a tank. Balding, with a doughnut of silvery hair circling his head. Always dressed in dress slacks, a white shirt, and a tie, but also always looking like it was five o'clock on Friday and he was wearing Thursday morning's clothes—wrinkled, sleeves rolled up, tie pulled loose. He reeked of cigarettes, one of the few people she knew outside of the modeling world who still smoked them. He was very nearly a walking cliché of the News Guy, as far as his look went, but London also knew that he was more competent than any person she'd ever worked for, and that despite his harried, stressed-out appearance, he was actually a calm, introspective boss who thought things through—even if it was just to assign her a fluffy piece on dating in New York City.

But that wasn't what he was contemplating now. He sat back in his chair behind his enormous desk and folded his hands over his slightly protruding stomach. Today's tie was blue and silver stripes, and it had been pulled askew all day. As he contemplated London and the idea she'd pitched, she wondered if he ever really tightened his tie properly or if he just put it on in the morning pulled loose so he didn't need to bother yanking on it later.

Another thing London had learned about her boss was that she didn't need to repeat herself. She didn't need to plead her case. He'd heard her the first time. She opened her mouth, then closed it again as she stood before him and felt like she could practically hear the gears cranking in his brain. She wanted badly to tell him more, to list all the things she'd come up with last night when her own brain wouldn't let her sleep. The muscles in her jaw hurt from keeping them tensed so she wouldn't ruin her case by overexplaining. After what felt like three hours, but in reality was about three minutes, Silas sat forward again, forearms on his desk. He reached for his favorite pen—a ballpoint that he clicked over and over again—and studied his computer monitor for a moment before meeting London's gaze. Then he glanced at his watch and said in his gravelly voice, "Come back in here at four."

That was it for now. He would say no more. She knew this from having worked here for over a year now. She gave one nod, turned on her heel, and headed back out into the common area where phones rang and the clacking of keyboards could be heard. Not a lot of people actually worked in the office anymore, at least not full-time. Even Silas was only in a few days a week. London mostly worked from home as well, but since she didn't want to subway all the way back home, only to have to turn around and subway all the way back later that day, she decided she'd go to one of her favorite Manhattan spots, get herself some coffee and a table, and do a little work. Or attempt to.

It was after she'd slung her messenger bag containing her laptop over her shoulder and headed outside into the bustle of Manhattan streets that she realized what a beautiful mid-March day it was and changed her plans. The sky was clear and blue, the sun was shining, the snow had disappeared weeks ago. She turned onto Sixth Avenue and blended in with other pedestrians, who'd apparently also agreed with her about the weather, and walked a few blocks until she reached Bryant Park.

It was one of her favorite places in Manhattan, and one of the first she'd discovered when she'd started working for *TN Squared*. Expecting the bustling newsroom she'd always seen in movies and on TV, she'd been shocked at the quiet. The sparse population of the office. The lack of the urgency she was expecting. The pandemic had changed all that, and now everything was done from home, over Zoom, offsite. It was completely different from her expectations, and she'd had to adjust hers in a big way. She'd slung her bag over her shoulder and gone walking and followed the sounds of bouncing ping-pong balls until she ended up at Bryant Park, at a small metal table for two near the table tennis. She'd found the sounds of the games that were near constant surprisingly relaxing.

She'd written sixteen articles for *TN Squared* so far, and any that had been written during decent weather had been written at the same table in the park. She stopped at the little kiosk and got herself a latte, then headed to her usual spot and took a seat.

"There's my good luck charm." His name was Howie, and that's all London knew about him. And she only knew that because she'd heard the other guys refer to him as such. She should've been surprised to see him outside in March playing table tennis, but she wasn't. He was a diehard fan of the game, and as long as it wasn't a blizzard or pouring down rain, Howie was there with his paddle. Today, he wore black sweatpants and a worn white Adidas T-shirt with a zip-up hoodie over it, the sleeves pushed up. London expected him to lose the hoodie before long. He'd gotten a fresh haircut, and his almost-black hair was trimmed neatly on the sides, a bit longer on top. He played during the day so often that London wondered if he worked a night shift somewhere, maybe in a restaurant or bar. Or maybe he was an actor on Broadway or off-Broadway. Something that kept his days free. He gave her a wink as she pulled out her laptop, then he served the ball. He was *good*, too. Almost magical to watch.

She set her laptop on the table and opened it, but it was a facade and she knew it. She wouldn't be doing much work. She was too excited. The fact that Silas hadn't shut her down and tossed her out of his office immediately boded very well for her idea. Well, Claire's idea. All she had to do now was wait for the official word, and she was way too keyed up to focus on anything else until she got it. So instead, she closed her laptop back up, put it away, took out her phone, and did a little surfing, all to the background soundtrack of the happy echo of bouncing ping-pong balls. And who knew? Maybe Sexy Jogging Chick would hustle by. That was always the sign of a good day.

She laughed softly to herself and shook her head, thinking she really should come up with a less reductive name for the woman she saw often jogging through the park. But she couldn't help it. The jogger was tall and lithe, athletic and strong, and, yes, absolutely sexy, though London had never actually seen her face, given the ever-present hat and sunglasses she wore, no matter the weather. But any time London caught a glimpse of her, something good happened. Weird but true.

She lost herself in TikTok for a while, jotting a few notes that sparked little nuggets of ideas for possible future stories, and the next thing she knew, it was time to head back to the *TN Squared* offices. As she packed up her stuff and glanced up from her little table, there she was. Sexy Jogging Chick. All long legs and dark ponytail sticking out the back of the hat pulled low over her sunglassed eyes. She glanced at London as she jogged past and gave her a killer smile that pretty much would've melted London's knees, had she been standing.

London could do nothing but watch her go by.

"Damn," she whispered as the gorgeous brunette jogged down the path and disappeared into the crowd. Taking a deep breath, she gave her head a shake, then gathered her things and headed back to her office.

As she hurried through the streets and back to the building, her stomach began to churn with nerves. Her palms started to sweat, despite the lovely, comfortable temperature. Silas could say no. Maybe he'd thought it over, decided it was a ridiculous idea, and would tell her to stop coming up with stupid stuff and write what he told her. She wiped her palms along her thighs as she rode the elevator up. Outside his office, she took a moment, fixed her hair, tugged the wrinkles out of her shirt, took a deep breath. Then she counted down in her head from five to one. It's what she'd always done before heading out onto a catwalk during a fashion show. The countdown calmed her, slowed her racing heart.

She knocked.

"Yep." That one gruff word was how Silas always answered his door. London pushed her way in. "Have a seat, Granger."

She normally preferred to stand when in his office, but she

did as she was asked and sat in one of the two black vinyl chairs arranged in front of his big desk.

"I like your idea. A lot. Got me thinking."

She gave one nod but knew better than to interrupt him. So she waited.

"I mean, really got me thinking. Lotta ways this can go."

Another nod.

"I'm kinda guessing you don't necessarily have access to a bunch of billionaires you can use as research subjects. Or maybe you do"—he quickly corrected himself—"from your modeling days..." He let it dangle, and she felt it was okay to speak then.

"Sadly, no." She shook her head with a smile. "I was hoping you could help me with that."

"I can." He said it so quickly that London realized he already had somebody in mind. "I reached out to Miranda Northbrooke." He dropped the name and let it sit between them.

"Oh my God." She hadn't meant to say that, but it slipped out before she could catch it. She knew she looked surprised because she *felt* surprised. "Seriously?"

"Yeah. She was very into it. Here's what we were thinking..."

❖

"You're shitting me." Claire smacked her open palm onto the table between them, rattling both their drinks in her disbelief.

"I am not shitting you," London said with a laugh, picking up her cosmo to prevent spillage. "I meet with her tomorrow to go over details and then we fly out on Friday morning."

"To fucking *St. Kitts*? I don't even know where that is, and I hate you." Claire's words held affection, though, as did her radiant, albeit astonished, smile.

"It's in the Caribbean," London told her. "I had to google it when I got home. It's, like, five-star hotels, luxury resorts, getaways for the super wealthy."

They were at their usual back corner table in McCusker's, an Irish pub near their apartment. It wasn't super busy, but it still buzzed, the after-work crowd stopping in on a Tuesday to shake off the day and loosen up before heading home.

"This is unbelievable." Claire signaled the waitress for another round. "I admit, when I gave you the idea, I wasn't really sure you'd run with it."

"Neither was I." London grinned at her. "And now I have to pack for my weeklong vacation at a luxury resort." The waitress arrived and deposited two more cosmos on the table. London picked hers up. "To my awesome roommate and her normally harebrained, once in a while *amazing* ideas."

"I will fucking drink to that." They clinked glasses and sipped.

"So, who are you accompanying on this *vacation?*" Claire asked, making the air quotes.

"Well, that's the interesting part." It was also the part London still couldn't quite wrap her head around. "Silas went to Miranda Northbrooke to bounce the idea off her." At Claire's furrowed brow and slight shake of her head, London explained. "The Northbrookes? They own the umbrella company that encompasses *TN Squared*, the NewsAmerica cable channel and all its subsidiaries, Coastline movie studios, and God knows how many other media outlets."

"A true media conglomerate, huh?"

"Exactly. Anyway, Silas went to Miranda because he thought, if she liked the idea, she'd know of some obscenely wealthy guy who'd go along with it as a favor to her and be my host."

"Makes sense."

London leaned over the table and lowered her voice, as if she and Claire were planning a bank heist. "Turns out, Miranda Northbrooke liked the idea so much, *she* wants to be my host. Hostess."

"No way," Claire said, louder than she'd intended, judging by the look on her face. She lowered her voice again. "You're going to a luxury island resort with a media mogul? How did this happen?" She made a show of looking around the bar. "Are we on a reality show? Are there hidden cameras in the ceiling?"

London laughed at her wide-eyed expression, but the truth was, she could hardly believe it herself. "Apparently, she hates traveling alone, prefers to have a companion to keep her company. Silas said she was all in on the idea of letting me see behind the curtain, as it were."

"You know she plays for the alphabet mafia, right?" Claire was on her phone, apparently googling. "She's an out and proud bisexual." She took a sip of her drink, then turned her phone so London could see it. "And, um, kind of attractive for an older woman. Like, seriously."

London nodded. She'd thought the same thing when she'd looked her up. Miranda Northbrooke had a bit of a Nicole Kidman look—tall, very thin, blonder than Nicole and with green eyes, but their builds were similar.

"I was expecting somebody in her seventies or something," Claire said with a laugh. "This says she's fifty-seven. When I think media mogul, I think old stodgy white guy, not sexy middle-aged cougar."

London barked a laugh. "Okay, so she just went from *kind of attractive for an older woman* to *sexy cougar* in the space of about five and a half seconds."

"Listen, she's growing on me." Claire continued to scroll on her phone, and London let her. She had gone from Silas's office straight to the subway, where she'd texted Claire to meet her at McCusker's for a 911, the code they used when one of them had the dire need to discuss something with the other. She hadn't even been home yet. And her brain hadn't really settled on what was happening. "This could be big, C." The words had been hanging out in her head for the past two hours, but she hadn't allowed herself to say them out loud. "This could be the real start of my career." She knew her face must've given away her sudden fear and worry because Claire reached across the table and gripped her forearm.

"It will be. I can feel it. And if anybody can take this story and run with it, it's you." Her grip tightened until London looked her in the eye. "You are a fantastic writer. You're gonna knock this out of the park. I just know it." She let go and downed the rest of her drink. "And when you write your book and you're on Kelly Clarkson or Drew Barrymore, you better damn well thank me."

London felt herself relax, the tension in her shoulders dissipating a bit. "I have to get through meeting with Miranda Northbrooke first. Let's hold off on the talk show appearances until I know for sure it's happening. Yeah?"

"Fine. But Kelly's my favorite, and if you don't get me some swag and an autograph, this friendship is over."

"That seems fair."

I just have to get through tomorrow. The words played over and over through her head for the rest of the night out and the entire time she tried to sleep. In all honesty, she had a good feeling about things, but thinking about having a good feeling seemed like a jinx possibility, so she tried to pretend she did *not* have a good feeling, all the while knowing she was lying within her own head about having a good feeling.

Yeah, she didn't get a whole lot of sleep.

CHAPTER TWO

How are we doing over there, Bo?" Kayla Tennyson spoke quietly, phone in her hand, AirPods in her ears. She could've easily texted, but the problem with texting was the receiver of the text had to actually look at the phone, which meant taking their eyes off their charge. And in the security business, taking your eyes off the prize could be detrimental.

"Her plane landed. Jake and I will meet them at the gate."

"Okay. I'm in her suite now, going over the whole thing. Looks all right so far. I'll keep you posted." She hung up and tucked her phone in her back pocket. They never said good-bye, her and Bo. They just hung up. They'd laughed about it once, said they were like a TV show where nobody ever said good-bye on the phone, but kept doing it, likely because they were very much on the same wavelength when it came to security.

She blew out a breath, hands on her hips, and turned in a slow circle. The suite was huge. Gorgeous. Expensive. Her client, Aria Keller, was Hollywood's current It Girl. She'd worked nonstop for the past two years and was taking a much-needed week off from rehearsals and filming and press junkets and talk shows to just chill here on the island of St. Kitts with two of her friends. Aria was barely thirty. She was talented. She was smart. She had boatloads of money. And she had a few fans that didn't understand boundaries.

That's why Kayla was there.

Normally, she'd send one of her crews, and she'd stay back in her New York City office and run things from there. But Aria trusted her and had asked for her specifically. So, here she was, standing in one of the most gorgeous suites she'd ever seen, and she'd seen many, checking for entry points or ways a stranger might be able to slip in unhindered. Even being able to take photos through windows was a no-go. That's why they were on a higher floor.

Her phone buzzed in her pocket, and she hit the button on her AirPod to answer, not checking first because she fully expected it was Bo with an update. "Tennyson Security," she said quietly.

"Hi, honey, it's Mom."

"Who else calls me honey?" Kayla said with a soft laugh.

"Listen, how would I know? You're a woman of the world. Maybe you have girls all over the place who call you honey. Maybe there's one in every port." Her mother's voice was gentle and tender, filled with love and humor.

"Who has the time for girls all over the place? Sadly, not your daughter." She stood at one of the glass doors and fiddled with the lock, testing its security. "What are you up to?"

"My pickleball tournament starts in an hour, so I'm getting ready for that. Where has this game been all my life?"

"In Florida, clearly." They laughed together, then Kayla added, "Be careful, okay?"

"Why? Think I'm gonna break a hip? Have a little faith in your mother!"

"I'm not worried about you. I'm worried about the opponents you're going to wipe the asphalt with. Go easy on them, okay? Don't make anybody cry."

Her mother made a *pfft* sound and Kayla laughed. "Where are you today?"

"St. Kitts. Guarding for Aria Keller."

"My daughter is so fancy."

"You don't even know who Aria Keller is, do you?"

"Not a clue."

Kayla grinned as she slid the door open and stepped out onto the private sundeck. "I won't bore you with the details. Just know I'll be here all week, working."

"All right, well make sure you allow yourself some downtime, okay? Self-care is important, Kayla Marie."

"Yes, Mother. I'll talk to you later. I love you."

"Love you more."

The conversation ended and Kayla clicked off, then stood still and took in the view. The stunning, breathtaking, so pretty it almost didn't seem real view. There was an infinity pool in front of her that gave astonishing views of the ocean and the island of Nevis across the water. The sky was a shockingly bright blue, and the thunderous sound of the rolling waves could easily lull a person into a calm, trancelike state of relaxation. Maybe she should come back here in a nonwork capacity. Her mother was always getting on her for working so much. And all that working had fattened her own bank account nicely. She could afford a vacation here.

Something to think about.

She stood for a few more minutes, then shook herself back into action and headed inside. The lock on the glass door wasn't super secure, but it would do. They were on the sixth floor and somebody would have to do some serious building-scaling if they wanted to break in this way.

Her phone pinged a text, and she pulled it out to read Bo's note. *Got the tiny package. Headed your way.*

"The tiny package." She snorted. While sometimes texting in code was necessary for security, Bo mostly did it to make her laugh. Aria Keller was about five foot two, and Bo was about six six, so to him, Aria was absolutely a tiny package.

She quickly swept through the rest of the suite. It featured three bedrooms and three bathrooms, one each for Aria and her two friends. Everything seemed to be in order. Next, she'd hang out in the lobby and near the bar, scanning the people there, seeing if anybody seemed out of place or overly interested in Aria once she arrived.

One last look out the glass wall at that amazing view, and then she slipped out and made sure the door locked behind her.

"Good afternoon, Ms. Tennyson," said the butler as he moved down the hallway.

She gave him a nod and a hello. The staff knew her well, which was one reason she enjoyed doing security work here. The Bella Grande had a fabulous manager who took security very seriously. Kayla guarded a client here probably four or five times a year, so she'd become a familiar face to the staff, and that was helpful if—and when—she needed something extra.

The lobby was bustling with guests arriving for their stays, lots of wealthy folks, some of whom Kayla recognized. There were a couple actors, a well-known basketball player, and the CEO of a financial institution she'd seen interviewed on CNN not long ago, to name a few. She moved through them confidently, having been around this caliber of people for much of her career. A nod here, a hello there, and she was through the crowd.

The hotel had several places to eat or drink or both. She headed to the bistro that was open to the outside and looked out onto the ocean. She needed to grab a quick lunch before Bo arrived.

Kayla liked Aria Keller. She was smart, and she seemed to have a good handle on her life and her career. She also took no shit, something else Kayla liked about her. She was never mean—not that Kayla had ever seen—but she also didn't allow herself to be walked on. She was a bit of a sex symbol in Hollywood, with her small stature and enormous green-brown eyes. Her brows were thick and dark, which only served to bring more attention to those eyes. Kayla knew her well enough now to discern the difference between her public smile and her genuine one, the one that lit up her whole face. She smiled that one now as she saw Kayla from across the lobby and hurried to her.

"Hey, Kay," Aria said as she reached up and wrapped her arms around Kayla's neck in a hug. "I'm so glad you're here."

"Good to see you, Aria," Kayla said, bending her five foot ten inch frame to accommodate. "I trust your flight was good?"

"It was super bumpy," said a woman to Aria's left. "I thought a private jet would be smoother."

Aria tried to suppress an eye roll, but Kayla caught it as Aria made the introductions. "Kayla Tennyson, this is my cousin Haley," she indicated the turbulence hater, "and my best friend from home, Cammie." Haley was a less attractive version of Aria. She had the same build and the same chestnut hair, but her eyes were small and set close together, and her mouth slightly crooked. She wore glasses that seemed too big for her face, giving her the essence of a bug. The other young woman was quieter than Haley, and she held out a hand to shake Kayla's, her auburn hair catching the sunlight coming in through the lobby's skylights. "Kayla's the one I told you about," Aria went on. "She runs my security detail. Bo and Jake work for her." She used her eyes to indicate the two men, standing just off to the side, sunglasses blocking anybody from seeing what they were watching.

"It's nice to meet you all," Kayla said, putting on her serious business voice. "You'll likely see us around during your whole stay. Bo and Jake and I will rotate shifts. I've checked the suite. Everything looks great." She turned her gaze to Aria. "You know how to reach me if you need something or if somebody feels off. *Do not hesitate.*" She enunciated those last three words. "And if one of us gives you an order, there's a reason for it, so don't argue. Just do what we say, and we'll explain later. Understood?" She waited for them to nod.

"Wow, Ar, your security chick is bossy." Haley meant it as a tease, but her tone was all wrong for that. Instead, it came out snarky. Aria threw her cousin a look that shut her up instantly.

For half a second, Kayla thought about explaining to The Cousin—which was how she'd refer to her in her communications with Bo and Jake—what kinds of things happen when a stalker or obsessed fan is allowed to get too close but changed her mind. She'd let Aria do the explaining. "If anything feels weird, let one of us know immediately. This is your vacation, and you deserve peace and relaxation. Okay?"

"You're the best, Kay," Aria said.

Kayla smiled. "I'll take the first shift so the guys can get some rest. We won't necessarily be posted outside your door, but we'll be around. As you know, we like to be more subtle."

Aria nodded as the bellhop approached to take their bags, and they all headed to the suite.

Kayla stood off to the side, hands clasped in front of her, sunglasses on, as Haley and Cammie took in the enormity of the suite, prompting several *holy shit*s from Haley as she went from room to room, bathroom to bathroom, balcony.

"Holy shit, is this *our* pool?" Haley shouted from out on the sundeck. "Like, just ours?" Even wide-eyed, her eyes weren't as big as Aria's.

"It is," Aria said, joining her cousin next to the sparkling blue of the infinity pool. She dropped an arm around her shoulders. "I told you guys I'd make this trip awesome, didn't I?" Cammie joined them and stood on the other side of Aria, who draped her other arm around her bestie.

"You sure did," Cammie said, and the three of them stood quietly, just gazing out at the view of the ocean and Nevis on the horizon. "God, it's beautiful."

Aria squeezed them both to her. "I'm so glad you guys are here with me. I've needed this so badly." And there was something in her voice then, something wistful and almost a little sad.

That was something people who worked for Kayla had to get used to—seeing behind the curtain of celebrities, observing them when they're not on display for the public, when they're just being people, being humans who cry and argue with their spouse and drink too much and burp and fart. Security detail was often invisible to the client—and that's how it should be. That's what Kayla strove for in her work. But being invisible to the client often meant the client threw off their public persona and left it in a crumpled pile in the corner of the hotel room like a dirty shirt.

After a few moments, the trio came back into the living room area of the suite. Haley announced she was going to unpack and put on her bathing suit. Cammie agreed and off they went.

"This is fabulous," Aria said to Kayla once her friends were gone. "You're happy with the security?"

Kayla nodded. "Yeah, I don't think you're going to have any problems."

Aria waited until Kayla looked her in the eye. "Thank you, Kayla. I feel safer when you're around."

It was the highest compliment a security firm could get, and Kayla nodded her thanks. "I'm glad you feel that way." She gave Aria the rundown of the shift schedule. "You guys enjoy the pool. Let me know when you order food and drinks. I'll catch it in the hall and bring it in, yeah?"

"You're the best, Kay."

With that, Kayla left the suite and headed to her own room. It was getting hot, and she wanted to change into something slightly less *I'm very clearly a security guard* and more *I'm here on vacation, you'll never notice me noticing you.* She did a presto chango into a flowy sundress in a floral print and, not for the first time, was thankful they'd shifted to wireless earpieces. There was nowhere to hide wires and such in the clothes you wore in a tropical paradise like St. Kitts. She pulled her dark hair back into a twist and slid her sunglasses back on.

With a nod to the mirror, she grabbed her tiny purse and headed off to find Bo.

❖

Miranda Northbrooke was exactly what London expected... and also not at all.

She had presence, that was the first thing that was clear. When she walked into a room, people took notice. Maybe it was because of her height—at least five ten, possibly a bit taller. Or maybe it was because of her look. If it was possible for a person to *look* rich and important, Miranda'd figured out how. From her designer dress to her perfect makeup and hair to the way she carried herself—head held high, confidence rolling off her in waves—she was a boss. She commanded attention, and she got it. London watched through the window as eyes followed Miranda through the main office space until she crossed into Silas York's office, her assistant trailing behind her.

"Silas," Miranda said, shaking his hand. "Good to see you

again." Without waiting for an introduction, she turned to London. "And you must be Ms. Granger. You are stunning. I can see why you were in the modeling biz." Coming from her, the comment somehow seemed neither inappropriate nor creepy. Simply fact. She held out a hand. "Miranda Northbrooke. Nice to meet you."

Her handshake was firm and solid. "Nice to meet you as well," London said.

"This is Ethan," she said, indicating the man who'd followed her in. He was dressed in a suit and tie, AirPod in one ear, iPhone in one hand. His dark hair was styled neatly, and he wore dark-rimmed glasses. London got the feeling he didn't miss a thing. "He monitors my schedule, takes my calls, and generally keeps my life running smoothly."

Ethan looked at her and gave a quick nod before returning his attention to his phone.

"So," Miranda said as she took a seat and crossed her long legs, "Silas has filled me in on your article idea. I like it. I like it very much."

London nodded. It felt a little strange to be standing over Miranda, but sitting also felt off. Like she hadn't earned it yet. So she stayed on her feet. "I think it could make for a very interesting read. Our audience loves being in someone else's shoes, especially if that someone moves in a completely different world than they do."

"A world they'll never be a part of." There was a slight edge of condescension in Miranda's tone, and when she punctuated it with a light chuckle, it made London bristle just a bit.

"I mean, not quite as simple as that." She knew in that exact moment that the other issues she intended to touch on in her article were things she wouldn't be mentioning to Miranda Northbrooke, because just that one statement was enough to tell London she wouldn't understand. "But yes."

"Well, Silas tells me you're one of his best writers, and he assures me that you'll handle things with the right blend of professionalism and fun."

She hoped she didn't look as surprised as the words made her feel. She shot a quick glance at her boss—she had no idea Silas thought she was one of his best—as the compliment made her stand a bit taller. "That's definitely my goal."

"Good. And I'll be happy to have a companion with me on this trip. It's been a while, and I really despise traveling alone." Then Miranda let her eyes roam down London's body, and it wasn't so much a leer as an assessment. She gave a firm nod. "You'll certainly fit right in."

London wasn't quite sure if that was a compliment but decided to take it as one.

"A couple of ground rules, if you don't mind."

"Sure." London glanced at Silas, who was watching the whole conversation with an interested expression on his face but had said next to nothing so far.

"First of all, there will likely be celebrities there. They're on vacation, just like me, and they don't appreciate being hounded for autographs or photos."

London nodded. "Of course."

"Since this is a place I vacation often, there may also be people I know there. Some friends, some not. Just be aware of that as well."

"Sure."

"Second, you won't have to be with me twenty-four seven. I'll definitely want some downtime, and I know you're going to want some writing opportunities." She waved over her shoulder where Ethan still stood, and it occurred to London that neither of the men in the room were much a part of the conversation, which she found interesting, since it was usually the other way around. "Ethan has reserved us a suite with two bedrooms, so you'll have your own space."

"I would like to be with you whenever possible, but you're right, I'll need time to write."

"Exactly. And third..." Miranda gave her a soft smile, and this one seemed more genuine than any expression so far. "I'd like you to enjoy yourself. So if you have questions or concerns, just ask me. All right? I think...we can't have people knowing you're a journalist or that you're writing a story about them and how they live, so let's keep that under wraps. As far as anybody's concerned, you're my traveling companion for the trip. And you're still a model. Yes?"

"Of course. Understood." It made a weird kind of sense, so London nodded. Okay, so she might have to play a bit of a role. She could do that. Please, in her modeling days, she'd perfected so many expressions, often standing in front of the mirror and making them over and over again until they were just right. So the moment a photographer shouted *Now smolder!* or *Look at the camera like you want to make love to it!* she could make the right face in a heartbeat. Part of modeling was acting, and acting like she was good friends with Miranda Northbrooke wouldn't be hard. If that's what she'd have to do for this article, she absolutely could. "Not a problem," she said.

"Wonderful." Miranda pushed to her feet. "Then I think we're good to go. Silas, Ethan has emailed you the itinerary."

Silas nodded as he also stood. "Got it. I'll go over it with London."

Miranda looked at London one more time. "Then I'll see you at the airport tomorrow. We'll take my jet."

Ethan opened the office door for her, and she breezed through. He gave a quick nod to London, then followed Miranda out, not having uttered one single word the whole time. London watched them leave, and the same thing happened on their way out—everybody present watched as they walked by. Once they'd crossed through the double glass doors and were out of sight, London and Silas both released breaths.

"Wow," London said. "She's…something."

"Right?" Silas asked. "Still wanna do this?"

"Oh, you better believe I do." The gears were already cranking in her head, ideas brewing and spinning. "Even more now."

"That's what I thought you'd say." Silas gave a husky chuckle and indicated the chair Miranda had vacated. "Sit. Let's hammer out the details."

CHAPTER THREE

Thank God for the Notes app on London's phone.

One thing she hadn't taken into consideration when preparing for this trip was how she'd remember what she saw. She was a huge notetaker when she was on assignment. Huge. But she couldn't exactly walk around next to Miranda Northbrooke with a notepad and pen in her hand, could she? Not when she was supposed to be her traveling pal and *not* a journalist. Luckily, being on her phone was perfectly normal—everybody else was—so she jotted as much as she could with her thumbs.

One of the first things she'd noticed was that Ethan did almost everything for her. Dealt with phone calls, ordered her food, got her drinks. On occasion, he'd ask her preference on something, and she'd answer, and then he'd be back on his phone. It was interesting. He seemed to work nonstop.

She stretched her arms above her head now, luxuriating in the softness of the zillion thread count white sheets on her bed. She had her own room in Miranda's suite, as promised. Her own bathroom as well. And it was all simply gorgeous, elegant and classy, and London had traveled quite a bit when she'd modeled, but this was a hundred steps beyond anything she'd ever seen, anyplace she'd ever stayed. Her room had double French doors that opened onto the private sundeck where their private pool was. Seriously. A private swimming pool! It was all so...*extravagant*. And rich. It was all just so rich. Miranda barely batted an eye when they'd arrived. Admittedly, it had been late and dark. And they'd all been tired.

Despite it being a private jet, there'd been a mechanical issue that had kept them on the runway. Miranda had been clearly irritated, but London had simply stared around her. A private jet! Her seat was like a damn BarcaLounger and cradled her body like it was made just for her. The flight attendants were more like a waitstaff at a fine restaurant, and the selection of drinks was astonishing to London.

They'd finally arrived by ten, all of them exhausted—Miranda, Ethan, and London—and they'd ordered room service from Chef Marco—yes, they had a personal chef!—and gone straight to bed. London would've liked to explore a bit, but she had to admit to her own exhaustion. Plus, she wanted to start Saturday fresh. She had a job to do.

And now, it *was* Saturday.

She'd slept with the French doors open—there was nothing quite like drifting off to sleep to the sound of the ocean waves rolling in—and now she stepped out onto the sundeck in her boxers and tank. The view sucked the breath right out of her lungs: the azure blue of the water, the trees blowing in the ocean breeze, the rumble of the waves as they crashed onto the shore, the other island visible on the horizon—something that started with an *N*, if she remembered correctly—and a huge bird floating by. The view was so perfect, it was almost unreal, as if she was looking at a computer rendering of what a perfect view would look like.

"Oh my God," she whispered as she stood there in awe.

"Gorgeous, isn't it?"

London gasped at the sound of Miranda's voice, and she pressed a hand to her chest with a small laugh. "I didn't see you there."

Miranda was lounging on a chaise, a cup of coffee in her hand as she gazed out at the vista before them. "It really never gets old, this view." She took a sip of her coffee before going on. "Doesn't matter how many times I come back, I'm still just speechless when I sit here."

"I've never seen anything like it."

And then they were quiet, just existing in the same space, looking at the same thing. London wondered what it must be like to be able to come back to something this beautiful again and again.

"I thought we'd have a beach day today," Miranda said. "Throw on our suits, slather ourselves with sunscreen, read, write, do whatever. What do you say?"

It sounded like the perfect opportunity to get started on her feature. She'd already learned so much, and it would give her a chance to organize her notes, arrange her thoughts, and figure out a layout for the article. "I say let's do it," she said with enthusiasm.

When London was a kid growing up in Ohio, her grandparents lived near a beach on Lake Erie. Every summer, they'd take a couple of day trips and spend the entire day at the beach, lounging in the sand, swimming in the lake, finding shells, listening to music. They'd eat Popsicles or ice cream, drink Cokes. She'd go home with sand in places she didn't know she had, her skin mostly bronzed, but with a few red splotches to remind her where she'd forgotten to put sunscreen.

Her memories of having a beach day were nothing like Miranda's beach day. Not even close.

She thought about that now as she lay back on a chaise lounge that was more comfortable than Claire's couch back home. Hell, it was more comfortable than her own bed. There was an umbrella if she wanted it. Miranda was under one, and she also wore a wide-brimmed hat, telling London she'd be bright red in a matter of minutes in this sun, no matter how much sunscreen she used. London didn't have that issue. She always used sunscreen—the higher the SPF, the better—but she'd also been born with skin that tanned easily. Claire liked to say that summer London was a bronze goddess.

"You really are stunning, aren't you?" Miranda's voice held a tinge of amusement, and when London turned to look at her, large sunglasses were hiding her eyes.

"Thank you," she said quietly, feeling suddenly self-conscious in her red one-piece bathing suit. She'd purposely not chosen the bikini because this was business, but it apparently hadn't made a difference. She could feel Miranda's eyes on her, even if she couldn't see them.

"What must it be like to be that effortlessly beautiful?" Miranda didn't give her a chance to answer, thank God, before she laughed and said, "I wouldn't know. I've been getting Botox injections since my early thirties."

A waiter came their way, balancing a tray laden with fruity-looking tropical drinks—another thing that reminded London this was not her grandparents' beach—and set them on the small table between their lounge chairs. How he trudged through the sand in the eighty-five degree heat, carrying trays of food and drink, and didn't seem to even break a sweat, London had no idea. He looked like he'd just woken up and put on his white uniform, his dark skin glowing in the sunshine. He smiled at them, nodded to Miranda, and asked if they needed anything more. Then he was on his way to the next customers down the beach a bit—three young women who'd arrived just after they had.

Miranda picked up one of the two drinks—frozen pink concoctions of some sort with bright green umbrellas and a straw—and took a sip, humming her approval. She glanced at London, who took that as her cue to taste her own drink. It was sweet, cold, and creamy. A little strawberry, but not quite a daiquiri. There was definitely rum, though—she tasted it immediately.

It was divine.

"Wow."

Miranda chuckled. "Yeah. The drinks here have always been fabulous." She indicated the water bottles, also on the little table. "Stay hydrated or you'll get lightheaded and sick real fast. The sun does not mess around here."

A good call, she was sure, and she took a long pull from the water.

Food and drinks hand-delivered by an impeccably dressed waiter. On the beach. It was almost surreal, and she pulled out her phone to jot some notes. When she finished, she glanced at Miranda, whose head was back against her lounge. She might have been resting with her eyes closed. She might have been watching every move on the beach. London couldn't tell, so she turned her gaze to the ocean.

It was hypnotic, in the most relaxing sense. The combination of the gorgeous blues of the water and the sky, the warmth of the sun, the softness of the lounge, and the way the rum had loosened her limbs was both intoxicating and invigorating, though that didn't seem possible. Down by the water, a woman jogged by looking very much like Sexy Jogging Chick from back home, though she was too far away to actually see. Still, her long legs, black tank that left her shoulders visible, and ponytailed dark hair made for a nice addition to London's ocean view as she jogged by and down the beach. London was contemplating that when a voice spoke, interrupting her thought.

"Miranda?"

London glanced up at the sound, shaded her eyes against the sun, and saw a man standing in front of them. He was maybe in his fifties, dressed in bright orange swim trunks. The hair on his tanned chest was white, but the hair on his head was a flattering salt-and-pepper. He slid his Ray-Bans down his nose as Miranda lifted her head.

"Oh, Keith," Miranda said with a cool smile. "Hi. How are you?"

"Not bad, not bad," Keith said. "You look fantastic."

Miranda made a *pfft* sound and waved him away, though something about the gesture made London think Miranda actually agreed with him. "The years are much kinder to men than women," Miranda said, and London wanted to nod her head in vehement agreement.

Keith pushed his Ray-Bans back on and looked around before asking, "You here on vacation?"

Miranda nodded. "Just taking a break, yeah." Her voice was breezy, like she hadn't a care in the world. Maybe she didn't.

"You always did talk about how much you love it here."

"I really do. Nothing relaxes me like this place."

The conversation seemed to stall then, and London jumped in. "Hi there. London Granger." She stuck out her hand.

"Oh God, where are my manners," Miranda said and jumped like she was poked. "London, this is my old friend Keith Masters. Keith, this is"—she paused for a split second before settling on—"my new friend, London Granger."

They shook hands, and London was slightly bummed that both Keith and Miranda still had their shades on. She was curious what was going on behind their lenses because something told her there was a history there. Maybe it was the wistful tone in Keith's voice or maybe it was the chill in Miranda's.

"What do you do, London?" Keith asked. He had a kind smile.

"She's a model," Miranda answered for her.

"Oh, interesting. Very cool."

"How about you?" London asked.

"I'm in finance," he said but didn't elaborate, and London wondered if that was some sort of code for *I have lots of money I didn't earn*. She immediately felt bad for making a judgment, but Keith went on. "Well. I'd better get back to it." He made a vague gesture down the beach but didn't define what *it* was. "Good to see you again, Miranda. Nice to meet you, London. Enjoy your stay." With a casual wave, he continued his walk down the beach.

"He seemed nice," London said.

"He is," Miranda agreed. "Super clingy, though. God."

London turned to look at her, and even with the sunglasses, she could sense a sort of smug satisfaction. "Oh! Is he…? Were you two…?"

"Believe me, it was very short-lived. But yes. We dated briefly."

"Should I not have…?" London realized maybe she shouldn't have jumped in the way she did. Her face must have registered her confusion because Miranda laughed softly.

"Oh no, you were fine." Miranda waved a hand between them. "Drink your cocktail and enjoy the sun." She lay back against her lounge once more.

The waiter came by again, this time with an array of fruit arranged on a platter, and left it between them. They hadn't ordered anything at all, but food and drinks just kept appearing. It was like nothing London had ever experienced. When she looked back out toward the water, Sexy Jogging Chick the Second was running in the opposite direction. It occurred to London that if she was going to be eating and drinking like this for a week, maybe she should consider a little activity to counteract it. Her gaze followed the jogger, and she popped a grape into her mouth.

I could get used to this.

The guys who worked for Kayla hated the excursions part of guarding. They didn't enjoy tagging along on boat rides or island tours or fishing expeditions, especially because they couldn't participate. Bo in particular was a huge fisherman, an outdoorsman, so Kayla tried to take the shifts on excursions that she knew he'd hate because he'd want to be playing, too.

This excursion, however, she took not because he'd want to participate and would be bummed out, but because he was horrendously afraid of heights.

Zip-lining would not be something he'd handle well. Oh, he'd do it. If there was no other option, he'd absolutely take the shift. He'd just be white as a sheet of paper the whole time.

But Aria and her friends were into it. Big-time. And she'd practically begged Kayla to come along, to zip-line with them. Since Kayla had—surprisingly, given all her travels—never done it, she'd agreed.

"It's gonna be so cool," Aria kept saying on the drive up. "It's five lines. We do the easy one, then we drive higher up and do three more. The last one is a race, two people zipping at once." Her excitement was contagious, and by the time they arrived at line one, the four of them were practically buzzing with anticipation.

Aria had paid extra for privacy, as she was a very recognizable face, so it was only the four of them.

The lead guide was named Raphael, and he explained all the ins and outs and rules. The rest of his team consisted of another guy with sandy hair whose name she'd missed, and a woman he introduced as Janine. Raphael went through some basics and gave them the rundown of how things would go, all pretty straightforward. They signed waivers, Aria looking to Kayla for what seemed like permission, and the next thing she knew, they were being fitted with harnesses.

Janine helped Kayla into hers, and her knuckles brushed against Kayla's breast.

"Sorry about that," Janine said, looking a bit chagrined, but also slightly arching a brow.

"That's the most action I've had in a long time. No worries," Kayla said, and Janine laughed softly.

"Well, that's just sad."

"It is, right?"

"In a big way." Janine gave her upper arm a squeeze, winked, and refocused on her job.

By the time they got to line number five, more than an hour and a half had passed, and they were all laughing, squealing, and absolutely pumped. Kayla watched Aria's face and was so happy with what she saw. Joy. Genuine, heartfelt joy. There were so many masks Aria had to wear as an actress. Fame did that to people. Kayla had run security for many celebrities and—with a few exceptions— most of them had an *on* persona, and then their actual personality. When the on persona took up a disproportionate amount of time, the actual personality could become stifled. Shut down. Seeing Aria being herself, enjoying herself, laughing genuinely with her girls was amazing.

"Okay, Kay, you and me," Aria said. "This is a race. Cammie and Haley, and then you and me. Yeah?"

"I'm gonna smoke you," Kayla teased.

She did.

Aria was small and tried to tuck herself into a ball, but Kayla lay back and made herself flat, like a human arrow. She shot over the rainforest at a height and speed that would've had Bo throwing up his breakfast all over the treetops, then pulled her feet back in just in time to be caught by Janine at the final checkpoint, where Cammie and Haley stood, cheering.

"Nice form," Janine said quietly, her dark eyes flashing.

"Why, thank you," Kayla said, unbuckling her helmet just as Aria came zipping up next to her.

"You kicked my ass," Aria whined, but she was grinning like a kid on Christmas morning.

"Told you I would."

Aria gave her a gentle shove.

"And now you're trying to push me off the platform and kill me."

"Runner-up takes the win if the winner can't fulfill her duties, right?" Aria said with a shrug, as they all began unclipping fasteners and stepping out of their equipment.

"This comes with duties?" Kayla asked. "What are they?"

"First round of drinks is on you," Aria said.

"Damn," Kayla said. "I should've checked that before I wiped the rainforest with your tiny little ass."

Aria tried to feign a gasp but ended up bursting out laughing instead. "You're hilarious, Kay."

Kayla shrugged. "I try."

"That was a blast," Cammie said. A bead of sweat ran down the side of her face, and her cheeks were flushed.

"So much fun," Haley agreed, and Kayla noted how not annoying she'd been on this excursion. Maybe she'd judged her too soon.

"It really was," Kayla said. Then to Aria, "Thanks for including me."

Aria leaned in to her like a little sister would. "Hate to break it to you, but you're part of my circle now."

"Uh-oh," Cammie said, eyes wide.

"Yeah, you should probably run," Haley added, deadpan.

Kayla laughed, then looked around. "All right, everybody ready? Seems I've got some drinks to buy."

❖

Kayla didn't stay with Aria and her crew. That would've been inappropriate. Much as she knew Aria enjoyed her company, she was there to work, not party with her client. She kept her promise, though, and bought the trio a round of drinks in one of the Bella Grande's lounges where they sat in cushy swiveling chairs surrounding a round table. The lighting was dim, mysterious. By the time she'd moved to sit at a corner of the bar where she could see them as well as the rest of the lounge, the girls were already looking at the menu. They'd be in this spot for a while, and Kayla found relief in that. Much easier to keep track of her client—and those around her—when she was in one place.

She sent a text off to Bo, who'd start his shift and take over in about an hour, and settled in.

"What can I get you?" the bartender asked as he polished a glass with a bright white cloth.

"Club soda with lime, please." She'd allow herself to have an actual cocktail or a glass of wine once Bo relieved her.

Taking a sip of her drink, she scanned the lounge, taking note of each patron. It wasn't terribly busy, but there were another lounge, three restaurants, a sports bar, and a club, all part of the resort, so the guests could easily spread out. Currently, there was a couple at the back corner table, their heads close together, nobody else seeming to even exist in their world. There were two men at another table, pretty clearly together—if Kayla's gaydar wasn't glitching—one of them an actor well-known for starring in several action blockbusters. There was a foursome of folks in their seventies—two couples, she surmised. Aria and her girls were the other occupied table. At the bar were an NFL quarterback and his wife, having what seemed to be a heated—albeit very quiet—argument. An older gentleman sat by himself, nursing what looked to be scotch, neat. Also sitting alone was a gorgeous blond woman, like, seriously stunning to look at, and Kayla chided herself for ogling her like a dude would, but wow. She wore a white sundress with spaghetti straps, and her skin was bronzed and held that warm glow of somebody who'd spent the day in the sunshine. Her blond hair had several different shades of gold, and it was pulled into a twist at the back of her head, a few escapee strands hanging in ringlets at the nape of her neck. She looked oddly familiar somehow. On the bar in front of her was a small notebook, a pen, and a martini. Kayla watched for several minutes as the woman stared off into space, then picked up the pen and jotted something down, then set it down and sipped her martini, then repeated the same thing again.

Watching her was fascinating.

Unfortunately, Kayla wasn't there to watch the pretty blond girl, and she had to consciously shift her focus to Aria's table, where the trio was laughing as their food was being delivered. A quick scan of the room told her everyone was still in their places. Nobody suspicious hung out in the dark or stared like a creeper.

"Hey, boss." Bo had arrived to relieve her and took a seat on the stool next to her. "All good?"

Kayla indicated the round table with her eyes. "Yup. They're having dinner. Zip-lining was crazy and exhausting and I bet they turn in early tonight." At Bo's snort, she laughed. "Or maybe they'll want to hit the club. Either way, they're all yours."

As she abandoned her seat, the guy sitting alone across the bar caught her attention. He slid off his barstool, took a moment to steady himself—how many scotches had he had?—and headed toward the blonde.

Oh, no, please don't, sir. She closed her eyes as she shook her head.

The blonde must've been deep in thought because the man's presence seemed to startle her, like she hadn't seen him coming.

"What's a pretty girl like you doin' at a bar all alone?" he asked her, a little louder than normal volume, and Kayla was surprised how clear his speech was. She'd expected slurring, judging by the way he was unbalanced.

The blonde smiled at him, and Kayla instantly recognized it as the same type of smile every woman plastered on her face when she was being hit on by a man she had no interest in being hit on by. The kind of smile that meant *I have to smile because he could do something terrible to me if I'm rude.* It was a fake, plastic smile, and he didn't seem to notice. Of course. They never did.

"I'm actually working, so…" The blonde let the sentence dangle, clearly hoping the man would take the hint.

He did not.

Instead, he took her words as an invitation and pulled himself into the seat beside her. "Work? Here?" He leaned close—too close—and looked at her notebook. "Whatcha working on?"

The blonde put her hand over her notes. "I'm sorry, but that's not really any of your business."

The man's bushy eyebrows met in a V above his nose, and he looked like she'd slapped him. "Well, you don't have to be a bitch about it."

Yeah, that was enough.

Bo made a move, but Kayla stopped him with a hand on his arm. "I got this," she said quietly, then walked over to them. "Hi there," she said to the man and held out her hand. "Kayla Tennyson." She waited for the man, whose confusion was clear, to let his manners take over. They did, as she knew they would, and he shook her hand.

"Bob Statler," he said.

"Bob. It's really nice to meet you."

He was disarmed by her, and that was the best part for Kayla. She loved watching the thoughts play out all over his face, trying to figure her angle. "Same," he said.

"Well, I don't meant to intrude, but my business associate here and I are about to have a meeting." She indicated the blonde, who looked up at her with the deepest blue eyes Kayla had ever seen, then said to her, "So sorry I'm late." Turning back to the man, she said, "Bob, let me buy you a drink for your trouble." A nod to the bartender, who nodded back and brought a new scotch, neat, to Bob's old seat.

Bob was clearly flustered and trying not to look it. He ended up grumbling a thank you and went wobbling back to his own chair.

Kayla threw an expression of thanks to the bartender, who winked at her and gave her a fresh club soda. As she took it and sat facing Bob so she could keep an eye on him, she said to the blonde, "I'm afraid I need to sit here for a bit to make my story plausible. Sorry about that."

The blonde smiled—a real smile this time—and said, "Why are

you apologizing? Thank you for the rescue. I deal with guys like that more often than I care to admit, but it was nice to have somebody else step in." She lowered her voice. "Poor guy didn't know what hit him. I almost felt sorry for him."

"Almost," Kayla said with a grin.

"Almost." It was the blonde's turn to hold out her hand. "London Granger," she said. "It's lovely to meet you."

"Back atcha, Ms. Granger. Can I get you another martini?"

"Actually, one needs to be my limit on these." Kayla tried to hide her disappointment, but then London said, "But I'd love a club soda. With lime. Please."

"You got it." Kayla signaled the bartender again and placed the order. Propping her chin in her hand, she asked, "So, what brings you to St. Kitts?"

"Work," London said, and something flashed across her face, zipped through her eyes. Kayla couldn't put a finger on it, though. It was gone too quickly.

"Oh? What do you do?"

"I'm a writer. I'm working on a book."

"A writer. Wow, that's amazing. I've always been in awe of people who write. Like, creating worlds and characters and plots." Kayla shook her head. "I can't even keep a journal."

London's smile was infectious. There was something about it that transformed her entire face, made her even more beautiful, and then she realized what it was: She had dimples. When London's smile was genuine, like now, her dimples showed. When she'd smiled at Bob, there had been none. She'd been dimple-less. But Kayla got the dimples and that gave her a little thrill. "I'm sorry, have we met before? You just…seem familiar to me."

"I was going to ask you the same thing, but I think I figured it out. Were you jogging on the beach this morning?"

"I was."

"That's where I saw you."

Kayla almost pointed out that since she hadn't seen London this morning, that didn't clear up why *she* thought London looked familiar. Before she could say anything, London went on.

"What about you?" she asked, pulling her back to the present. "What are you doing here on the island?"

"Oh, I'm working, too," Kayla said. "I'm in security."

London's brows rose. "Security, huh?" She glanced around the lounge. A few more patrons had shown up since Kayla'd first arrived. "Lots of famous faces here, so I'm not surprised. Are you allowed to tell me who you're…securing?"

Kayla tilted her head to the side, in Aria's direction. "Actress."

London was tasteful enough to glance, not to stare. "Oh yeah, I recognized her. She's good. She'll get an Oscar before long."

"I think so, too."

London held her gaze then. Something clicked—Kayla literally felt it somewhere within her, like some kind of swirl in her blood, and it was both exciting and alarming.

"So, security, huh?"

"Yes, ma'am."

"But your eyes have been on *me* for the past fifteen minutes…" London left the sentence dangling, but there was a spark in her eyes that told Kayla she was teasing.

Kayla moved her gaze to Bo and back as she said, "That's because my shift is over, and my colleague is watching our client." She sipped her club soda. "Can't have you thinking I'm incompetent."

"Oh, I suspect you're anything but." London's eyes held hers over the rim of her glass as she sipped.

Kayla felt her face heat up and a throbbing begin between her thighs. God, it had been a long time since she'd flirted with anybody. She forgot how much fun it could be.

"How'd you get a job in security?" London asked. "Seems like uncommon work for a woman."

"I built my own company," Kayla said, sitting up a little straighter, as she always did when talking about Tennyson Security.

London's light brows rose toward her hairline. "Really? That's impressive."

"Thanks. I'm proud of it." Kayla signaled the bartender. "I think I'm ready for a glass of wine. You?"

London glanced down at her empty club soda and nodded. "Okay. One glass."

Once they each had a glass of one of the bar's house reds—a lovely, rich zinfandel—Kayla asked, "What about you? Writing a book, huh? How'd you get into that? Can you tell me what it's about?"

A shadow of something zipped across London's beautiful face before she smiled softly and said, "I'm afraid I can't. I don't like to share anything about my work before I'm ready. As for how I got into writing, it's always been something I've enjoyed, and been pretty good at. I modeled for a few years, but that life was..." She shook her head as she gazed off into the distance.

"Boring? Horrible? Awesome?"

"Well, it definitely wasn't boring. I traveled quite a bit. But the pace was brutal. And I never felt thin enough. There were some drugs and *a lot* of smoking—both methods of appetite suppression. After a couple years, I was just unhappy and so, so tired. So I decided to make a change." Kayla waited for more, but London sipped her wine and lifted one shoulder in a half shrug.

"I admire that. It's not easy to change careers. At any age. Do you miss modeling?"

London scratched at a spot on her neck as she seemed to seriously contemplate the question, and Kayla watched her long fingers as she did. "I really liked having hair and makeup people all the time. That was pretty cool. The travel was cool. The designer clothes I got to wear. I do miss all of that a bit. I do not miss being written off as an airhead. Left out of conversations. Not taken seriously."

Kayla liked the little spark that seemed to ignite when London talked about her experiences. She had spunk. "Oh, I didn't even think of that. It really happens, huh?"

"Ugh. You'd be surprised. And it wasn't only men. Women would look right through me at times. Photographers. Producers. Agents. They'd literally talk around me like I was a toddler or something. It was infuriating." She sipped her wine. "And anytime I called somebody out on it, they'd go all wide-eyed and be mortified and fall all over themselves apologizing. Because they hadn't even realized they'd been doing it." She tipped her head to the side. "Also infuriating."

"You'd call them out?"

"God, yes."

"Okay, that's awesome." Kayla held up her glass. "To you and your…gumption."

"I love that word." London's dimples were back as she touched her glass to Kayla's. They sipped, and their gazes held fast.

Again, there was that swirling feeling that had Kayla slightly off-balance, in the best of ways. She was just about to mention it, to ask if maybe London felt it too, when London suddenly set her glass down and slid off her stool. "I'm afraid I need to call it a night."

"Well, that's too bad." Kayla tried to hide her disappointment as well as her surprise at the sudden end to their conversation.

"Thank you for the wine," London said, and the appearance of the dimples gave Kayla at least a tiny inkling of relief.

"You're welcome. Maybe I'll see you again."

"Maybe I'll come jogging with you in the morning."

"You'd be more than welcome."

There was a beat where London didn't move, just looked at her. Then she blinked rapidly, as if coming out of a trance, smiled briefly, and left.

Kayla watched her go, feeling an odd mix of disappointment and possibility. When she glanced toward the corner of the bar, Bo was watching her with a knowing grin.

He held up his glass of water in salute.

CHAPTER FOUR

Sleep had not come easily to London on Saturday night, which hadn't been the case for Miranda. By the time London returned to their suite, Miranda had already turned in for the night, having had an online meeting with some of her employees. That was why London had had time to herself—and it wasn't lost on her that Miranda'd held a meeting on a Saturday night. Maybe days of the week didn't matter when you were rolling in money?

She'd headed straight to her own room and tried to go over the notes she'd taken so far. Observations from the day at the beach, dinner, how people seemed to know what Miranda wanted before she asked for it. It was all kind of surreal, and she'd relished her time alone at the bar, a chance to breathe and remember who she was and where she came from.

And then Kayla Tennyson entered the picture.

London lay in her bed now—her giant California king, sheets so soft she probably couldn't count high enough to reach the thread count—doors open again so she could hear the roar of the ocean waves, and the only thing her mind would let her focus on was Kayla.

First of all, what right did the woman have to be that imposingly good-looking? She was very tall—had to be six feet—and so damn sexy. Dark hair that skimmed her shoulders. Deep, dark eyes that London could drown in if she let herself. Her voice was low, a little husky, stupidly sexy. London had had to make a conscious effort to *not* stare at the woman's mouth every time she spoke.

She was so London's type. She loved that athletic build. That subtle strength that told her Kayla could pin her to a wall. Or a bed...

She groaned. Quietly, but still. The clock on the bedside table said it was four seventeen in the morning, and London was pretty sure she'd been awake, tossing and turning and having sex fantasies for about ninety percent of the night.

This was so *not* what she needed.

Well.

It actually was *exactly* what she needed. She hadn't had good sex in a long time. Hell, she hadn't had any sex in a long time. Yeah, she could certainly use that. But it was so not what she needed in relation to what she was doing there. In that resort. On that island. With Miranda Northbrooke. Kayla Tennyson was a complication and nothing more.

"A very sexy minor complication," she whispered into the dark as she slipped her fingers between her legs and found a shocking amount of wetness there. "Damn it."

She came hard and fast.

❖

She beat Miranda to the sundeck Sunday morning, and Miranda's surprise was clear on her face.

It was five thirty, and London had been in the lounge chair for nearly an hour, still unable to get any sleep, even after the orgasm that nearly blew the top of her head off and had her biting down on her pillow to keep from screaming out her pleasure.

Fantasy Kayla sure was good in the sack. Wow.

She was grinning about that when Miranda appeared, wrapped in a fluffy white robe.

"Goodness, you're up early." She took the lounge next to London and sat with a steaming cup of coffee. As she held it up, she said, "Room service brought a fresh pot, and Chef Marco made croissants if you're hungry."

Chef Marco was baking this early? Once again, London was

surprised by the level of service. How early did the staff of the Bella Grande get up?

"I'm too comfy to get up." Miranda pulled her cell out of the pocket of her robe, and somehow, London just knew she was going to wake up Ethan and ask him to bring breakfast out onto the sundeck, so she reached over and put her hand on Miranda's arm. "It's okay. I'm good. I'll get up and get something in a bit." When she felt Miranda stiffen, she added, "Thank you, though," and smiled.

Miranda seemed to relax.

She thought she should ask how the meeting went the night before, but it was so peaceful and quiet on the sundeck that she kept the question in. Instead, they sat in the silence and watched the sun rise up over the ocean. It was breathtaking.

"You're good company, London," Miranda said, finally breaking the silence. "You know when to talk, and you know when to keep quiet."

London squinted as she gazed out over the water. What a weird compliment. Wait, was it a compliment? If nothing else, it was a little taste of what Miranda Northbrooke expected from a partner—knowing when to shut up. "Thank you," she said because what else could she say?

"How do you feel about doing a little shopping today?" Miranda asked a few moments later. "There are some lovely boutiques in Port Zante. We can go there and wander around, then have lunch. There are some wonderful local crafts you might find interesting."

A chance to get out of the resort and into the actual culture of St. Kitts sounded terrific. It would also help her make sure to have a well-rounded setting for her article and book. With a nod, she said, "That sounds great."

They made a plan, deciding they'd come back to the Bella Grande for the afternoon so they could both work, Miranda telling her she had a handful of calls to make and an assistant to check in with. One thing London was finding interesting was her own assumption that a vacation with a supremely wealthy person would be just that, a vacation. She hadn't expected Miranda to work as much as she had, even two days in.

"I'll text Ethan," Miranda said as she hauled herself out of her lounge and headed inside.

Poor Ethan. This was certainly not a vacation for him, was it? She wondered if she could find some time to chat with him, just to get some insight into what he did for Miranda, how he did it, and how he felt about it.

The sun had fully crested the horizon, and London sighed as she pushed to her feet, sad to leave such a beautiful view, even knowing she'd come back to it later. In her room, a simple glance at the bed had her reliving her early morning fantasy and its result. A gentle throbbing began low in her body, and she gave herself a shake. She hoped getting away from the resort for a while would take her mind off a certain tall, dark, arrestingly beautiful woman because this kind of distraction was the last thing she needed.

She was here to do a job.

Damn it.

❖

The stretches Kayla, Bo, and Jake worked were very doable, eight-hour shifts. Because Kayla'd had the night off, she took the first shift on Sunday. She'd be off by two, and Jake would take over. Bo was a night owl and very much preferred the overnight shifts, the weirdo.

So she sat now, outside in the morning sun, a table away from Aria, Cammie, and Haley, keeping an eye on them, hearing their voices but not actively listening in on their conversations. That was a talent you had to work hard on in security. No client wanted to think they were being eavesdropped on, but when you had to stay close, it was hard not to listen in, even unintentionally. Kayla had learned to tune out most of it while still paying attention. She sipped her coffee and kept an eye not on the girls, but on the people around the girls. Security was more about who was nearby, who was close, who was too close.

This was going to be a pretty easy gig, though. So far, there'd been nobody even bordering on suspicious. She was familiar with a couple of Aria's fans who were a bit too much, ones that didn't understand boundaries, ones that felt they knew her, even though they didn't. She, Bo, and Jake all had photos on their phones in case one of these people—three men, one woman—had somehow managed to figure out where Aria was. Not that it would be hard, given the photos she'd posted on her Instagram account yesterday. Kayla was still debating whether or not to talk to her about that. Damn social media made it way too easy to track somebody down.

The waiter stopped by and refilled her coffee, asked if she wanted anything else. She didn't, but as she sipped the much hotter beverage, her mind wandered to the alarmingly gorgeous woman from last night. London Granger. What a cool and unique name. It felt good in her mouth. And yes, she'd gone right to the social media she cursed and googled her. There wasn't a whole lot of personal data—which she was secretly proud of London for—but a bit of professional stuff. She hadn't been lying about her modeling days. Kayla had spent far too long searching for photo shoots and ads London had featured in. Perfume, makeup, designer clothing. She'd done a lot for what seemed to be about five years, and then it just stopped. She worked for *The New and The Now*, writing what seemed to be fluff pieces about dating and which running shoes were best and which astrological signs were most compatible. And despite having no idea what kind of a writer London was, Kayla was immediately indignant for her.

Then she'd searched for articles and had spent a couple hours reading her work.

She was a damn good writer, even when she was writing fluff.

The irony of what she'd been doing was not lost on her, basically cyberstalking a woman just as others cyberstalked her clients, and now she shook her head and smiled to herself as she sipped her coffee and wondered if she'd run into Ms. Granger again this week.

She hoped so.

"Kay," Aria called, yanking Kayla out of the beginnings of

a very nice fantasy. Probably for the best. She moved to the table where the trio sat. "Wanna go to the rainforest today?"

"Aria. You don't have to ask me what I want to do, you know. This is your vacation. I'm just tagging along." She said it gently because she wasn't trying to chastise her client who was becoming a friend. It was more a reminder.

Aria's grin was cute, as was the slight blush that tinted her cheeks pink. "I know. I just don't want to drag you there if you'd rather not."

"Do you want to see the rainforest?" she asked, looking from Aria to Haley to Cammie and back.

"I really, really do," Aria said, and her girls nodded with enthusiasm.

"Then let's do the rainforest."

About forty-five minutes later, the foursome met up in the lobby and waited for the ride Aria had ordered. She'd also gotten them a guide, saying she was kind of a nature buff and wanted somebody to tell her about the plant life.

"I wouldn't have pegged you as a tree lover," Kayla said as they headed toward the front doors. "You seem like such a city girl."

"Oh, I love the city, don't get me wrong. Living in LA is fine, and if I could live in New York? I'd be in heaven." She sighed a dreamy sigh. "One day. But I grew up in the country. My parents have fifteen acres, and it's mostly woods. I've climbed more trees than I can count. Country roads are in my blood."

"I have new respect for you," Kayla said with a laugh, and then the sound died in her throat as she caught a flash of a reflection in the window. No, it couldn't be. She glanced over her shoulder quickly, and sure enough, the glimpse was enough to confirm that she had indeed seen what she'd thought she'd seen. Or *who* she'd thought she'd seen. Miranda Northbrooke, standing near a pillar, looking down at the phone in her hand.

Goddamn it.

What were the chances? Like, fucking seriously, what were the odds of Miranda Fucking Northbrooke being on St. Kitts during the very same week Kayla was working there? *Really, Universe? We're playing this game now?*

"Hello? Earth to Kayla?" Aria's voice brought her out of her mental disappointment.

"Yeah. Yeah, sorry. What?"

"I asked if you've been to the rainforest here before?"

Her brain tossed her an image then, walking hand in hand through the lush green, listening to sounds that you'd never, ever hear back home in New York, stopping beneath a huge tree and finding her back pressed against the trunk while she was soundly, thoroughly, passionately kissed.

"Just once," she said, then praised the stars above when their ride pulled up. "A long time ago."

It was a time she'd shoved way back into a deep, dark corner of her mind, and she tried hard not to go there. Revisiting led her nowhere good.

"And?" Claire asked, her voice sounding so close and normal that London almost forgot there was a four-hour flight and a sea between them. "How's it going? What's it *really* like to be a billionaire?"

London chuckled into her cell as she sat on the patio of one of the restaurants in the resort and sipped a lovely green tea. "It's only been two days, so it's hard to say, but God, Claire, it's freaking gorgeous here. The views are all of the ocean. On the horizon, you can see the island of Nevis, which is sort of a sister island to St. Kitts. The resort is stunning." She lowered her voice. "There are several celebrities here."

"I read it's a popular vacation spot for them. Who have you seen?"

She lowered her voice even more and rattled off the names of several famous people she'd noticed, including a couple athletes, a famous chef, and three actors.

"Wow. That's so cool."

London was used to seeing famous faces, given where she worked, but Claire was always a little starstruck, even after living in New York City for more than five years and working in the literary world. "It's fun."

"And how is the obscenely wealthy Ms. Northbrooke? Has it been weird spending time with somebody you don't know? It must be."

"She's actually pretty easy to hang with." She told Claire about the gentleman on the beach and how he was an ex of Miranda's. "And she's…" God, how did one describe Miranda Northbrooke in a few words? "Interesting. A little cool. Used to getting what she wants when she wants it, no matter the time of day or day of the week. She's been nothing but nice to me, though. And she's been nice to all the staff so far."

"It's still early in the trip."

"True." London realized both she and Claire sounded like they wanted Miranda to exhibit some undesirable behavior. It *would* spice up her story, that was true, but she knew she'd also be disappointed if she saw Miranda treat somebody poorly. She thought of poor Ethan. "She does have an assistant who I think might be a robot."

Claire laughed softly. "Oh, really?"

"His name's Ethan and he's literally at her beck and call. Like, she thinks nothing of texting him in the middle of the night to have him do something for her."

"I mean, maybe he gets paid enough to warrant that?"

"Huh. I suppose that's possible." London looked down at the notes she'd been jotting before Claire called. "I met this woman last night." The words were out before she even realized she was going to say them.

Claire gasped. "I'm sorry, what?"

London chuckled. "I met a woman last night. In the bar. Miranda had a Zoom meeting, and I didn't want to get stuck in the suite, so I headed to the bar for a martini."

"Oh, I could go for a martini right now." Claire's voice was wistful.

"It's not even noon there." London laughed.

"Listen, it's Sunday and brunch is a thing. Tell me about the girl. I demand it."

London relayed the story of being hit on by the drunk guy and how Kayla had come to her rescue.

"Oh, she's the chivalrous kind," Claire said. "I love that."

"God, Claire, if you could've seen her. I'm not sure I've ever seen a woman this beautiful."

"You were in the modeling world, so that says a lot."

London scoffed. "Models are way too thin. They're like stick figures. This woman? Solid. Lean but solid. I could tell by looking at her arms that she could bench-press me in a heartbeat and still be pretty while doing it."

"Oh my. Tall or short?"

"Taller than me."

"Wow, that's tall. Light? Dark?"

"Dark. Dark hair, deep tan, dark eyes. God…"

"You sound smitten, my friend. Will you see her again?"

London let herself sigh, knowing it would give away much of how she was feeling about her one meeting with Kayla Tennyson. "I don't know. I'm here working. She's here working. It may not be possible. Plus, I'm supposed to be here for Miranda. I can't exactly be on the prowl, you know?"

"Sweetie, you wouldn't know how to be on the prowl if I gave you a how-to manual."

"Shut up. I can prowl."

"No. You cannot. You're a hopeless prowler."

London conceded with another sigh. "You're right."

"What does she do? How is she there working?" A little intake of air came over the phone as Claire asked excitedly, "Is she a bajillionaire, too?"

"I don't think so. She's in security. In fact, she's doing security for Aria Keller."

"The actress? The one who was in that movie about the stalker?"

"Yep. Kayla's her bodyguard. Well, one of them. While Aria is here on vacation."

"That is *so cool*. I'm so jealous of you right now."

"Please. You're jealous of me all the time."

"I mean, it's true."

They talked about a few more things, mundane life stuff, and then hung up. London thanked the waiter when he brought her another pot of hot water and a selection of tea bags. If she drank more tea, she'd float right off the patio, but she wasn't ready to leave the stunning view quite yet.

She glanced around several times, trying not to appear to be looking for anybody, though that was exactly what she was doing. She hoped she'd maybe see Kayla Tennyson again, wandering around or lurking in a dark corner, keeping an eye on her client, but no such luck. She frowned just as her phone pinged a text.

Was thinking. You never talk about a girl you just met like you did about this one. Might be worth pursuing. Just sayin'...

Was it? Worth pursuing? The logistics were not ideal. She wasn't here to hook up. And somehow, she was pretty sure Miranda Northbrooke wouldn't be all *Sure, go find yourself a date while you're here as my traveling companion. Be my guest.*

She might need to let this go.

And then she thought about sitting next to Kayla Tennyson last night, thought about her dark eyes, how they'd never left hers, how closely she'd paid attention to everything London had said, how London had felt like there was nobody else in the world right then for Kayla, how *seen* Kayla had made her feel.

It had been a long time since somebody had been that focused on her.

And as she sat there and thought about the last time anybody had made her feel that important—had anybody *ever* made her feel that important?—she realized something else: She wanted to know much more about Kayla Tennyson. What was her favorite color? What did she love about her job? If she could go anywhere in the world, where would she go? What were her dreams? What was her favorite snack food? Where did she see herself in five years? She wanted to know so much more.

She wanted to know everything.

A small groan escaped her lips as she understood how impossible it would be to get all her questions answered. At least here. No, she had to put it out of her mind. She had to send Kayla to the spot in her brain where stuff she'd deal with later went. Things like calling her mother. Finding a new dentist. Learning how to cook. Kayla would be in good company.

The waiter returned to check on her, and she told him she was finished. Because she was. With her tea and with this entire train of thought.

She had to be.

Picking up her notebook and her bag, she stood, took a last look at the breathtaking view, and headed inside the Bella Grande. It was time to find Miranda Northbrooke and get to work. It's why she was there. It was time to do her job.

The rainforest had been just as gorgeous as Kayla remembered when she'd been there two years ago. The sounds, the smells, the colors. All the same. All rich and lush and beautiful.

She couldn't wait to leave.

Kudos to the guide Aria had hired, though. He really knew his stuff. He answered all Aria's questions about this plant and that tree. Cammie and Haley were clearly in awe of the place. It was the quietest Haley had been since Kayla had met her. She simply looked around, wide-eyed, and paid very close attention to everything the guide said. Nice to know some things that weren't electronic could still capture the attention of young people.

God, she sounded like her mother.

That thought made her grin, and she managed to get through the rest of the guided tour without whining. Or rolling her eyes. Or crying. Once their ride pulled back up to the front doors of the Bella Grande, she had to consciously stifle her sigh of relief. The tour had taken up the entire morning, and they were well past lunchtime now. She texted Jake to see if he could take over soon so she could do some work in her room. As she knew he would, he stepped right up, then she bade a temporary farewell to the trio of girls and headed to her room.

She didn't have a suite like Aria did. She had a more modest room. While it didn't have its own private pool, it did have a balcony and a lovely view of the ocean and beach, so she ordered some iced tea along with some cheese, crackers, and fruit from room service, took her laptop out onto the sundeck, and set herself up to do some work. The beach was sparsely populated, something else she loved about the Bella Grande. It had its own private stretch of beach, so you could walk it or lie on it or build a sandcastle and never have to worry about feeling crowded.

God, the view here was…beyond. Kayla had traveled to a lot of different places on the job. Paris. Vancouver. Madrid. Istanbul. And they were all gorgeous in their own way. She'd never really considered herself a beach girl, but there was something about the ocean here. The rumble of the waves and the shade of blue of the water and the clean sand and the swaying trees. It was easily one of the most peaceful places she'd ever been.

Room service came quickly and set up a second table next to the one she was at. The waiter spread out her food in an impressive show of presentation—cheeses and crackers and spreads—poured her iced tea into a clear highball glass, and asked if she needed anything else. She tipped him, thanked him, and settled in to get some work done.

Kayla didn't always take the lead with a client like she had with Aria. More often than not, she delegated things to her nearly fifty other staff members. As her company had grown, it had become clear there was no possible way she could be personally involved in every operation. As she sat, there were ten other clients on three continents being taken care of by Tennyson Security. Actors, politicians, musicians, athletes, businesspeople, she had a wide variety of clients. Word of mouth was key in that world, so she was super particular in who she hired. So far, she'd gotten nothing but raves about her people.

Calling up her finance app, she got to work on invoicing. It was both her favorite and least favorite part of owning a business. She loved getting money in but hated asking for it, even if it was earned.

She nibbled cheese and sipped iced tea as the warm ocean breeze lifted her hair off her neck and rearranged it. She finished invoicing and was answering an email when she glanced up at the beach and saw a familiar figure wandering along the sand.

And that was weird, wasn't it? That she knew in a glance that it was London Granger? Granted, her room wasn't on a higher floor like Aria's was—she was only on the third—but still. She recognized the blond hair being tousled by the ocean breeze. She recognized the gait, the stride of long legs that she'd barely seen the night before. How was it possible that she knew it was London?

But she did.

It was absolutely her. She knew it in her soul.

And before she even realized what she was doing, she had closed up her finance app and was shutting down her laptop. She took everything inside, locked her laptop in its case, and stopped in front of the mirror. With a glance down at her sundress, she wondered if she should change, but there was no time. Maybe London wasn't staying on the beach. Maybe she was simply out for a walk and was actually headed back to the resort right now, tired of the sand and sun. Maybe she was crossing the beach because she was meeting someone. Kayla fluffed her hair, not letting herself think about that. She slicked on a quick coat of lip gloss, stepped into her sandals, and muttered, "It's gonna have to do."

She was out the door five seconds later, not bothering to wait for the elevator, instead taking the stairs, which she had located as soon as her room was assigned. Then she passed through the lobby and headed for the beach exit of the resort, hoping hard that London was still strolling through the sand. A glance back up at the building oriented her to where her room was and gave her a rough idea where she'd seen London walking and in which direction. She hurried that way.

Toward the end of the stretch of beach owned by Bella Grande was yet another bar—a tiki bar, this time, complete with tiki torches and coconut shell decor. Totally hokey. Absolutely fun. And there at the corner under the thatched roof in the shade, a coconut shell in front of her with a purple umbrella sticking out of it, sat London. She didn't see Kayla right away, so Kayla quickly slowed her pace, put on her *Who, me? I was just wandering this way and hey, what a fun coincidence that you're here, too!* face, and strolled up.

"We meet again," she said once she was closer to London, who looked up, wide-eyed and…was that happiness? Delight even? Might've been. Might've also been Kayla's wishful thinking.

"Hi," London said, her smile wide, and yeah, it was definitely delight. Kayla felt her insides warm as London patted the seat next to her. "Sit with me?"

"As long as I'm not interrupting anything."

London held up her coconut shell drink. "It's just me and my tropical umbrella drink. Nothing to interrupt. Sit. Please."

Kayla sat, and the bartender came over.

London looked at Kayla and held up her drink. "Don't let a girl drink from a coconut alone."

"Oh, we can't have that." She pointed to London's drink and to the bartender said, "One of those, please." He gave a nod and went to work. "So, what brings you to the end of the beach?"

London seemed to ponder the question. "Curiosity? A desire to walk? Boredom?"

"Boredom? Here in paradise?"

London's sigh was wistful. "I know. Silly, isn't it? This beach is just gorgeous, but I've never really been a lie in the sun girl."

"With that skin and that tan?" The words were out of Kayla's mouth before she could think about them.

But London laughed. "The tan is lucky genes. The skin is from a very diligent skin care regimen."

"That you learned in the modeling world?"

"From my mother, actually."

"Really?" Kayla's drink arrived, her umbrella pink. The liquid inside was white and creamy looking.

"I have no idea what it is, but it's delicious," London offered.

Kayla held hers up. "To moms who know skin care." They

touched coconut shells together, then each sipped from her straw. "Oh, wow. You weren't kidding. That's yummy." She sipped again. "So, you were saying your mom helped you with your skin care?"

"She's an aesthetician. Knows everything there is to know about skin and skin care. I was never let out of the house without being slathered with sunscreen."

"Smart of her."

"I think skin cancer is her biggest fear. Like, it's almost laughable. My dad teases her mercilessly."

"I bet he's got great skin, though."

"People are shocked when he tells them he's sixty." London slipped her phone out of her small bag and scrolled through her photos until she found what she was looking for and held it up for Kayla to see. The man had sandy hair shot through with a bit of silver. He had crow's feet around his dancing blue eyes, likely made more prominent by his wide smile, but no other wrinkles to be seen. "Wow. I'd have put him in his late forties. And you look just like him."

London grinned. "Been told that my whole life." She put her phone back in her bag. "What about your parents? Are you close?"

"It's just me and my mom. And yeah, we're very tight. Talk every day. Spend time together. She's awesome."

"That's great. I have so many friends who just can't relate to their parents at all. Makes me sad. What about your dad?"

It was a question that always came up eventually when she was talking to somebody new. And it was always a little uncomfortable. But not this time. Not with London, for some reason. "I never knew my dad. He was a fling my mom had in college. They were both drunk. He wasn't interested in being a father, so he wasn't."

London grimaced. "I'm sorry about that."

Kayla shrugged, her standard response to the subject. "Don't be. My mom took great care of me, and we have a great relationship."

And then London laid a warm hand on her bare arm, and the contact was like a gentle sizzle of electricity. "Still."

"Thanks." That sat quietly for a moment, and Kayla was also surprised by how easy it was. Not an uncomfortable silence.

She didn't feel the need to fill it. It was…what was that word? Companionable. That was it. A companionable silence. She suddenly had a vision of the two of them on a couch. Opposite ends, so their feet were mingling in the center. Each of them had a book. Quiet instrumental music played from some unseen speaker. She glanced up from her book to see London looking back at her, nibbling on a thumbnail, one eyebrow arched…

"Hey, you okay?" London's voice brought her back to the beach. "I didn't mean to offend you. I'm really sorry if I did."

"Oh God, no. Not at all." She smiled at London. "There's nothing to be offended about. No worries." London's relief was obvious, and that made Kayla feel good. She sipped her drink. "It's always been just me and my mom. Her parents divorced when she was young. Her dad moved to England and started another family, so their relationship was always kind of surface. My grandmother died when I was a teenager. So, really, it's just been my mom and me for most of my life."

London raised her coconut shell. "To only children."

"Ah, you, too?" Kayla touched hers to London's again.

"Yup. I was a rough pregnancy and my mom had to have a hysterectomy not long after I was born. So it's just me."

"Did your mom want more kids?" Kayla asked the question gently, as she knew it was none of her business.

London tipped her head. "I don't honestly know. My parents always talk about how perfect I am, and they did one and done." She laughed then, and it was a pretty, musical sound that Kayla instantly adored.

"No more needed."

"Right?"

They sat in silence again, and again, it was comfortable and peaceful. Kayla's drink was nearly gone, as was London's, and they sipped together.

"Wanna walk?" London asked suddenly. And suddenly, Kayla wanted nothing more.

"Absolutely."

London signed the drinks to her room, and Kayla noticed the

room number without meaning to. Memorized it. Filed it away in her brain. Occupational hazard. "Ready?"

"Yes, ma'am."

Kayla could honestly say that when she created the contract for Aria Keller and booked her room at the Bella Grande, walking on the beach with a beautiful woman who interested her beyond measure was the farthest thing from her mind. The least expected thing. And yet, here she was, her sandals dangling from her fingers, walking next to one of the most magnetic humans she'd ever met. How did she get here?

She glanced at London out of the corner of her eye, not wanting to look like she was gawking—which was what she really wanted to do. She wanted to rake her eyes over every inch of London Granger. Take her in. Memorize every slope. Every curve. Instead, she settled for glimpses here and there. A toned calf. A freckled shoulder. Blond hair being stroked by the ocean breeze. London had slipped her sunglasses back on, so her eyes were shuttered, but the rest of her was glorious, right down to her feet, her toes painted a deep burgundy.

"I love to walk," London said, snapping Kayla back to her face.

"Yeah? Me, too. It's a good way to clear your head."

"Exactly. And I live in New York City, so walking is part of life."

"You do?" Kayla tried to hide her excitement. "Me, too."

London turned to face her, smile wide, straight white teeth gleaming. "Seriously?"

"Seriously. Honestly? I wouldn't live anywhere else. I love it."

"Are you from there?"

"I'm from New York, but not New York City. Upstate. A little town called Northwood. My mom's still there but is headed to Florida soon for the winter." London grimaced, which made Kayla laugh. "Oh, I agree. Trust me. The politics there is crazy right now. And it's so humid. Don't get me started on what that state does to my hair."

London laughed again. "I find it hard to believe that you are ever anything but gorgeous." Then her eyes went wide, as if she hadn't meant to say the words out loud, and Kayla burst out laughing. London flushed the most beautiful shade of pink, circles blossoming on her cheeks. "I'm sorry, that was…inappropriate."

"Listen, I'm not the least bit offended, so don't worry." She glanced down at her feet as they sank in the sand. "Thank you."

Conversation stopped for a bit, and they walked and listened to the roar of the ocean waves. There were very few other people on the beach, which was odd and awesome at the same time, because Kayla felt like it was just the three of them, her and London and the ocean. And the level of peace it gave her was astounding. She had no idea what the hell that was about, but she also didn't want it to end. There was something about being around London Granger that made everything in her…settle. In the best of ways.

They reached the part of the beach leading into the resort, and London waved absently in the direction of the building. "Well, I should probably go inside, get some work done."

"Yeah, me, too," Kayla said, then rolled her eyes at herself because she'd left that work just to sprint down to the beach to see London. And yeah, she really should get back to it. But neither of them moved or seemed in a hurry to. She was just about to ask London if she could see her again when London's phone buzzed. She grabbed it out of her bag, looked at it, and frowned.

"Oh God, I really need to go," she said, and with a quick little wave and an "I'm so sorry," she turned and hurried into the resort before Kayla could say another word. She could only stand there and watch her go, everything she wanted to say stuck in her throat.

When the doors drifted shut behind London, Kayla inhaled deeply and sighed. "Well, damn."

❖

Later that night, London was seated at the dinner table with Miranda, Ethan, and a couple named Anna and Richard Stevenson. According to Miranda, they were old friends of her parents, and they just happened to be on St. Kitts the same time Miranda was. Her mother had asked her to dine with them.

"My mother is always trying to marry me off, always hoping I'll find a nice guy and finally settle down," Miranda said as they got ready earlier. "Let's give her something to wonder about." London wasn't exactly sure what that meant, and then Miranda'd cackled evilly—yes, actually cackled, like Ursula in *The Little Mermaid*—at the thought. "Follow my lead."

Initially, London had balked internally at fooling these poor elderly folks. Anna walked with a cane and Richard was slightly stooped. They had to be in their eighties if they were a day. Anna had gorgeous silver hair, done up in a French twist. Richard was bald but sported a goatee that actually looked perfect on his face. She heard Claire's voice in her head saying, *Yeah, very few men can pull off a goatee, you know. Kevin Costner can. My dad cannot.* But Richard Stevenson totally could.

Miranda had introduced London as her date for the week. "She's a model and very successful writer." Well, half right. Almost. Okay, not really. She was a former model and a writer who managed to pay her bills, but who was she to argue. Miranda had told her to follow her lead, and that's essentially what she was being paid to do, so she would.

It didn't take long for her to see the true colors of the Stevensons, though, and they were not bright and celebratory ones. They were dark and ugly. The first shocking example came when Anna referred to a member of the waitstaff—the majority of whom were Black—as *those people.* After that, Richard and Miranda got into a debate about housing insecurity. Richard's attitude could not have been more old white guy stereotypical if he'd been trying his hardest. Because according to him, they should just get jobs, for cryin' out loud. He was about to launch into a soliloquy about how Ukraine was getting what it deserved when Miranda thankfully cut him off by inquiring about her parents.

"How are Mother and Daddy anyway? I haven't seen them in ages. I owe them a phone call soon."

It was the perfect segue, and Anna began telling a story of how she'd been at a charity luncheon recently with Miranda's mother. That's exactly when Miranda decided to reach for London's hand

and entwine their fingers. Anna's eyes went right to them like a magnet to metal, but she never faltered in her story, never missed a beat. As Richard talked of his latest round of golf with Miranda's dad, Miranda let go of London's hand and, instead, draped her arm across the back of London's chair. It was a possessive move, and the Stevensons both saw it as such, London could tell by their expressions—though she might not have if she hadn't been looking. A slight widening of the eyes. A clear of a throat. A glance down at their hands.

Dinner with this couple would've been excruciating if London hadn't been utterly fascinated by them. They were old money, clearly. Anna talked endlessly about her charity work, but never about an actual career. Richard was the same. He ran a foundation—the basis of which London was absolutely confused by—but that was about it, and it made her wonder how they identified. She herself was a former model and a writer. Miranda's family owned a media conglomerate, and yes, she'd inherited her wealth, but she also worked. Hard. London had seen it. She also couldn't help but bristle at the irony of Anna's charity work, while she simultaneously made racist comments. London wondered if she even understood. While she couldn't exactly take notes, she did her best to memorize everything she heard and to formulate some topic headings based on this evening.

Later, after having bid farewell to the Stevensons, Miranda suggested they move to the bar, then ordered them very dirty martinis.

"My God, those two," Miranda said quietly, shaking her head as she took a sip of her cocktail.

London nodded, not sure how free she was to speak, given the Stevensons were old family friends.

"They're insufferable, aren't they?" London nodded again, and this time, Miranda looked at her. "Safe space here, London. You're not going to hurt my feelings if you call them walking, talking stereotypes of wealthy, racist white folk."

London exhaled loudly and said, "Oh my God, they were total walking, talking stereotypes of wealthy, racist white folk." They both laughed, and London went on. "Holy shit. I have never seen people miss the irony train so spectacularly. Wow." She took a slug of her martini, because good Lord, she needed it.

"Awful people, both of them. I swear, Anna does charity work just to make sure she gets into heaven."

London barked a laugh.

"It's true. Do you think she actually gives a crap about the plight of *those people*?" She made the air quotes.

"God, I couldn't believe she actually used those words," London said.

"She wants to write a check so she can check that box. That's all."

"Well, you ladies seem to be having a lovely time." The gentleman who'd been sitting two stools down decided to slide closer to them, his forearms on the bar. He waved a finger at the bartender, and it wasn't long before two more martinis appeared. "Where are you from?"

London felt Miranda bristle next to her, and she put a hand on her arm before turning a smile to the man, her manners winning out. "New York. You?"

"Philly. Not far from you at all."

"No. Not far."

"We could meet up. I could take you to dinner." He seemed to realize he was only talking to London and leaned back to see Miranda. "Both of you."

Miranda sipped her martini and didn't look at him.

He leaned in closer to London. "Kinda unusual to come across single women in a place like this." He made a show of looking at London's hand. "No wedding rings. On either of you." He looked extremely satisfied with himself at his observation, and he sipped his drink without breaking eye contact.

That's when London felt Miranda's arm slide around the small of her back, similar to what she'd done at dinner but far less subtle, and pull her closer. She put her other hand on London's forearm and leaned forward so she could meet the man's gaze. London realized she was getting a taste of Miranda Northbrooke at her finest.

"What makes you think no wedding ring means we're single?" The man opened his mouth to speak but closed it again. This happened two or three times until he looked a bit like a fish out of water. His face turned red, and he glanced down at the bar. "I'm so sorry," he said. "I didn't think that you two…it didn't occur to me that…" He shook his head. "Forgive me. So sorry." Not only did he slide back down the bar, but he downed the rest of his drink and hurried out of the room.

London watched his exit. "I think you made him cry," she said quietly.

Miranda's laugh was soft, and she let go of London. "I'm sorry about that. I just…" She shook her head with a sigh, and London was surprised to realize that she was bothered. Not so much angry as uncomfortable. Slightly shaken. "This is part of why I don't like to travel alone."

"I never thought of that," London said, and it was the truth. "I think I'm just so used to it." She grimaced and took another sip of her drink. "How sad is that?"

"It's infuriating." They were quiet for a moment before Miranda spoke again. "What if…" She turned to look London in the eye. "Listen. I'm very much enjoying your company, but I need you to understand that there's nothing more than that."

London squinted at her. "*Okay.*" She drew the word out, not sure where this was going.

"No, no." Miranda wiped a hand in front of her as if erasing her words. "No, I mean…what if we presented as a couple? Just for instances like that? For deterring Mr. Philadelphia and men like him?" She jerked a thumb over her shoulder. "Like we did at dinner."

"Oh!" London laughed and sipped her drink. "Sure. That's a great idea. If one of us needs rescuing, we swoop in."

"Exactly." Miranda held up her glass. "To rescuing each other when necessary."

"I will drink to that."

They clinked glasses.

"Speaking of dinner, my next call with my mother will be interesting." Her grin seemed very satisfied to London.

"Do your parents not know you're…bi?" She hazarded a guess, based on the guy on the beach yesterday and Miranda's performance at dinner tonight.

"Oh, they know. Of course they know. I've told them a million times. They just don't like it. My mother thinks if she's not aware of my dating life, it doesn't exist. Trust me, Anna will make sure she's aware of it." She sipped. "And you?"

London smiled. "I like girls."

"I thought so." Miranda didn't say anything more or explain how she knew, so London accepted she must have exceptionally good gaydar.

They finished their drinks and headed back to their suite. They were quiet the entire elevator ride, London suddenly very tired. As they exited and walked down the hall, they passed Aria Keller and two other girls with her, plus the very large and imposing man from the bar the other night. One of Kayla's employees, London recalled.

Miranda turned her head to follow them so fast, London was surprised she didn't get whiplash. "That was the actress," Miranda murmured.

London nodded and kept her voice low. "Aria Keller."

"She's even more striking in person." Miranda's voice had a slightly dreamy edge to it. "Gorgeous."

"She's super attractive. Agreed."

The elevator dinged and the foursome got on. As the doors slid closed, Miranda handed her bag and her wrap to London. She stood up straight and her voice took on an authoritative tone this time. "I think I'm going to go down and grab a nightcap at the bar. Be a dear and take my stuff back to the suite with you, would you?" She didn't wait for an answer, just turned on her Jimmy Choo heel and hustled to the elevator.

London stood there and blinked for a moment as Miranda got on the elevator without so much as a glance back. "Well, okay then," she muttered. With a sigh, she headed into the suite.

❖

Kayla had the night off.

She never really knew what to do with that when she wasn't at home. Should she rent a movie on the hotel TV? Should she read a book? She always had her Kindle with her, and reading was a favorite escape. But she didn't really feel like reading tonight. Her brain was too busy with other things, and she didn't think she'd be able to concentrate on a story. When she felt like this—full-headed—she knew it was best to just sit quietly and let her thoughts play out until they calmed.

So, she poured herself a scotch from the bottle she'd purchased downstairs, took it out to the sundeck—which her brain now renamed the moondeck, as it was fully dark—made herself comfortable on a lounge, and simply relaxed. Listened to the ocean. Felt the warm breeze on her bare legs. Gazed at the stars—God, so many stars here!—and let her mind wander.

She knew exactly where it would go, and it didn't disappoint her. London Granger's face materialized in her head, those sparkling blue eyes and full lips and blond hair blowing gently in the breeze. How this woman had managed to affect her so intensely, she wasn't sure, and she found it slightly disconcerting. Kayla Tennyson was a woman in control. Of everything. Her business. Her life. Her heart.

Okay, clearly not that last one.

Before she could analyze further, her phone pinged an incoming text. Bo.

Thought you should know, your ex is here hitting on the tiny package.

Kayla inhaled deeply and blew it out. She was hoping not to have any run-ins with Miranda. She really would've liked to not deal with her at all. As it was, Miranda hadn't seen her, and she honestly wasn't sure if she'd recognize Bo. If you didn't affect Miranda's immediate world, she barely noticed you existed, and Bo fell into that category. She texted back.

Aria can take care of herself, but keep an eye on things. If she starts to look uncomfortable or needs rescuing, let me know and I'll come down.

She knew Aria and her girls had wanted to have drinks at the bar and sit outside to watch the ocean at night. She felt bad that she was now being annoyed by Miranda, and she could totally picture the whole setup. Miranda would've sent drinks first. For the table, because she wouldn't want to alienate the friends of her target. She'd send something expensive, like a bottle of Dom Pérignon. Miranda knew her wines and bubblies and she'd know exactly which year to request. Once her gift was delivered and poured, she'd make her way over to the table and educate them on the wine she'd picked and why. Of course, Aria would ask her to join them. She was unfailingly polite and Miranda was attractive and charming, so why not?

Kayla didn't know much about Aria's sexuality spectrum. She wasn't sure if she was super straight or if Miranda would pique her curiosity. Miranda could do that. She'd done it with Kayla. Yes, Kayla was gay, but Miranda Northbrooke wasn't even a little bit her type. And yet...

Ugh. She didn't want to think about her now.

No. She wanted to sit here on her very lovely moondeck, listen to the roar of the ocean, feel the evening breeze in her hair, and think about somebody who was the polar opposite of Miranda Northbrooke.

CHAPTER FIVE

For whatever reason, sleep had been elusive for London Sunday night. She'd drift off into a very light slumber, only to be woken up by some sound, either outside her open French doors or somewhere in the suite. She'd heard Miranda come in and had glanced at her phone. Nearly two in the morning. She'd found herself wondering if Miranda had managed to seduce Aria Keller, and a big part of her hoped not. She wanted to have more respect for the actress.

By five a.m., she gave up on trying to sleep and decided to sit on the sundeck and catch the sunrise. For once, Miranda was not out there, and she was able to sit in peace, wrapped in a light blanket, and simply enjoy the show.

And what a show it was. The sun took its time and made sure to chew all the scenery on its way up, using reds and oranges as its entry colors. It was a spectacular display, and London felt goose bumps break out on her arms as she watched. Stunningly beautiful.

Speaking of stunningly beautiful things, her gaze was caught by a figure running on the beach, and she knew immediately who it was.

She didn't recall Kayla Tennyson saying anything about running, but that didn't mean it wasn't something she did. Clad in black leggings and a neon-green tank top, dark hair pulled back into a ponytail, hat on, she sprinted along the beach, close enough to the water that the sand was packed and gave her some traction.

The way her body moved…God. She was beauty and grace personified. A prime example of the gloriousness of the human body and what it could do. London found herself frowning in disappointment when Kayla had run out of view.

Well, she had to come back, right?

She'd wait.

Rather than bother room service, she scooted into her bedroom and used the coffee maker on her dresser to brew herself a steaming cup. Her mini fridge held actual cream, which surprised her, and she doctored her coffee, then took it back out onto the sundeck and waited.

Sure enough, not ten minutes later, Kayla Tennyson came running back in the opposite direction. There was nobody on the beach but her, and she slowed her jog until she stopped. London looked on as Kayla pressed a hand to her neck and looked at her watch, clearly monitoring her heart rate. Then she grabbed a piece of what must have been driftwood and set it in a spot in the sand. She found a second piece, carried it about thirty or forty yards away from the first, and set that down. Then she did something on her watch, crouched, and ran.

This was not jogging. This was sprinting.

London watched in amazement as Kayla ran from one piece of driftwood to the other, crouched to touch it, then sprinted back to the first piece.

London's volleyball coach in high school had called those suicides, though she was pretty sure there was another name for them. All she remembered was they were fucking brutal.

Back and forth, Kayla ran. Sprinted. And she was fast. London was beyond impressed. She ran between the two pieces of wood ten times by London's count before she stopped and bent at the waist, hands on her knees. She suddenly had a water bottle, which London had missed somehow, and she drank deeply from it. Then, much to London's surprise, she repeated the entire process. Ten times, back and forth, stop, catch her breath, look at her watch, drink some water, and then round three.

The woman was a machine.

A gorgeously fit, amazing to watch machine.

She was too far away for London to make out details like whether

her cheeks were flushed or how her face was likely glistening with perspiration, but she let herself imagine just the same.

What a glorious way to start her day.

Finally, Kayla took her water bottle and left the beach, walking out of London's sight. Her disappointment was real and heavy, and she was just sighing it out when Miranda came out onto the sundeck, carrying her morning cup of coffee and her phone.

"Morning," she said, her voice a bit hoarser than usual.

"Morning," London said. "You were out late. Have fun?"

Miranda looked like she was trying to hide her grin, but failed. "I did. The actress was lovely, as were her companions."

London noted that she didn't call the actress by name and found herself inexplicably irritated by that. Without prompting, Miranda went on.

"I sent some drinks, and they invited me to join them at their table. There was a jazz band playing that was quite good, so we sat together and listened to the music for a while. Talked. It's the actress—"

"Aria," London supplied before she could stop herself.

"Yes, sorry. Aria, her cousin, and a friend. It's her first legit vacation in a couple years. She loves it here."

It was more info than London expected. Too much, really, and she felt a strange sympathy for Aria Keller, but she wasn't sure why. "Well, I'm glad you enjoyed yourself."

"Oh, I did. I may see her again. We'll see." And this time, Miranda didn't hide the grin. And this time, it seemed almost smug, more of a smirk than a grin.

"I'm going to shower," London said because for some reason, she couldn't get away from Miranda fast enough. Under the spray of hot water, her mind replayed a little movie of Kayla running from driftwood to driftwood, muscles flexing, legs pumping, and goddamn, what a sight. Even in her mind.

When she came out of her room a bit later, dressed and ready for the day, she found Miranda asleep in her lounge chair on the sundeck. Unsurprising, given she'd gotten about three hours of sleep the night before. She thought about waking her but changed her mind when she recalled the smug smile, the way she'd talked about Aria Keller as if she was prey rather than an actual woman with a personality and worth.

Apparently, women can be just as gross as men.

She slipped out her phone and jotted the thought into her notes.

With a shake of her head, she moved toward the door, her rumbling stomach sending her in the direction of breakfast.

❖

Kayla always felt better when she got in a morning workout. It wasn't always possible, given her schedule. Sometimes, she was needed first thing. Sometimes, her surveillance was twenty-four seven, and there just wasn't time to get any exercise in. But this morning, she'd been able to do some sprints on the beach. It had felt amazing to get her heart pumping, get her heart rate up, feel her muscles strain. And the beautiful sunrise had been a bonus.

A beautiful start to a beautiful day.

The thought had barely run through her head when it was followed by another one almost immediately.

Speaking of beautiful…

And there was London Granger, walking into the restaurant— no, gliding. London Granger didn't walk, she glided, and Kayla wondered if that was a holdover from her modeling days, the way she moved. She wore a simple summer dress in white, which accentuated her tan, making her look like some bronze goddess moving through the mortal realm. She was just leaning in to speak to the hostess when her eyes locked on Kayla's, and Kayla did not imagine the way London's smile widened at the sight of her.

Kayla had her elbows on the table, her coffee cup held in both hands, and with her eyes, she indicated the empty chair at her table.

London wasted no time waving the hostess away and crossing the restaurant floor toward Kayla's table. The heads that turned as she passed were not lost on Kayla, but London didn't seem to notice.

"Well, isn't this a nice way to start my day," London said as a waiter appeared out of nowhere to pull her chair out for her.

"I could say the same," Kayla said. "Hi."

"Hello there, you." London sat back as the waiter unfolded her napkin and laid it across her lap, then asked if she'd like coffee. When he left, she frowned. "I don't think I'll ever get used to that."

"The napkin thing? Yeah, it's strange, isn't it? Like, I can do this myself, thanks."

"Exactly. I thought you were on guard duty in the morning."

"I usually am, but my client had a late night and is sleeping in, so I get a bit of a break." She glanced at her watch. "My colleague will text me when they're up."

The waiter returned with London's coffee, then took her order for some fresh fruit and yogurt. Kayla watched as she added creamer to her coffee and stirred. As she lifted the cup to her lips, her eyes met Kayla's and she said, "More time for you to run on the beach."

Kayla couldn't hide her surprise. Or her blush. She felt the heat creep up her neck and move into her face.

London's grin only grew. "And she blushes. The super tough bodyguard is a blusher, folks. Who knew?"

Kayla laughed softly. "Super tough? How would you know?"

"Because I watched you run on the beach."

This conversation had skidded quickly into the category of flirtatious, and Kayla was there for it. She kept her voice light and teasing as she said, "I see. So, you were spying on me?"

"Oh, no, spying implies secrecy and mystery. I was openly ogling from my sundeck. No mystery about it."

Kayla's turn to smile widely. "I see," she said again. And the idea of London watching her while she worked out on the beach? Yeah, she didn't hate it.

"Maybe I'll join you next time."

"I'd love that." The idea of London in workout gear, running next to her on this breathtaking beach, was one Kayla could barely handle.

The waiter brought London her breakfast, an assortment of pineapple, mangoes, and kiwi with what looked like freshly made yogurt and a sprinkling of ground nuts and shredded coconut. "Man, I love how fresh the fruit is here," London said, and it was so quiet,

Kayla wondered if she'd said it to herself. But then she glanced up at her and asked, "Don't you?"

"I had the exact same thing for breakfast before you got here. Plus a protein shake. Pineapple coconut."

"Well. It's delicious. And your shake sounds good, too."

"You should get one."

"I didn't do sprints on the beach."

"Oh, you saw the sprints, too?"

"They were my favorite part." Again, London sipped her coffee and held Kayla's gaze over the rim.

"I'll keep that in mind." Kayla wasn't going to lie. She very much liked the idea of London watching her from her sundeck. The thought of it gave her a little thrill and sent a gentle throbbing between her legs.

London popped a piece of mango into her mouth and studied Kayla as she chewed. "Tell me what you love about what you do."

"Well." Kayla picked her cup up again, reset her elbows on the table, and held it in both hands as she gave the statement some thought. "First and foremost, I like being my own boss. I like that I don't have to answer to anybody, that I make the rules, that I decide who I work with. Second, I travel. A lot. My clients are very wealthy, and they travel all over the globe, which means I go with them. I've seen more of the world than I ever thought I would."

"Excellent reasons," London said. "Have you ever had a client you hated?"

Kayla snorted a laugh. "Oh God, yes. Too many. Remember the part about my clients being wealthy?"

London tipped her head to the side. "Are you saying all wealthy people are terrible?"

Kayla blinked at her. "No. No, of course not."

London's face split into a smile, and her eyes honest-to-God twinkled. "I'm just teasing you. Though I bet there are some."

"Here's the thing," Kayla said. She set down her cup and folded her hands on the table. "With wealth comes great privilege. Oftentimes, people forget that. My clients can be...expectant sometimes. A little entitled. They expect preferential treatment. They expect the best of things. Rooms, cars, food, service. Don't get me wrong, they pay for it. But that expectation can leave a bad taste with some people."

"Understandably." A shadow crossed over London's features, and Kayla felt her stomach churn just a bit.

She reached over and closed a hand over London's forearm. "I'm sorry. That was really presumptuous of me. I didn't mean to insult you. I don't know you at all and—"

London cut her off with a bark of a laugh. "Oh God, no, you didn't insult me. I am not wealthy, trust me. I'm just here…" She trailed off and blinked several times before finishing with, "On my publisher's dime." She waved a hand around, gesturing at everything around them. "I can't afford this on my own. No way."

"Oh." Kayla studied her but couldn't put a finger on what it was about what she said that seemed…off. "Okay. Well, I just didn't want you to think I was trashing you."

Another laugh, and London laid a hand over Kayla's, still on her arm. "I wouldn't think that about you. No worries at all."

And just like that, the tension eased and the moment passed.

"What about you?" Kayla asked, working to redirect the conversation to more pleasant things. "What do you love about being a writer?"

Just like that, London's face went all whimsical, a little dreamy, and Kayla knew she'd asked exactly the right question. More than that, she really, really wanted to hear the answer.

London dabbed at the corners of her mouth with the napkin before she spoke. When she did, she looked at Kayla, and her blue eyes sparkled like they were ringed with tiny diamonds. "God, I love words. I love the written word so much. It's hard to describe. Which is ironic, given the subject." A little giggle that was adorable. "I love how you can write a description of something and the person reading it can get exactly what you're talking about. I love that there are so many different ways to say the same thing. I still have the first thesaurus I ever got. From my grandmother. It's all worn and dog-eared, but I take it everywhere." She pointed at the ceiling. "It's in my bag as we speak."

Kayla propped her chin in her hand, absolutely loving listening to London speak about something with such passion. "What else?"

"I love that I can make up people. Just make 'em up. That they can be exactly who I want them to be. Have you ever adored a fictional character so much they felt real to you?"

"Kinsey Millhone," Kayla said instantly, recalling the mystery series that she'd discovered in college and read through until the author, Sue Grafton, had passed away in 2017. "I still can't believe she wasn't a real person."

"That's the beauty of writing in a nutshell. Right there." London sat back in her chair. "You ask what I love about writing. That's exactly it."

"So, you write fiction."

London nibbled on the inside of her cheek. "Not always. No. In fact, the book I'm here to work on is nonfiction."

"But you can't tell me about it." Kayla shot her a sly grin to keep it light.

"I can't, no."

"Can you tell me what you love about writing nonfiction?"

"That I can do." London sat forward again, and that sparkle in her eyes was back. "Nonfiction is about truth. It's about getting to the bottom of it, getting down to the bare bones of a story, the nitty-gritty, uncovering all the secrets and lies and facts people may not know, and then sharing them."

"That's a fantastic explanation." And it was. What was more, London's passion for the subject had kicked up about twenty notches, which Kayla hadn't thought would be possible, given how lovingly London'd spoken about writing fiction. "Wow. You really love what you do."

"I do. Very much. I'm incredibly lucky to have a job that I'm so happy doing." London's face was radiant when she talked about her work. Kayla noticed that in the first moment. Her eyes were bright, there was a healthy flush in her cheeks, and she leaned slightly forward as she spoke.

"Looks like we both lucked out when it comes to our careers. You were smart to get out of modeling. Look where it got you."

"Agreed." There was a moment of quiet where they each sipped their coffee, and while Kayla couldn't speak for London, she was perfectly happy just to sit there with her. "So," London said after a few minutes, "what have you done since you got here?" She gave her head a shake and amended. "I mean, what has your client done that you've had to sit in a corner and watch her do?"

Kayla laughed at the choice of words. "We went zip-lining."

"We?"

"Oh yes, Aria wanted me to go with her." At the questioning tilt of London's head, she explained, "I've worked for her several times now and we've become friends. Sort of."

"Oh, that's fun. And so she corralled you into sliding over a deep ravine on nothing but a string."

Kayla snorted a laugh and set down her empty cup. "Methinks somebody is afraid of heights."

London grinned. "Not normally, but that would make me nervous."

"Well, I assure you, it's more than a string, and there are tons of safety precautions taken. I wasn't worried."

"You are a braver woman than I." London looked her in the eye and their gazes held.

Kayla's throbbing intensified. She was just about to speak when her phone beeped. A glance told her it was Bo, and she sighed deeply. "I have to run," she said, and the clear disappointment on London's face made her morning. She settled her bill, tossed her napkin to the table, and stood. Then she stopped, snagged by those blue eyes, and just looked at London for what felt like a long time. And somehow—she couldn't explain how—she just knew they'd see each other again. It was the strangest feeling, but she ran with it. With a grin and a quick squeeze of London's shoulder, she headed off to meet up with Bo.

❖

The Bella Grande threw occasional dinner parties for its guests. This was something London hadn't known and hadn't really expected, so when Miranda announced that afternoon that they'd be attending one in a few hours, she was surprised.

One of the significant benefits of her short-lived modeling career was her wardrobe. She knew fashion, knew how to dress, and had dresses and outfits for just about every occasion. A dinner party with wealthy people—some of whom Miranda knew—was no exception. She'd packed a couple dresses that would work, and she chose the draped one-shoulder gown in red. It had a slit up one side, and her strappy silver heels were the perfect accent to the subtle sparkly sequins that decorated the bodice and flowed down the gown. She put her hair partially up and left the rest down around her shoulders. Modeling had also taught her about makeup, and she'd applied an evening base of it.

When she stepped out into the main living area of the suite, she knew she'd hit a home run by the way Miranda completely shut up, then looked her up and down. "Wow," was all she said. Ethan stood in the corner, glanced up from his phone to see her, looked back down, then shot his head back up again in a double take that was almost comical.

Okay, so the dress works. Good to know.

There was a fine line between seeing in the faces of other people that you looked good and being ogled. And while what Miranda and Ethan were doing was *just this side* of ogling, she didn't mind.

Miranda didn't look so bad herself, if London was being honest. She wore a black evening gown with capped sleeves and a plunging V, and even London found herself drawn to a peek at the cleavage. Her light hair was up, which made her sharp cheekbones even more prominent. She'd had a manicure that afternoon, and her ruby red nails popped against her black clutch.

"You look amazing," London said because it was true.

"Thank you," Miranda said with a soft smile, and London could tell the compliment had flattered her. "So, tonight, there will be several people I know, both friends and clients."

"Got it. I shall stand close and be quiet." She grinned to show she was teasing.

"Perfect. And you aren't a writer. You're a model."

A nod. "Yes. Currently a model. Got it."

Miranda held out an elbow in a show of chivalry. "Shall we?"

London tucked her hand in, and Ethan—looking surprisingly dapper in a tux—held the door. They were off.

London tried to pretend she didn't hope they'd see Kayla here tonight. Seemed like a party Aria Keller would attend, which might mean Kayla would be tucked in a corner, looking all sexy dressed in black, talking into her sleeve and touching her earpiece with a finger. Yes, she realized she had no idea if Kayla had an earpiece or a sleeve microphone, that those were things she'd seen in the movies, but envisioning it all was fun, just the same. And she might have crossed her fingers, just in case.

She realized fairly early into the party that it was for people like Miranda…business folks, entrepreneurs, finance people. The rich and not necessarily famous. Absent were any of the celebrities or athletes she'd seen so far during her stay, and present were a few new faces she didn't recognize, but whose importance was clear simply by the way they were approached by others. It was fascinating, and she wished she could take notes, but her phone was tucked away in her tiny purse that had room for little else, and grabbing it out to type away on it now would look gauche. Instead, she did her job, holding on to Miranda's arm and smiling as Miranda stopped and spoke to various people—the majority of whom were male. She introduced London as her companion for the trip. London bristled at that because, despite being the truth, it made her sound like an escort, and she absently wondered if that was Miranda's intention.

Thankfully, as the night went on, Miranda dropped the *for the trip* and introduced her simply as her companion. Much more palatable.

London wasn't exactly sure what she expected from the obvious wealth surrounding her. Name-dropping? There was a little of that, yes. Networking? There was a lot of that. The hedge fund guy was clearly open for new clients, while the computer duo were angling for investments for the newest arm of their company. It was fascinating to watch and listen to.

What was more fascinating, though, was watching Miranda at work. As one of the few woman present who wasn't there as somebody's arm candy, she moved through the crowd with confidence, her head held high. It definitely helped that she was tall, but there was an air of assurance and poise that she carried off like few people London had ever met. She turned heads all night. People gravitated toward her. It was impressive, to say the least.

A couple hours in, London had excused herself to the ladies' room. When she came out, Miranda was surrounded by a circle of men, and the idea of working her way back in and standing there quietly, while Miranda talked about the state of media today and the men looked at London in ways they thought were subtle but were absolutely not, felt super heavy on her shoulders. Instead, she turned and headed for the bar in the corner and ordered herself a glass of white wine.

"Is that the sauv blanc?" a man asked in a British accent as he sidled up next to her and leaned his forearms on the bar. "It's surprisingly good."

"It is and I agree," she said. Over the years, she'd learned just the right tone for this type of situation. Friendly, but not inviting. Firm, but not dismissive. It was a fine line to walk sometimes, but she'd become a pro.

She observed him as he ordered himself a scotch, neat. The man was a walking, talking cliché of tall, dark, and handsome. His brown eyes were kind. His dark skin had a healthy glow, his black hair cropped close, following down his sideburns to a precisely trimmed beard. He turned so he leaned his back against the bar's edge, one elbow on the surface of it while he cradled his drink in the other, and he scanned the large room. "I hate these things," he said quietly. "Don't you?"

"Parties?" London asked. "No. No, in fact, I kind of like them."

He grinned, revealing very straight, very white teeth. *He's almost too handsome.* "Funny. No, I meant parties with rich businessmen milling around trying to out–bank account each other."

"*Oh*," she said, and drew the word out. "I see. Actually, this is my first such party, so I really haven't formed an opinion yet."

"Fair enough. Fair enough." He smiled and held out his hand. "Rick. Rick Bennett."

London put her hand in his, making sure to give a firm handshake. "London Granger."

"Oh, that's a very cool name."

"Thank you. All credit goes to my parents."

"And what do you do, London Granger?"

She caught herself about half a second before saying she was a writer. "I'm in the modeling business." She'd always phrased it that way because going around saying she was a model felt somehow obnoxious to her.

"Seriously? Wow, that's got to be a very interesting career. You travel a lot?"

"Quite a bit, yeah. Been to a lot of different places." She was starting to feel the slightest bit uncomfortable, but only because Rick Bennett was asking questions she had to lie about. Miranda's orders. It wasn't like she was outright making up crap—using her past experience was serving her well—but she felt bad. Rick seemed like a nice guy, and she felt guilty she wasn't being honest with him. Maybe she could redirect the conversation. "What about you? What do you do?"

"Oh, Rick earned his money the old-fashioned way." Miranda was suddenly there, suddenly appearing next to London like a magic trick, placing herself between the two of them. "He inherited it." She ran her hand gently down London's arm before settling a hand on the small of her back. The move felt intimate. And possessive. Judging by the startled look on his face, Rick Bennett felt the same way.

"You're one to talk, Miranda," he said, his gaze moving from London to Miranda, though his expression went much darker and much less friendly. "Pretty sure your money ended up in your account the same way."

"Yes, but my father didn't swindle anybody." Miranda delivered the line as if she was reporting the weather, with little inflection or emotion. Then she sipped the martini she held and watched him over the rim of her glass, like she was observing her insult hit its mark.

He blinked at her once. Twice. Then he slugged back the remainder of his drink and pushed himself off the bar. Setting down his empty glass he pointed at London. "It was nice to meet you, London Granger." His eyes indicated Miranda, and he frowned and shrugged and added, "Good luck to you."

They both watched him walk away. Miranda's hand was still warm on London's back. "Ex of yours, I assume," London said.

Miranda gave a nod. "Six months. Nice guy, but God, so fucking clingy." She shook her head, but her eyes were still on him. "Dynamite in the sack, though."

London took a large gulp of her wine. "So, how many exes do you have? And how many are here?"

Miranda tipped her head to the right and pursed her lips. "I guess that depends on how you define an ex. Because I have exes, but I also have conquests. And they're very different."

"Conquests." London didn't think she had anybody in her life that she'd consider a conquest, but she made it a habit not to judge the sex lives of others. "And which was Rick again?"

"Oh, six months definitely puts him in the ex category."

"I see." London's confusion must have registered on her face because Miranda laughed then. Loudly.

"I have *so* much to teach you, darling." She moved her hand around from London's back and gave a little tilt of her head. "Come on."

For the next two hours, Miranda led London through the partygoers, introducing her, telling them she was a model, and then steering the conversation to business or politics. London had to consciously change from wine to club soda because she felt herself getting tipsy. Plenty of partygoers looked at her, plenty were polite, nobody really seemed interested in talking to her, and she was reminded once again why she disliked her modeling career so much. With little conversation to be had, she found herself sipping her wine fairly quickly. The change to club soda was a necessary one if she didn't want to end up sloppy.

The whole time, the entire stretch of the party—which somehow turned from dinner party to after-dinner cocktails to some kind of late night happy hour—she kept her eyes open, scanning every few minutes, checking the restrooms, the corridors, the corners for a tall brunette with a high cheekbones and a killer smile. When she couldn't find her, she scanned for Aria Keller. If Aria was there, Kayla might be. But as she'd noticed earlier, this seemed to be more businesspeople and not so much the celebrities she'd seen the past couple of days. No Aria.

Her disappointment was real, and heavier than she'd expected. Ah, well. Maybe it just wasn't meant to be. She recalled her thoughts from earlier, reminding her why she was there, what she was being paid to do. She wasn't here to frolic, as her grandmother would say. She wasn't there to date or flirt or anything of the sort. She was there to work. And she couldn't let Kayla Tennyson's sexy smile and sexy voice and sexy hands get in the way of her job. And then her brain took her away on a roller-coaster ride of a fantasy that involved her and Kayla and hot fudge.

"You seem tired." Miranda's voice was right in her ear and made her flinch. "It's late. I've got some more mingling to do, but if you're ready to leave, feel free."

A glance into Miranda's eyes registered no sarcasm or irritation, so London gave one nod. "I think I will, as long as you don't mind."

"Not at all. A bunch of the guys are going outside to smoke cigars. I think I'll join them."

"You will?" London couldn't catch the words—or her surprise—before they left her mouth and showed on her face.

Miranda gave a sly grin. "That's how the men like to cut the women out of the conversation. They figure going outside for cigars is a guy thing, and none of the ladies will follow." She drained her Manhattan and set the glass on the tray of a passing waiter. "They underestimate me. They always have." With a squeeze of London's shoulder, she turned and headed toward the doors that led to the patio.

London shook her head with a smile. Miranda Northbrooke was not a woman to be trifled with, that was for sure. She might have some behaviors and attitudes that London didn't share, but she couldn't deny the confidence and business savvy Miranda exuded in waves. It was impressive, she had to admit it. She set her glass on the bar, slid her phone out of her clutch—how the hell was it after one a.m. already?—and headed for the door that led to the lobby and the interior of the resort. She wanted to jot down what Miranda had said about being underestimated before she forgot it.

Her intention had absolutely been to go back up to the room, but she found herself taking a left-hand turn instead. A patio on the other side of the lobby was open and quiet. She found a table and took a seat, watching the reflection of the moon on the water and listening to the never-ending roar of the waves. When a staff member asked if he could get her anything, she took a chance.

"Do you, by any chance, have any hot tea available?"

"Of course, madame." He left and was back in less than ten minutes with a teapot of hot water, a cup and saucer, and a box with a shockingly large selection of tea bags. She chose a decaf Earl Grey, made herself a cup, and settled back in her chair.

It was the most at peace she'd felt all night.

Clubbing was one of Kayla's least favorite things when she was on assignment. And she didn't mean she went clubbing. She meant when that's what her client wanted to do. There were so many reasons why it was a bad idea, especially when a client was confronted by a person who had no concept of personal boundaries. Clubs were loud. They were dark. They were crowded. Protecting somebody in a club was one of the most difficult assignments for security detail.

Luckily, she wasn't all that worried about Aria. While she definitely got looks and garnered some head turns, nobody seemed on the brink of overstepping. And she and her two companions were having a great time, if their laughing and dancing were any indication. She'd decided to give Bo and Jake a break, let them grab some dinner and watch Monday Night Football. Bo's Jaguars were playing Jake's Bills, and for all Kayla knew, she might find out they'd killed each other while watching and she'd be on her own for the rest of the week.

The thought made her grin. Once they returned to the resort, Bo would take over, and Kayla would be free until tomorrow afternoon.

She was surprised when Aria danced her way up to Kayla and told her they were ready to go. It was almost two a.m., and she'd expected them to be there for at least another hour.

"Yeah? You're sure?"

Aria nodded, her forehead glistening with perspiration. "I'm beat. And I have a Zoom with my agent in the morning."

"I'll get our ride."

Not long after that, they were pulling around the side of the resort, where there were people visible out on the patio. A cloud of blue smoke hung over them, telling Kayla several somebodies were smoking cigars.

"Oh," Haley suddenly cried, startling them. "I think that woman from last night is out there. Let's go see."

"Ugh," Aria said on a groan. "I'm so tired."

"*Please?*" Haley asked and drew the word out to about four syllables, like a child begging her mother to stay up late. "She was so fun."

"Please," Cammie chimed in, "you just like that she flirted with you."

Haley's sly smile said that's exactly what it was. "Hey, she's a cougar. And she bought all our drinks."

Kayla was pretty sure her tongue was bleeding from so much biting of it. She knew exactly who they were talking about. Miranda Northbrooke. And it wasn't her place to offer up opinions on people unless they posed a threat of some sort. And much as she wanted to warn them away, she couldn't.

"Fine." Aria finally gave in. "But only for a few minutes. I'm dead." She turned to Kayla. "Your shift is over, yeah?"

Kayla nodded and managed not to add *thank fuck*. She pulled out her phone and sent a text. "Yeah, Bo will take over." Thank fuck.

It was Cammie's turn to become a lovestruck schoolgirl. "That Bo is fire. God."

She was only thirty-six years old, but Kayla found herself fighting the urge to shake her head and say, *Kids these days.*

They hung out in the lobby for a few minutes until Bo arrived. Kayla briefed him, gave him the clean report from the club, and then lowered her voice as she asked him to please keep an eye on things. She didn't know what could possibly happen or what she expected him to do about it, but he seemed to understand her concern and gave her his one-nod acknowledgment.

"No worries. Get some sleep."

She stood and watched as the foursome walked away, the girls in their club attire—a lot of tiny clothes and high heels—and Bo in his trousers and black polo shirt, the sleeves of which strained trying to cover his massive biceps. Then she sighed and found herself suddenly entertaining a little fantasy in which she was headed up to her room where London Granger was waiting in her bed, adorably half asleep, having tried to stay up and wait for her. Kayla would undress, utterly exhausted until she slid under the covers. And then London's naked body would have her suddenly wide-awake, buzzing...

"Ugh. Stop it." She scolded herself aloud, turned on her heel, and headed for the elevator bank. The resort must've had a night setting on their hall lights because everything was dim. Quiet. The solitude was nice...until she rounded a corner and ran hard, directly into a person coming from the other way. "Oh my God," she said as she reached out and grabbed upper arms to steady the person, their heads close enough to almost be touching. "I'm so sor—"

She focused, and blue eyes sparkled back at her in a combination of amusement and...something else. Something dark and sexy and erotic, and Kayla swallowed hard. Golden waves cascaded around shoulders—one of which was bare, God help her—and yes, it was London. She couldn't believe it. London Granger. Right here, in the dim hallway, wearing—oh, her heart!—a red one-shoulder evening gown. She silently asked the Universe what it was trying to do to her. London's arms were bare, warm as Kayla held them. She couldn't seem to make herself let go, not that London made any sort of move to extricate herself. No, they simply stood there, noses nearly touching, gazes held. Until London licked her lips, and this time, Kayla spoke aloud.

"Oh God," was all she could manage, and then she crushed her mouth to London's. A whimper came from one of them, but Kayla wasn't sure who. All she knew was that London's lips were achingly soft, her mouth tasted sweet, and then London's arms were around her neck and she was pulling Kayla closer, kissing her back, and for the love of everything holy, how had she lived her entire adult life without ever kissing this woman? How? It was like she finally found oxygen. Or sunlight.

She shifted them, turned them so London's back was against the wall, and pushed into her. Tongues were at play now, the kissing deep and thorough, no sound except the soft smacking of their lips. Kayla was lost. God, this woman. She was just lost.

And then, suddenly, London was pulling away. Her hand on Kayla's chest, she pushed gently. It took Kayla a moment for the message to reach her brain. Stopping. London was stopping the kissing. So sad. But when Kayla met the blue eyes, she saw confusion in them.

"We shouldn't," London said softly. "I'm so sorry. I just…we shouldn't."

The words took a moment to register, and she blinked rapidly at them.

But London didn't pull away immediately. She lingered. She touched her fingertips to Kayla's lips, kept them there for a moment. Her focus was on Kayla's mouth, the anguish in her eyes clear, but she seemed torn. She moved her fingers and placed her palm flat against Kayla's chest, near her collarbone, the warmth seeping through her shirt. And then there was a small whimper, the origin of which Kayla couldn't quite define. Sadness? Frustration? Both? London kissed her again, still lingering, and just as Kayla was about to let herself sink into this woman, London pulled back quickly, whispered, "I'm sorry," and hurried away.

Kayla could only watch her go, her legs feeling like jelly and keeping her from walking without the very real worry that she'd crumple to the tile floor. Her lips burned in the best of ways. She could still taste London, and now she wondered if she was glad about that, glad she'd gotten a sample, or if that only made it worse, made her desire crank up to unbearable levels.

She stood there for a long time. So long, she was actually surprised to find herself still there after what felt like an hour. Just standing there, back against the wall, staring after London, who was long gone by now. She brought her own fingers up to her lips, touched them where London had touched them, where she'd kissed them, and they still tingled.

What the hell had just happened?

❖

Oh God, that was so stupid. So incredibly stupid. What had she been thinking?

London slammed the door of the suite and leaned her back against it. Just stood there, eyes closed. She could still feel Kayla's mouth. Her hands. She could still feel Kayla's body under her own hands. Could still smell her, that clean, fresh scent that seemed to follow her everywhere. Could still taste her.

What had she been thinking?

She was here with Miranda. For all intents and purposes, she was here as Miranda's companion. What if somebody had seen them? What if one of her entrepreneur friends had been headed for the elevator and had run into them? What if somebody *had* seen them, and she didn't even know because she'd had Kayla's tongue in her mouth?

Miranda would likely be furious at the way it would make her look. It could throw London's entire project into the garbage disposal.

"Oh God." She closed her eyes. What the hell had she been thinking?

She hurried into her room and shut the door. She didn't want to have to face Miranda. Even if Miranda had no idea, London knew she probably looked guilty as hell. Claire was always telling her she had no poker face.

In the bathroom, she caught her own reflection. Her eyes were still slightly hooded. Her lips were a bit swollen, and she brought her fingertips to them, touched them lightly, and remembered touching Kayla's. How they felt, the softness. How she tasted, tangy, like lime.

I haven't been kissed like that in forever.

God.

She hadn't been kissed like that in forever.

She stared at the woman in the mirror looking back at her. Her eyes were wide, like she was in a permanent state of surprise. Which, in and of itself, was not at all a surprise.

"All right, Granger," she whispered to her reflection. "Pull yourself together. What the fuck was that? Are you a horny teenager? No, you are a grown-ass adult with a job to do. Pull yourself together."

Her entire college career, she'd given herself little pep talks in the mirror. Before a test. Prepping for a presentation. In the moments before a date. And they always helped. They gave her a boost of confidence, a little shot of adrenaline. But this time, the woman in the mirror just stared back with her big surprised eyes and her kiss-swollen mouth, and London scoffed at her and waved a hand in disgust as she turned away.

"Ugh. You're useless."

It was so late. She hadn't realized it and was surprised Miranda was still out. How much could she have to say to a bunch of old, mostly white, cigar-smoking men?

"Apparently, a lot," she said aloud as she stepped out of her gown and into the shower. Part of her was hesitant to wash away any traces left of Kayla on her body, but it wasn't like they'd had sex. Of course, the second that thought crossed her mind, her brain decided she should fantasize about just such a thing and tossed her an image of what they might look like. "Oh God," she whispered, laying her forehead against the cool tile of the shower as visions of a naked Kayla writhing beneath her filled her head. Before she even realized what she was doing, she'd unhooked the shower head from its brace and aimed it between her legs.

She came in seconds.

That was twice, she thought later as she slid, naked, between the cool sheets of her bed. Her skin was hot to the touch, and she felt like her body was on fire. Pajamas might make her spontaneously combust. That was two times she'd taken care of herself while envisioning Kayla Tennyson. This was becoming a problem. And now, instead of being relaxed and sleepy, as an orgasm should have made her, she was wired. Wide-awake, as if she'd just had an espresso. Or five.

Her doors were open—probably the thing she loved most about this room—and the ocean breeze was lovely. Salty, a little cool. She had just started to relax, her eyes finally growing heavy, when she heard the door to the suite open. Miranda must be back.

But then there was conversation. More than just Miranda's voice. She picked out one other—no, two. Was it three? No. Two. There were definitely at least two people with Miranda. She thought about getting up, putting on her clothes, and making an appearance, but that went away quickly. She did get up and pad quietly, nakedly, across the room to her door to listen, though.

"So, your family owns the whole conglomerate?" a woman's voice asked.

Miranda's laugh was husky. "My grandfather was the original *media mogul*," she said, and London could almost see her making the air quotes. "There are a handful now, but he was the first."

"So, you've just always been rich." It was the same voice that asked the first question, and London detected a slight slur in it.

"Haley, Jesus," came a different voice. Embarrassed. Irritated. Also with a slight slur.

"What? I'm just asking." That was Haley again, sounding like a petulant child.

"You're being rude." The first voice again. "I'm sorry, Miranda. Please excuse her. I probably should've cut her off a while ago." The last couple of words were said through gritted teeth.

"*Pfft*," came Haley's response.

"I was going to offer drinks, but maybe water is better?" London closed her eyes and shook her head, knowing Miranda was about to make somebody bring her room service at three in the morning.

"Oh no, we're fine. We can't stay. Aria will kill us if we take up too much of your time." Realization set in. *It's Aria Keller's two companions.* That, of course, made her brain zip right back to Kayla Tennyson territory. Was she here, too? Would security be needed if Aria wasn't around?

"How about just one?" Miranda again.

London pictured the women looking at each other, and then Haley said, "It's not like we're driving. And this is vacation!" Again, she sounded like a child. London felt bad for her friend, who was clearly ready to go.

London heard the tinkling of glass and the fridge in the kitchen being opened, and she realized in surprise that Miranda was actually serving her guests herself. *Small miracles.* She only lasted about three minutes before she had to know if Kayla was literally in the next room. She threw on some clothes but didn't want to announce herself. Seriously, what would she do if Kayla was here? They'd just made out in the hall—a full on make-out session. What would she do if she saw Kayla standing in her suite right now? No, she couldn't make herself known. So, instead of opening her bedroom door, she tiptoed out onto the dark sundeck, just far enough so she could peek into the living room through the windows of the closed doors.

She'd been right about the two friends of Aria Keller's, and it was easy to tell which one was the drunker of the two—the one with the glasses. She was wandering around the suite slowly, but her balance was shaky, you could tell just by looking at her. The other girl, the one with the auburn hair, watched her with concern. Miranda's back was to the deck doors, and soon she turned with two martinis in her hands.

"Here we go," she said as she approached the two women and handed them each a glass. The redhead thanked her, then grimaced slightly, clearly not wanting the drink. The one with the glasses slurped loudly, then made all kinds of noises of approval. London scanned what she could see of corners and shadows. Not only was there no Kayla, there was nobody else, and she wondered if Kayla's team was only responsible for Aria, not Aria's companions if they were separate from her.

Miranda turned back to them with a martini of her own and a big smile, and for some reason, London felt weird. Whether it was the fact that she'd brought two—from what London knew—complete strangers back to her suite at three in the morning or that she was extolling her family's wealth or that she was mixing drinks for a woman who was clearly already drunk, she wasn't sure. But she turned and went back to her room a bit confused about what she was feeling.

She liked Miranda. She did. She didn't think they'd ever be friends if London wasn't on an assignment, but she'd found Miranda interesting and intelligent and funny. She wasn't sure why what was happening beyond her bedroom door left a bad taste in her mouth, but it did.

Once she was back in bed, comfortably ensconced between the kajillion thread-count sheets, she found herself wishing she could talk to Kayla about it. And that led to visions of Kayla's face. Her eyes. Her hands. Her mouth. And then flashbacks ensued, and her body was on fire. Again.

Yeah. Just what she needed.

She grabbed a pillow and covered her head with it.

Screaming into it was almost too tempting.

CHAPTER SIX

By the time her phone read four seventeen a.m., Kayla couldn't take it anymore. She'd tossed and turned and tossed some more. She'd scrolled on TikTok. She'd answered email. She'd invoiced three clients. All from her bed. On her phone. Because she couldn't sleep. Because her head was full.

Full of London Granger.

What the hell had she been thinking, kissing her like that? God, what an idiot she was. Who did that? Who ran into a person in the hallway and just started making out with them? It was practically assault. She'd half expected London to scream for help. Jesus, what had she been thinking? London probably hated her now.

Okay, calm down, crazy-pants. She kissed you back. Remember?

Yeah. There was that, wasn't there? London Granger had most definitely kissed her back.

God, did she kiss me back.

That was the thought that had kept her up pretty much the entire night. She was hot. She was cold. She was hot again. She'd taken care of herself three times, a fantasy of her and London playing out in her head—so realistic, she had to stop and remind herself that it had never really happened. And she wanted to again.

This was bad. This was really, really bad. She couldn't be this distracted. Not with her job. She had to pay attention to everything. Locations. Faces. Vehicles. She couldn't be daydreaming sexual fantasies about a woman she'd met barely three days ago and had spoken with exactly three times.

She needed to blow off some steam. And there was only one way she knew to do that. Well, two ways, but since London wasn't naked and in her bed, she was going to have to go with door number two.

It didn't take her long to dress in her workout clothes and head down into the lobby. There was always a snack set up in a corner—which Kayla found odd for such an upscale place, but she was thankful as she snagged a banana on her way by.

The morning was gorgeous. Not quite light, but the sun was beginning to make its entrance stunningly, if the bright pink peeking over the horizon was any indication. She absently wondered if people who lived here year-round ever got tired of such perfect weather. Oh, she was sure there were storms. Probably hurricanes, even. And she imagined it could also get uncomfortably hot. But anytime she'd been there, it had been nothing but beautiful. She'd exercise outside all the time at home if New York City had this kind of weather.

"All right, enough endless thoughts about the weather," she muttered to herself as she reached the beach, tossed her banana peel into the trash, and pulled off her zip-up hoodie. She dropped it in the sand, along with a towel and her water bottle, and began to stretch. Physical fitness had always been important to her. Ever since she was a teen, she'd had some kind of workout routine. If she went longer than a day or two without exercising, she started to get cranky, as if her body was rebelling. She stretched her back first, always. Having suffered an injury a couple years ago, she was always extra careful with it and stretched her core thoroughly, even if she had little time. Then it was on to her legs. She'd pulled a hamstring once in high school because she hadn't stretched properly before a basketball game. It was incredibly painful, and she'd vowed never to skip stretching again if she could help it.

She hit a couple buttons on her watch and started down the beach on a slow jog. Running in the sand made things a hundred times more difficult, so she didn't spend nearly as much time on her workout here as she did at home in her gym. She could run for miles on her treadmill. On the beach? Only a few.

It was early enough that the beach was pretty much deserted. With the exception of a few fishermen and one other early-morning jogger, she felt like she was the only person on the island. It was quiet—or as quiet as a place could be beside a roaring ocean. But there was no music, no hum of conversation, no buzz of children playing in the sand. Just the sound of the waves, the pounding of her footsteps, and the rush of her own breath in and out of her lungs.

It was her favorite way to center herself.

And she needed to center herself after last night.

Again, the first thought that hit her was what the hell had she been thinking? What was it about London Granger that made her so irresistible? Because that's essentially what it was. Kayla hadn't been able to *not* kiss her, and that was the troubling part. She was not a woman who lacked control, who didn't understand boundaries, so this was alarming. And once again, her brain reminded her that London hadn't exactly struggled to get away.

God, could she kiss…

And she was off on the sense memory train, chugging along in her brain as she ran on the beach, starting up a throbbing between her legs, dampening her leggings, making her sweat more than the run was. She gave her head a literal shake, and it helped a little. Not much, but a little. That little didn't do much to ease her frustration, though. Sexual and other. She needed to talk things through. She knew that. Once she'd turned around and run back to her starting point, she took out her phone and sent a text to her mother, asking if she had time for a chat later. Of course, her mother said yes.

Relief. Okay. That was good. Her mom was great at helping her look at things from angles she might be missing. She'd have some guidance.

She stretched some more, deciding to forgo the sprints today and maybe do a second run instead. The sun had crested the horizon and was now showing off, reflecting all its gorgeous color off the water, making for a spectacular sunrise. She picked up her towel and patted the sweat off her face, her neck. She tipped her head back and took a long, cool drink from her water bottle.

And there she was.

"Hi." London was suddenly next to her, dressed in leggings and a black tank top, her blond hair pulled back in a ponytail, looking absolutely delicious. "I thought I might run with you, but it looks like I'm a little late."

"I…" Kayla had to stop and clear her throat of the surprise that was still lodged there. "I was going to do another lap, down and back."

"Oh, great. Mind if I tag along?"

"Sure."

They stretched together for a few moments and then, by unspoken agreement, began to jog. Silence reigned for several moments until London spoke.

"Did you see that sunrise?"

"I did. I was right here when it happened."

"I know. I was watching you."

And that did things to Kayla. Knowing London was up on her sundeck and watching her run…it made her legs quiver and her heart rate pick up, and she tried her best to smother the goofy grin that wanted to break out across her face. They ran for another few moments, and then London said it.

"So, about last night…"

"Oh, my God, I am so sorry." Kayla stopped running and put her hands on her knees to catch her breath. London realized she'd stopped and walked back to her. "I was so out of line."

"No, listen…" London gazed out over the ocean, her blue eyes matching the turmoil of the waves. She took a deep breath and blew it out. "It's complicated. That's all. I just…" She glanced down at her feet. "It's complicated."

"Okay. I can accept complicated. As long as you understand that I like you." She coupled her words with what she hoped was a soft smile to take the intensity out of them. The sun had grown brighter as it rose, and she pulled her sunglasses out of a pocket and slid them on.

London's eyes went wide.

"What?"

"Oh my God, it's you," she said with a laugh. At Kayla's look of confusion, she added, "You jog in Bryant Park."

Kayla took the shades back off and squinted at her, trying to make sense of her words, and then it hit her, why she'd thought London looked vaguely familiar. "You sit by the table tennis!"

"Yes!" And then they were laughing. "You smile at me every time you jog by."

"Why wouldn't I? Have you seen yourself?"

Gazes held then, until London laughed. "I can't believe I didn't recognize you until now."

"Same." Another beat of silence and gazing, and Kayla had so many questions and things to say swirling in her brain. But all she asked was, "Shall we continue?"

"Yes." London smiled up at her.

They ran. Side by side.

Jogging with Kayla had been more sensual and erotic than it should've been. London knew Kayla had dialed her pace down a notch—or twelve—so she could keep up, but that hadn't stopped the sounds of her breathing or the perspiration that made her skin glisten in the sun or the flexing of the muscles in her legs from teasing London as they went. She'd had no idea sexy jogs were a thing, but she knew now.

They hadn't talked much once they got going, and when they finished up, Kayla got a text from one of her colleagues and had to go. She said she hoped to see London again and that she'd be there jogging the next morning. It was a definite invitation, and London tucked it away.

She returned to the surprisingly quiet suite fully aware of the goofy grin that had plastered itself on her face, which she quickly wiped *off* her face because this was not something to smile about. Again, she thought about the night before and how somebody could've seen them. She was here working, not looking for dates. And she was here as Miranda's...what the hell was she? Companion? Flavor of the month? What if somebody had seen them? What if somebody had told Miranda they saw her companion making out with some other woman in a dark hallway? It would be humiliating. For both of them.

No. This had to be erased from her mind. From her heart. She liked Kayla. A lot. But the timing was all wrong and she needed to remember that. She was here to work.

She took a quick shower, dressed, and headed out into the still surprisingly quiet living room. No Miranda. No Ethan, even.

Miranda didn't seem to be a person who slept in, even if she had been up until the wee hours. At least, that was London's opinion. She was busy. She helped her family run a media empire. Sleeping in seemed like a luxury London had trouble associating with those other things. Yet her bedroom door was closed and it was going on nine.

To be honest, she was kind of relieved. She had no idea how long the two women had stayed the night before, but they'd still been talking and drinking and laughing when London had finally drifted off just after four.

A soft knock on the door and a voice calling, "Room service!" pulled her back to the present. She let the pleasant smiling man and his wheeled cart in. Okay, maybe Miranda was awake, as she'd clearly ordered breakfast. The scent of bacon wafted out from under one of the silver domes, and her mouth watered.

The waiter left just as Miranda's door opened and she stepped out, looking and smelling freshly showered, then pulled the door closed behind her, which was new.

"Good morning," Miranda said, her voice husky, and her gaze went straight for the coffee.

"Morning," London said, pouring two cups. "How'd you sleep?"

"Not long enough, but well." She grinned as she brought the cup to her lips. "I was thinking we do a food and drink tour today," she said then, as she gazed out the open French doors at the view. "I have a contact who fancies it up for me. What do you say?"

"Sure," London said. "Sounds great." In her head, she made notes on the fact that Miranda said the tour was *fancied up* for her.

She'd need to look up a standard tour and see what kind of better treatment they got. "What time?"

"We can play it by ear. Maybe midafternoon?" With a smug smile, she picked up a plate that had pancakes, scrambled eggs, bacon, and some fresh fruit on it and carried it into her bedroom, then shut the door once again with a soft click.

And then London heard voices. Plural.

"Are you kidding me?" she whispered out loud to the empty living room. It took everything in her not to run over and press her ear to the door. She sighed and snagged a piece of bacon off the plate left behind. One of the girls had stayed the night. Hell, maybe both of them had. That was something she hadn't seen coming.

Snagging another piece of bacon, she set down her coffee and decided she didn't really want to be there when whoever was in that bedroom with Miranda came out. She could get coffee downstairs on the patio, work on her notes, watch the water, and not be subjected to seeing how Miranda had bedded a woman likely half her age that she'd known for exactly less than a day.

And then she was annoyed with herself.

Once she was in the hallway and headed for the elevators, she gave herself a little mental talking-to for being judgy. If one—or both—of those girls wanted to sleep with Miranda, that was no concern of London's. Everybody was a grownup and, she assumed, consenting, so she needed to take off her judge's robe and put down her gavel and let people be who they wanted to be. Yes, she'd turned away Kayla in favor of not embarrassing Miranda because being here *was her job*. Those girls last night? They were on vacation. If London was on vacation, things would be different. But she wasn't.

She sighed as the elevator doors opened. "I'm not," she whispered. Then she followed her nose to the freshly brewed coffee.

✦

Kayla had the early shift that day, so after her workout, she showered—her mind on London and jogging with her the whole time—dressed, and headed up to Aria's suite to relieve Bo. When she got there, Aria was pacing and Cammie looked like she'd been run over by a bus, and also like she might throw up at any moment.

"I can't believe you just left her there," Aria was saying to Cammie as Kayla closed the door behind her.

"I'm sorry," Cammie said, her voice high-pitched, her face slightly gray. "I was drunk, and I didn't want it to turn into a threesome! It seemed kinda close a couple times. And Haley's a big girl."

"She's a big stupid girl when she's drunk," Aria muttered, more to the carpet she was wearing a trench into than to her friend. She seemed to notice then that Kayla had arrived. She ran to her and grabbed her hands. "Kay. Kay, can you go get her? I texted her, and she read it but hasn't answered me back."

"What are we talking about?" Kayla asked, hoping her calm tone would bring Aria's down a notch. Or seven.

"Haley. Last night. Remember, we went out to join that party?" Kayla glanced at Bo, who gave one subtle nod. "I got tired—it was three in the morning by then and you guys knew I had a Zoom call this morning." She shot a look at Cammie, who glanced down at the floor, clearly chastised. "So I came back up here and left them with that woman."

"What woman?"

"That one from the media family. North…something. Land? Wood? Lake?"

"Brook," Kayla said with a sigh. "Northbrooke."

"Yes. Her. These two"—Aria waved absently in Cammie's direction—"didn't want to come back. They wanted to stay and party, and apparently, they went back to her suite. Where Haley proceeded to spend the night."

Kayla looked to Bo once again. This time, he gave a subtle one-shoulder shrug. They both knew his job was to guard Aria. Sure, they'd guard her friends as well, when they were with her. But if they went off on their own, they were no longer under the watchful eyes of Tennyson Security. They weren't being paid by the friends. Aria Keller was the client.

"Please, Kay? She's probably following the woman around like a puppy at this point. I just want her back here." As she turned and walked toward the windows, she muttered, "So I can slap the shit out of her for doing this."

The last thing in the world Kayla wanted was to traipse to Miranda Northbrooke's suite and pick up her one-night stand. Luckily, Bo also knew this and stepped in at exactly the right time.

"I got it," he said, moving to the door. "I'll bring her back here and then hit the hay."

"Awesome. Thanks." Kayla tried to keep her voice light, while using her eyes to send Bo her eternal gratitude. He gave her a quick grin on his way out the door that told her he got it completely. Thank God.

"Thanks, Kay," Aria said, then shot Cammie another look.

"What do you want from me?" Cammie said, and it was clear she'd reached her limit of taking the blame. "*I* came back." She turned on her heel and stomped off to her room. The door slammed loudly, leaving Aria and Kayla standing in the living room looking after her.

"Well." Aria sighed as she flopped down on the buttery white leather couch. "I guess that's what I get for bringing my friends on vacation with me." She glanced up at Kayla, who still stood near the door. "Come on, Kay. I know you're my security detail, but we've done this long enough that I think we're friends. Don't you?"

"We are," Kayla said, moving farther into the room.

Aria indicated the chair across from her. "Good. Sit. Tell me what you think."

Kayla perched on the edge of the overstuffed chair, elbows on her knees. "I think Cammie's right. Haley's a big girl. She can make her own decisions." She frowned. "They might be…questionable decisions, but they're hers to make."

Aria nodded as Kayla spoke. "You're right. I know. I just…she's my baby cousin, and I've always looked out for her. I shouldn't have left her last night, but she gets stubborn when she's been drinking, and she was just determined to stay, and I was *so* freaking tired. So I left."

"I don't think you did anything wrong. Plus, it's not like she went home with some creepy guy from the neighborhood. She went home with a very respectable, very well-known woman. I'm sure she took good care of Haley."

"Why do you look like you ate a worm as you said that?"

Kayla burst out laughing. She couldn't help it. "Let's just say I'm familiar with Miranda Northbrooke and leave it at that."

Aria held her gaze for what felt like days, her big eyes capturing Kayla's, and Kayla was sure she was going to ask questions. She must've decided against it and just gave a nod instead.

"Hey, how did the Zoom call with your agent go?"

If Aria recognized her very obvious attempt to change the subject, she didn't let on. She sat up a little straighter as she said, "Fantastic. Greta Gerwig's directing a new drama and asked for me specifically. The script will be at my apartment when I get home."

"Oh wow, that's amazing."

"I'm excited about it. Could be good."

The door opened then, and Bo ushered a disheveled-looking Haley through it. Well, disheveled and royally pissed off.

"Really, Aria?" Haley's eyes were flashing behind her glasses. "You had to send the babysitter to come get me?"

Bo looked at Kayla, eyebrows raised to show what he thought of *that* descriptor.

"I wouldn't have had to if you'd answer your fucking texts," Aria shot back. "I didn't know if you were dead or alive."

Haley snorted in response, then stomped away toward her room. The door slammed just as loudly as Cammie's had, leaving the three of them in the living room blinking at each other.

"Jesus, it's like I brought my two teenage daughters on this trip with me," Aria said, shaking her head.

Kayla crossed the room to Bo.

"As much as I'd like to see what happens next," he said quietly, "I'm heading off to get some shut-eye. Enjoy your handful." He winked at her as she gave him a playful shove, and then he was out the door.

Back in the living room, Aria had pushed herself up from the couch and wandered out onto the sundeck. Kayla followed her but gave her space. Old habits had her scanning the corners of the sundeck, even though she knew nobody could get to it without coming through the front door and getting past Bo, who was built like a human brick wall. Still, her gaze wandered over every shadow, peeked behind every plant.

"Wanna just go shopping today?" Aria asked suddenly.

Kayla glanced behind her, wondering if one of the other girls had made an appearance.

"I'm asking you," Aria said with a laugh. She gestured toward the suite with her chin. "I've known those two long enough to know they're gonna be babies for a few hours. If we go into town, then they can come out here and enjoy the pool, and we'll all be out of each other's way for a while. By the time we get back, everything will be fine."

Kayla was surprised by the assessment. "You think so?"

"Please. I've been fighting with those two forever. I know so." She shrugged. "What do you say?"

"Aria, I work for you. If you say we're going shopping, we're going shopping."

Tuesday was hot, hotter than the previous days had been by a good ten degrees, and London found herself unexpectedly grateful for the air-conditioning in each of the stops during the food tour. And Miranda hadn't been kidding about it being fancied up. London had researched the tour they were on, and on their second stop now, they'd had nothing that was listed on the public menu. Also, the website said the tour included drinks, but not alcohol. Well, this tour certainly did, she thought, as a waiter handed her a French 75. And it wasn't a sample drink, just to give them a taste. It was a full-sized flute filled almost to the brim. There were seven stops on this tour, and if it kept going like this, she was gonna be *lit* by stop number four.

"Oh, thank God," she said quietly as their host set a plate of saltfish between them. The last place had brought them a bowl of goat water stew. London's grandparents had four goats on their land, and she'd grown up loving them like pets. There was no way she was eating goat meat. Her relief over the fish was palpable.

Miranda gave a soft chuckle. "No goldfish at home, then?"

"No, thank God." London chuckled back. Miranda had asked the names of the goats her grandparents had raised, then proceeded to only take one bite of her stew before pushing it away and claiming she didn't really like it. London knew she was lying but appreciated the gesture just the same.

"This is delicious," Miranda said now, chewing a piece of the fish.

That, London had to agree with, and she ate quite a bit, along with the Johnny cakes, which were little balls of dough, almost doughnutlike, hoping to get out in front of her impending drunken afternoon. She left half the French 75 in her glass as they moved on to the next stop.

This time, they were seated outside, on a shaded patio out front, and they were able to see straight down the street, all the shops, and the people bustling in and out of them. London didn't miss how the servicepeople fawned all over Miranda.

"Do these places know you're coming?" London asked.

Miranda looked momentarily surprised by the question, as if she'd never thought about it. "I mean, my travel agent sets it all up, so yes?"

"No." London cleared her throat. "I mean, do they know *you* are coming. Like, who you are?"

"*Oh...*" Miranda drew the word out with understanding. "I imagine so, yes."

Again, not really the answer she was seeking. She imagined Miranda's travel agent, though, explaining to the hosts of each place exactly who she was and what was expected. That made sense, because it was clear at each stop that the staff was expecting her and had been told to grant her every wish. She made a mental note to get an interview with the travel agent, if possible.

The drink here was the house rum, served on the rocks. It went in strong and with a bite, like lighter fluid at first, but then London found that it mellowed nicely on the back and sat on her tongue with a bit of a burnt-sugar finish. More Johnny cakes and a lovely stew—vegetable and completely free of goat—were set in front of them, and London dug in again.

"You have a very hearty appetite for a model," Miranda said. The words surprised London, especially coming from another woman.

"Former model," London said, correcting her. "And that was a big part of what I hated about the modeling industry—the body-shaming." She took another bite of the stew, a prickle of irritation crawling up her spine. She should stop there and let it lie. She should shut up. But she couldn't because remarks like the one Miranda had just made had nearly ruined her, health-wise. She met Miranda's eyes across the small table. "I saw the effects those kinds of comments had. I saw women starve themselves to the point of tanking their health, losing their periods. More than once, a model passed out during a shoot because she'd had nothing to eat for hours and hours, sometimes days. I saw anorexia develop and thrive. So many models are smokers because it curbs the appetite. And I admit, this isn't across the board. Lots of models have found ways to be healthy and still stay as thin as the agencies want them to be. But believe me, it could be horrifying. When everybody tells you that you have to be thinner or you're going to lose jobs, you do whatever you have to, and almost none of it is good."

Miranda had been watching her, and as she'd said more and more, she'd stopped eating, just set her fork-holding hand down on the table and listened, her eyes on London's face. London instantly wished she could take back half of what she'd said, at least until this job was over.

"Crap," she said, going for sheepish. "I'm sorry, I didn't mean to get up on my soapbox. I can get a little carried away on the subject. I apologize."

Miranda waved a hand like she was erasing a whiteboard with one swipe. "No need, no need. Never apologize for speaking with passion about something. Never."

Well. That was surprising. London let herself smile. "Okay. I won't."

"And I'm sorry. My comment was out of line."

"Forgiven."

"I imagine you heard that type of thing a lot from men," Miranda said, taking a bite of her stew.

"You might be surprised to know that it came mostly from women. Agents, producers, editors, photographers. Even other models."

Miranda scoffed. "I'm actually not surprised. Women would much rather tear each other down than lift each other up. In my opinion, anyway."

"I found that to be a sad but true fact." She took a sip of her rum and studied Miranda for a moment. "But you…you're in such a position of power and wealth. You can pretty much surround yourself with whatever people you want, right? People who lift you up instead of tearing you down?"

"Correct. And I do." Miranda shot her a smile over the rim of her glass, and for the first time since they'd first met several days ago, London thought maybe she and Miranda might actually end up being friends.

London couldn't speak for Miranda, but she seemed very content just sitting there and watching the world go by. Across the street from them was a panhandler. He had a guitar and was singing something London didn't recognize. Several doors down from him was a man sleeping in a doorway, his legs up against the frame.

Panhandlers and unhoused people. Not so far from New York City after all…

And over Miranda's shoulder, farther down the street, was a pair of women about to cross. Both carried bags that indicated they'd been shopping. London would recognize that gait anywhere—which was such a weird realization, recognizing the way somebody you hardly knew walked—and she sat up a bit straighter as she watched Kayla and Aria Keller enter a shop.

"What are you looking at?" Miranda asked as she turned to look behind her.

"Nothing," London said, even as she could suddenly feel Kayla's lips on hers. "Nothing at all."

Their car pulled up then. "Ready for the next one?" Miranda asked. And then they were in the car and pulling away, away from the restaurant and away from Kayla.

God, she had it bad.

❖

Kayla had run security for a lot of clients. She'd run security for both men and women. She'd even become friends with a few of them over the years. But she couldn't name a single one who shopped like Aria Keller. Holy shit.

Once they'd stopped for lunch, they'd hit about a dozen stores, and Aria wasn't even close to done. They shopped for three more hours, and by the time they were in the car headed back to the resort, there was barely room for *them* among all of Aria's bags. They needed the bellhop and a wheeled cart to get everything up to the suite.

"I'm gonna have to have the hotel ship this stuff back home for me," Aria said as they walked down the hall toward her suite.

"You think?" Kayla teased, as she texted Jake that she was back, and he could come take over. "Man, you can shop."

"One of my many talents," Aria joked back at her.

The suite was quiet, and both Cammie and Haley were on the sundeck on lounge chairs. Aria headed out there to see them and corralled them back inside so she could show them her purchases. Of course, being Aria, she'd bought them some gifts as well. The girls wandered into the living room, Haley looking a bit pale and tired, but okay overall. A knock on the door and then Jake arrived. Kayla gave him the report and gathered her things.

"We're about to have a fashion show, Kay," Aria said, her arms full of bags. "Sure you don't want to stay?"

Kayla laughed. "Already saw it all. But thanks." She gave a quick wave. "See you all in the morning."

Out in the hall, she felt herself relax. It was always like that at the end of a shift. Even when the assignment was simple, like this one had been, she was always on alert. Let's face it, it was her job to be on alert. She was on alert so her clients didn't have to be. That's exactly what they paid her for, handsomely.

In the elevator, she rubbed at the back of her neck, pressed into the flesh with her fingertips, and wondered if she had time to book herself a massage. She made a mental note to check with the concierge later on.

She took a quick shower, then dressed in simple shorts and a tank and went out onto the sundeck to call her mother.

"Well, there's my daughter the bodyguard," her mother said, her tone warm and sweet like honey. Kayla felt everything within her relax.

"Hey, Mom. How's things?" She pulled her lounge chair back a bit so it was in the shade, then sat, stretched out her legs, and crossed them at the ankle.

Her mother told her about her latest pickleball win, in which she trounced her best friend Maggie.

"You realize you sound absolutely delighted that you squashed your bestie, right?"

"Listen, she said pickleball was for people who had gotten too old to play tennis and that it was super easy. *She* challenged *me.* Clearly, I had no choice but to wipe the court with her."

"Clearly," Kayla said on a laugh.

"How are you, my girl? How's island life?"

"Not gonna lie, it's pretty sweet. My client wanted to shop today. I'm not sure she left anything for anybody else to buy."

"Girl after my own heart," her mother said. Then, "What's up?"

"What do you mean?"

"Sweetie, do you think I haven't known you for thirty-six years? Something's on your mind. Do you need me to coax it out of you using a very intricate series of trick questions until you finally spill it without even realizing it? Or do you just want to tell me?" Kayla heard her take a sip of something and swallow. "Either is fine."

She laughed. "Okay, okay. Fine. I'll tell you. Because the truth is, I could use your advice. Also, I'm gonna need wine for this."

She was off the clock until tomorrow, so she headed inside, popped open the bottle of chardonnay the resort had left for her, and poured herself a glass. She took a sip as she headed back out to her lounge. Not her usual varietal, this one was buttery and delicious and she took a quick photo of the label for future reference. Once she'd settled back down in her chair, she spilled. All of it. Every detail. She and her mother had that kind of relationship. Her mother knew the first time she'd kissed a girl, when she'd lost her virginity, the first time she'd smoked pot. So she didn't hold back here either. She told her about the first time she'd seen London, how interesting and fun their conversations were, how they kept running into each other. Then she told her about the ambush kissing and London's reaction to it and about jogging together that morning, and also learning the coincidence that they actually saw each other in Bryant Park on an almost weekly basis.

"Wow," her mom said once she'd finished her story. And that was all she said for a long moment.

"That's it? Wow? Not terribly helpful, Mom." She took a big sip of her wine.

"I'm taking it in. I'm taking it in. Give me a minute."

She heard her mother sip again and swallow and pictured her with a glass of iced tea, her favorite drink in the world.

"Tell me about the kiss," was what her mom finally settled on.

And Kayla couldn't help it. She sighed. A big, wistful, dreamy sigh.

"Oh wow. That good, huh?"

"Mom, I don't even know how to describe it. It was hot and sexy and sensual and…"

"She kissed you back?"

"Hell, yeah, she did." She frowned and took a sip of her wine before adding, "At first."

"Oh. Uh-oh."

"Yeah. She stopped it. She stepped back a tiny bit and said she shouldn't."

"She shouldn't what?"

"She said we shouldn't. And she apologized and then left."

"Ooh, ouch. What do you think she meant?"

Another sigh. "I don't know. Could be any number of things."

"True. She could be married or maybe she has somebody."

Kayla didn't like that option.

"She could be recovering from a breakup and isn't ready for something new."

"I suppose."

"She could be straight."

"Yeah, she's not straight," Kayla said with a snort. Then she told her about London watching her workout on the beach and then joining her, how hot their flirting was. "You don't have chemistry like that if you're not both interested."

"So? What are you going to do?"

"I don't know. That's why I'm calling you."

Her mom laughed softly. "Can you call her? Or text?"

"I don't have her number."

"Seriously?"

"Mom! I have been out of the game for a while." But she laughed because she knew her mother was just teasing her.

"Since Miranda."

"Who is here, by the way."

"What? She is? Ugh. What are the odds?"

"I know, right? Yeah, I saw her but she didn't see me, thank God. I'd like to keep it that way."

Her mother audibly inhaled slowly and then breathed out just as slowly. "I don't know what to tell you, honey. You might need to just hope you run into her again. I doubt the concierge would give you her room number—"

"Oh!" Kayla said, sitting up quickly enough that she sloshed a bit of wine out of the glass and onto the chair. "I already have it."

"Have what?" Her mother's tone said she was clearly confused.

"Her room number. From when we had breakfast at the same time. I saw her write her room number on her check." Her adrenaline hit in a surge that had her jumping up from the chair in excitement. "I know right where she is."

"Okay, hang on there, Casanova," her mom was saying into the phone. "What's your plan?"

"Plan?"

"Yes. Plan. You can't just go knock on her door and then kiss her again. She said no, remember? What if she's got somebody? You can't be showing up with flowers and champagne. Okay? You need to think this through." Her mother paused. "And you also need to accept that this may be something doomed from the start."

Kayla did not like that statement one little bit, but she had to hear it, had to take it in and accept it, because the reality was, her mother might be right. "Okay. Fine."

"Don't get sad. You never know."

"True."

They talked a bit longer and then hung up, Kayla feeling a little melancholy, like she'd just found out the dog she wanted to adopt had been adopted by somebody else. Maybe her mother was right. Maybe she simply needed to let go of this idea of London. The truth was, she didn't know much about her. Of course, that's what dating was for, to get to know somebody. But she couldn't take London on a date if she wasn't interested.

She went inside and refilled her glass, vowing to go downstairs to one of the restaurants and get herself a nice dinner as soon as she was done.

For now, though, she'd sit on her sundeck with her wine and listen to the ocean.

❖

"How do you stay so fit?" London asked the question before she could think about it, the words just tumbling out. Come on, she'd had five or six drinks put in front of her that afternoon, and even though she didn't finish them, she was definitely feeling them. Tipsy was a good word.

"Me?" Miranda asked, pressing a hand to her chest. Then her smile grew and she said, "My secret weapon is Raoul. Personal trainer. Body like an Italian statue. He works me out in more ways than one, if you know what I mean."

Good God, did Miranda sleep with everybody with two legs? She was starting to wonder and, thank Christ, was able to keep her lips closed around *that* question.

"And thank you for the compliment." Miranda picked up her phone and began to type. "I'm going to see if the girls want to come over again." She didn't ask if London minded, probably because it didn't matter if London minded.

"I think I'm going to go downstairs and do some work, if it's all the same to you."

"Of course," Miranda said without looking up.

In her room, London downed an entire bottle of water, then cracked open a second. She ate some crackers and a protein bar and drank the second bottle and finally started to feel human again. She took a shower, dressed in a simple mint-green sundress, pulled her hair back, and gathered her notebooks and pen and slipped them into her shoulder bag. Miranda didn't seem to notice her good-bye, and then she was out in the hall, hoping to skedaddle and not have to see Miranda's company.

She hit a new bar today. The resort had several, and she chose one with small tables for two outside, making herself comfortable in a corner out of the sun—she could hear her mother's voice lecturing her on the importance of sunscreen—with a spectacular view of the water. The sound of the ocean waves crashing against the shore had become a soundtrack at this point, one she'd grown used to and found soothing. When the waiter came, she ordered herself a glass of unsweetened iced tea with lemon and an order of Johnny cakes. "Kind of addicted to them at this point," she said to him.

He smiled knowingly. "Happens all the time."

She wasn't hungry for dinner, but she did want something a little sweet, and they'd be perfect. She took out her notebooks and her phone and opened everything she had so far.

One of the things that had struck her that day had been sitting at a bistro table on the sidewalk, being waited on hand and foot, eating and drinking very expensive things, all while a man slept in a doorway not thirty yards from them. There had been several more apparently unhoused people, sleeping in doorways along the street. London had had trouble eating at that particular spot. Miranda didn't seem to notice, but lots of people didn't notice, so that wasn't necessarily on Miranda. It just…was.

She opened her notebook and gazed out onto the water as her thoughts zipped around her head. So far, Miranda had never been rude to any waitstaff or service people. She hadn't been particularly warm, but she hadn't been rude. She didn't seem to be a rude person. She'd been…expectant. That was the thing London noticed most so far, in all of this comparison of very wealthy people to regular middle-class folks. The expectation. The entitlement. Miranda had…it was almost an aura of sorts, something that made it clear she expected to be waited on, taken care of, and given top of the line treatment without saying a word. And the service folks and waitstaff saw it, and they acted accordingly. True, they also knew who she was, were often given a heads-up prior to her arrival. But she didn't seem to throw her weight around. It really was almost a thing that hung in the air. She'd noticed the same in some of the others staying at the resort, especially the more noticeably famous. It was hard to describe, and she sat at her table for a long while, pen in hand, and stared out over the water as if the words might float to the surface for her.

The waiter interrupted her train of thought by setting a glass of white wine next to her. "From the gentleman," he said, indicating a man sitting across the patio, alone at a table. He wore mirrored sunglasses and a Seattle Seahawks baseball hat, and he lifted his glass in salute to her.

She sighed, and that weird, uncomfortable feeling settled in the pit of her stomach. This was where she always struggled, because she was brought up to be polite, not to be rude. And this type of situation always made her angry because now she felt like it was expected that she would thank the man, possibly talk with him.

The word *expected* stuck out in her brain then, and she glanced down at her notes. Expectation was such a damaging thing, wasn't it? It could make you horrendously uncomfortable. It could destroy a dream. It could wreck a relationship. She grabbed her pen and quickly jotted down her thoughts, then wondered how Miranda would handle this strange man sending her a drink. Would she invite him over for a chat? Would she tease him? Sleep with him? Belittle him? She could actually picture Miranda doing all of those things, and it made her laugh through her nose.

"I hope that wasn't too forward," came a deep voice, and when London looked up from her notes, the man was standing next to her table. He kept his sunglasses on as he said, "I just saw you from across the room and thought, God, she's beautiful." He gestured to her notebooks, phone, and pen with his chin. "I see you're busy, so I won't bother you. Just wanted you to know somebody noticed you. Enjoy the wine."

And just like that, he was gone.

Okay, that was the weirdest interaction of this sort she'd ever had with a man. She'd been hit on plenty. She'd had dozens and dozens of drinks bought for her, sent to her from across the room. Guys always took that as a reverse invitation. They bought you a drink, now you had to talk to them. Didn't matter that you didn't ask for the drink. But this guy? The fact that he'd noticed she was working and decided *not* to interrupt? Nearly unheard of.

She took a sip of the wine, which was delicious, and refocused on her notes.

❖

Naps were not Kayla's thing.

She wasn't a person who normally napped. Oh, she tried. She loved the idea of a good afternoon nap in the sunshine. Or even a power nap. Bo could close his eyes for fifteen minutes and be as refreshed as if he'd gotten a full eight hours. Kayla couldn't even fall asleep that quickly. And when she did nap, she slept too deeply and woke up cranky and annoyed. No, naps were not her friends.

And despite knowing that fact, she'd tried to nap anyway. She was tired. She was a little bit sad about the conversation with her mother and the whole London thing, having decided she probably needed to leave it alone. She must've needed it because she opened the sliding door to her balcony to let the breeze in, lay down on her bed, and promptly fell asleep.

She'd dreamt about a gorgeous blonde in a flowing white dress, walking barefoot on the beach. When she called out to the blonde, she looked up, and her face burst into clear happiness to see Kayla as she began to run through the sand and into Kayla's waiting arms.

She woke up cranky and annoyed.

There was paperwork to be done. More invoicing. An estimate for services. She needed to check in on three of her other teams and make sure everything was okay. She hadn't heard from them, so they were likely fine, but still. She was the boss and she should know.

A room service dinner crossed her mind, but she knew holing up alone in her room would not help the shitty mood she was in. No, she needed sand and surf and blue sky. Work could wait. The sun would be setting before long, but there was still time. And for God's sake, she was on St. Kitts! The place was gorgeous. She should soak it in every chance she had. She got dressed in some lightweight casual ivory pants and a royal-blue button-down tank, slipped on her sandals, and headed for the elevator.

Halfway down, her phone buzzed, one of her team leaders checking in. She texted him back as the doors opened and spilled her into the lobby, where she promptly banged into somebody walking the other way.

"Sorry," the man muttered, adjusting his ball cap on his head.

"My bad," Kayla said with a quick wave, and then she returned her gaze to her phone. A beat went by and something niggled at her, like a tiny pine needle in the collar of her shirt, poking at her neck. She turned to take another look, but the guy was gone, the elevator doors sliding shut. With a shrug, she headed out toward the beach.

"Kayla!" a voice called, and she veered to her left where Aria and Cammie lounged on chairs, a table between them littered with wineglasses and the remains of what looked to be a charcuterie board. Farther off to the left and a little bit behind them, Bo sat in his own chair, taking everything in behind his Ray-Bans. Kayla gave him a nod.

"What are you guys up to?" Kayla asked, glancing around. "You're down one."

Cammie rolled her eyes, and Aria shook her head. "Don't get me started. But sit. Join us. There's some cheese left. This one with the little hot pepper bits in it slaps. A little bit of dried fruit…"

"You're very sweet, but I think I'm gonna take a walk on the beach and then grab some dinner at one of the bars."

"You're sure?" Aria was disappointed, she could tell. And much as she liked her and enjoyed her company, she also needed to keep a line between business and pleasure.

"I'm sure."

"All right, well, we're probably gonna be here awhile longer if you change your mind. Somebody's gotta keep an eye on Bo." Aria glanced over her shoulder and winked in Bo's direction. He quirked an eyebrow but remained stone-faced. Aria looked back at Kayla. "Damn, he's *good*."

"Tell me about it." Another nod to Bo and she headed off toward the water. Walking had always been a way to clear her head. Ever since she was a girl, when she got upset or frightened or confused, she'd go for a walk. Sometimes, it was just around the block. Sometimes, it was for miles. One time when she was home from college and snowed in by a blizzard, she walked laps around the dining room table until she felt better. There was something about the simple movement of her legs, of putting one foot in front of the other, of the certainty that no matter what was going on, she could walk until she felt better, that grounded her and helped her to think more clearly.

She turned to her right and began to walk the beach. Focusing on her breath was something she'd learned recently, so she did that, trying to clear her head of anything else that was stressing her out. Walk and breathe. Walk and breathe.

The sun was beginning to sink toward the ocean, ready to put on a show. Kayla walked as the colors went from yellow to orange to a deep pink the color of the pomegranate juice she'd had with breakfast the other day. She stopped and faced the water, faced the sunset, and just watched the performance. You could think whatever you wanted about the people who walked on this planet, but the planet itself was beautiful. She inhaled deeply, exhaled slowly, and let herself feel it, that beauty. She let it fill her eyes and her lungs and her soul, and that little part of her she tried to keep quiet wished she had somebody standing next to her, somebody special to share such a glorious sight.

By the time she got back to the resort, the sun had made its curtain call and dusk had fallen. The breeze had picked up a bit, warm and salty, and she tossed a wave to Aria, Cammie, and Bo, all still sitting in the same place she'd first seen them.

The lobby had picked up, people milling about, heading out for the evening or deciding where in the resort they were going to dine. There was a sports bar of sorts on the other side of the resort she hadn't been to yet, so she thought she'd see if she could get a simple burger and fries—probably not a dish commonly ordered here, given the upscale nature of the resort, but she'd give it a try. As she was passing the bank of elevators and the small crowd of guests getting on or off them, her eye was caught by a flash of pale green and blond, and there was London, stepping onto the elevator. As she did, something fell out of her bag, but she didn't seem to notice, and the doors slid closed. London never saw her.

Kayla walked over and picked up the item. It was a pen, but a really nice one, heavy and solid, with the initials *LEG* engraved on it, and she wondered if it had been a gift.

London would probably be sad when she realized she'd lost the pen, which meant Kayla would need to get it back to her somehow.

With a smile, she slid it into her own small bag and zipped it up tight so it wouldn't fall out. The smile stayed as she continued on her way to find dinner, because she knew she was going to see London at least one more time.

Because now, she had an excuse.

CHAPTER SEVEN

L ondon couldn't believe it was Wednesday already. This trip was going so fast. She was enjoying herself—please, anybody who couldn't enjoy themselves here in the lap of freaking luxury was hopeless—and she was also garnering a lot of information for her article. While she was still in the early stages of organizing, she was going to be able to start writing it in earnest pretty soon, and that had her excited. And being excited about a project was one of her favorite feelings in the world.

She knew she'd told Kayla that she'd jog with her that morning, and she had stood on the sundeck waiting to see her on the beach, but she hadn't shown. And maybe it was better that way, depressing as it was to watch the beach and see no sign of Kayla at all. After all, they both lived in New York. Maybe she could just…sit in Bryant Park and wait for her to jog by, then jump up and ask her out. The ridiculous romanticism of that plan had her smiling, despite not seeing Kayla jogging.

She and Miranda hadn't made a solid plan for the day, so London remained in the linen pajama pants and tank top that she'd slept in and put her hair in a messy bun. She came out of her room just as Miranda was closing the front door of the suite, clad in her silk robe. Her hair was down and slightly tousled, and she looked younger, somehow. She wore an amused smile and was subtly shaking her head.

"Everything okay?" London asked as she headed for the room service cart with the coffee. Yeah, she could definitely get used to having *really good* hot coffee ready for her the second she came out of her bedroom. She'd miss that.

"Oh yes. Everything's fine. You know, I thought I would've had my fill of that one by now." Miranda poured herself a cup of coffee, as she continued to smile and shake her head. "I've enjoyed her and was sure, at this point, I'd be about done with all the inane chatter." She used her hand like a mouth and opened and closed it several times, a wide-eyed expression on her face. "But I'm not. I'm enjoying her company. I'm enjoying *her.*" Then she laughed softly and pulled out her phone, and London found herself wondering at that soft laugh, that amused smile. Then, a moment later, Miranda put the phone to her ear, and it was clear she was talking to Ethan about business as she took her coffee out onto the sundeck.

And just like that, Miranda became a little bit more human in London's eyes. Not that she hadn't been, but this turn of events was surprising, and London mentally reminded herself that you never could tell what was below the surface unless you took the time to actually look.

Coffee on the sundeck was a thing she'd been looking forward to when she woke up, but she had sort of hoped to have the sundeck and some silence. With Miranda out there chatting to Ethan, she'd never be able to concentrate. She grabbed her laptop from her room and made herself comfortable on the huge couch in the living room. Maybe she'd go down to the beach later today, do a little work, and then maybe read. People watch. Chat up the staff. That was something she really wanted to do—who would have more inside information on what it's like to be of service to the very, very wealthy than the waitstaff who served them?—but she wasn't sure how to approach them. Maybe she'd give Silas a call later. She owed him an update anyway.

She was typing herself a note when she heard Miranda's raised voice through the open doors to the sundeck. "Well, I don't care about that, do I? I've told you a hundred times what needs to be done there."

London grimaced to herself. Poor Ethan. Interviewing him would be huge, but she wasn't sure how she could without either putting him in jeopardy from Miranda or having him tell Miranda the kinds of things she'd asked. She was mulling over her options when there was a knock on the door.

That's odd. She looked at her watch—it was still fairly early—and she pushed to her feet. Probably the concierge or housekeeping dropping something off. Or maybe Miranda had ordered breakfast. She heard Miranda behind her, coming in from the sundeck. "Just get it done, for fuck's sake."

London pulled open the door.

And froze.

"Hi." Kayla stood there, looking absolutely edible in her casual clothes—lightweight black pants, a purple tank that left her delectable shoulders in full view, her dark hair in a ponytail, her face freshly scrubbed and free of makeup.

"Hey." How she managed to even push out that one syllable, London had no idea. God, it was good to see Kayla. Her brain tossed her a quick flashback of kissing those lips that were now smiling uncertainly at her. She could almost feel those straight white teeth as they nibbled at her lower lip.

Kayla's expression, which had been bright and happy when the door had opened, faltered now, stumbling into hesitant, unclear. And then she held up a pen. London's favorite Montblanc that her father had given to her as a gift when she'd first started writing. "Um, you dropped this yesterday. I saw it happen but couldn't catch you before the elevator closed, and well, after our last meeting..." Her voice trailed off and London hated the insecurity on her face, wanted to wipe it away. With a kiss. Okay, with several kisses.

She took the pen, and just as she opened her mouth to speak, Miranda's voice cut through the air, brittle and icy.

"Well, well, well, what do we have here?" She moved in close, stood next to London—not even next to her, practically on top of her—and then her arm was around London's shoulders and she squeezed her close. "How nice to see you, Kayla."

London wanted to shove her away. She wanted to be annoyed and ask her what the hell she was doing, but the look on Kayla's face kept every word lodged in her throat. She watched in horror as Kayla's eyes went soft, then hardened, as she blinked several times as if in disbelief, as she took in both their states of dress— London still in her pajamas, Miranda in a robe that left little to the imagination—and came to conclusions. Not correct ones, but conclusions that Miranda clearly wanted to broadcast. And honestly, probably the same conclusions London would've come to if their places had been reversed.

What was simply no more than a moment felt like it lasted a year. Finally, Kayla cleared her throat and spoke. "Nice to see you, too, Miranda." She turned back to London, but her gaze fell somewhere around London's chin, like she couldn't bear to look her in the eye. "Anyway, just wanted to get this back to you." Just as she practically shoved the pen into London's hand, Miranda leaned over and spoke very close to London's ear.

"Should we order some breakfast?"

London turned her head and met Miranda's gleeful gaze. She felt Kayla turn on her heel and hurry down the hall, but she couldn't bear to watch her go. The pen she held was still warm from Kayla's body heat, and there was a lump in London's throat the size of a golf ball. She wanted to leave, wanted to duck out of Miranda's embrace, which felt cold and icky this time, but she couldn't seem to make her feet move.

"Well, that was fun," Miranda said with a small laugh as she closed the door. "Did you see her face? Priceless."

"I…" London cleared her throat and finally unglued her feet from the floor. She clutched the pen as she sat back down on the couch. "Who…?"

Miranda poured herself another cup of coffee. "That's Kayla Tennyson. We dated for nearly a year until she decided we weren't working. *She* decided." Then she scoffed, as if that was the stupidest thing she'd ever heard. "Ridiculous." She shook her head and doctored up her coffee. "I had no idea she was here this week." She said it almost to herself. "Must be working." She raised her cup in salute to London, clearly oblivious to her shock. "What was she doing here anyway?" Miranda sipped and watched London over the rim of her cup.

London held up the pen. "I lost this. Downstairs."

"Ever the Good Samaritan." Miranda said it laced with sarcasm, like it was a bad thing, being a decent person. "Thanks for playing along. I hope we run into her again." And then she was dialing her phone, and then she was talking into it as she headed back out onto the sundeck, and London had never been so relieved in her life to watch somebody leave a room.

She sat there. Just breathing. Just blinking. Her brain felt overloaded. Not just by the crystal clear hurt that had been plastered all over Kayla's beautiful face, but by this new information she couldn't seem to compute. Miranda and *Kayla*? Kayla and *Miranda*? Had been a couple? Seriously? For almost a year?

"It makes no sense," she whispered to the empty room.

Kayla was sweet and kind and gentle. Miranda could be harsh and brittle and cold. How in the world had they made it work?

They hadn't, her brain reminded her.

But still. Nearly a year, Miranda had said.

She wanted to ask Miranda for more details, but she also didn't want to know. She wanted to go find Kayla, but she also didn't.

Kayla had found her. She'd made a conscious effort to get her pen back to her—a pen with significant sentimental value. She got points for that.

She heard Miranda's voice again. *She decided* she'd said, then snorted like it was unheard of that somebody else would choose to break up with her. The ego was large, that was for sure. And something about Kayla doing the breaking up made the whole thing just slightly more palatable for London. Slightly…

She pulled her laptop onto her lap and began typing.

❖

Kayla slammed the door to her room, fell with her back against it, and burst into tears as she slid down to the floor.

It was unlike her, this level of emotion. She normally prided herself on her ability to keep a lid on her feelings at all times. But this had been a one-two punch she just hadn't seen coming, Miranda being in the suite *and* being with London. The possessiveness was just nauseating. When she'd leaned in so close to London's head, Kayla was almost certain she'd throw up right there in the hall on the very expensive ceramic tile. And God, that satisfied look on Miranda's face. Did she know? Did she have any idea that London had been making out with her less than forty-eight hours ago? Maybe she did. Maybe London was the kind of person who would tell her girlfriend everything.

Ugh. She hated that word in her mouth, associating London and Miranda. Girlfriends. Ugh.

And then she cried a little more. Let herself get it out. Her mother always told her crying was a good thing. It released both toxins and tension, and while Kayla thought of herself as a very strong woman, she heard her mother's voice and let herself cry it out. She'd known that London had affected her, but not nearly as much as her tears were saying. Still, she let them come and, after a while, told herself it was time to get it together.

Maybe this was the Universe's way of telling her to let it go. Yes, she felt an outrageous connection to London, one that had happened instantly and was stronger than anything she'd felt in a very long time. But clearly, it wasn't meant to be. At least not now. In some other life? Past? Future? Maybe.

She pushed herself to her feet, only to cross the room and flop face down onto her bed. She hated this. *Hated it.* She barely knew this woman. Yes, they'd talked. Quite a bit. They seemed to have a lot in common. Kayla really, really enjoyed chatting with her, had wanted to again the moment they'd parted, wanted to talk to her all the time, get to know all of her. And the kissing…God, don't get her started on the kissing.

"All right. Enough." She stood up, gave herself a full-body shake. One thing she'd learned about herself was that if she started to wallow and let it go too far, she'd wallow all day and be of no use to anybody. No. She wasn't doing that here. She had a job to do. She needed to move. She'd been on her way to the beach to work out when she'd decided to drop the pen off.

Stupid fucking pen.

She hadn't worked out yet that morning, but she'd be damned if she was going back to the beach now where London could see her. Or not see her—which Kayla would also notice and then have to overanalyze just like she was doing now.

No. The Bella Grande had a very nice fitness center off the lobby. She'd go there.

She drove her body into the ground and it felt great. A good workout always soothed her head and calmed her racing thoughts. She lifted some weights, did some stretches, then ran, doing HIIT until her legs felt like they were made of rubber. The whole time, London's very pretty face floated around in her head, but she didn't let her speak. That was an accomplishment.

Back in her room, she showered and dressed and did her best to focus on work. One of her team leaders called with questions about the awards show they were working, and she sent out a few invoices, then checked in with her banker, and before she knew it, it was time to relieve Jake.

Aria's suite was on the same floor as London's, but at the opposite end, and so she took the stairs up, not wanting to risk running into either London or Miranda—mostly Miranda—at the elevators. She got to Aria's place and asked Jake for the rundown of how the night had gone.

"Fine. The usual." He lowered his voice and leaned down a bit. "Listen, I caught a glimpse of a guy last night on our way through the lobby." He hesitated. "It could've been our dude, but it was just a glimpse, and then he was in the elevator, and I couldn't get a better look." He subtly shrugged his enormous shoulders.

"Okay. Thanks for telling me." She sent him on his way to get some rest, then immediately texted Bo to let him know what she'd just learned.

Aria came out of her room and grabbed herself some coffee. "Catamaran today, Kay. I'm so excited!"

Kayla was glad for today's excursion. It would get her off the island for a solid seven to eight hours, thereby eliminating any chance of her running into London. Or Miranda. Or, God, both of them. Together. Holding hands or something worse.

Aria knocked on one of the other bedroom doors. "Cammie, you ready?"

"Just a sec," came the reply.

Then Aria tapped lightly on the third door, let herself in, and closed it behind her.

A few minutes later, Cammie came out, beach bag in hand, big sunglasses on her face, her red hair pulled up into a ponytail.

"You smell very coconutty," Kayla told her.

"That's my sunscreen. If I don't slather myself, I will fry like an egg. The curse of the freckled redhead." She shrugged and sighed, and then Aria came out of the third room and shut the door again, followed by Haley, who was practically floating.

Aria shook her head, and her expression was a mix of amusement and a little concern. She met Kayla's expectant gaze, and her face said *Tell you later*, without her having to use any words at all.

Forty-five minutes later, they'd made it through the lobby and down to the pier without running into Miranda or London, and Kayla sent up a little prayer of thanks. It wasn't long before they'd set sail and were on their way across the Narrows toward the island of Nevis. There was really nothing for her to do until they got to Nevis and off the boat for a bit, so she found a comfy spot in a corner, settled in, and let the sun toast her nicely and the wind play with her hair, as they sailed along.

The captain announced that they'd stop halfway to the island to do some snorkeling, but to relax for a bit. Aria came over and flopped down next to her.

"Hey," she said, bumping Kayla's shoulder with hers.

"Hey yourself. All good?"

Aria sighed and laid her head back against the boat cushion behind her. She looked gorgeous, if not a bit skinny for Kayla's tastes. But such was the life of an actress. Kayla worked for several and they were all alarmingly tiny. Nature of the business. Her dark hair was loose and blowing in the wind, and when she pushed her sunglasses up onto her head, Kayla was struck by the unique hazel-green-brown color of her enormous eyes, as she was every time. "Did I tell you I hesitated to bring Haley on this trip with me?"

Kayla shook her head. "You didn't, no."

"She's my cousin and I love her. I really do. We practically grew up together. But we're very different people."

"I can see that."

"She's impulsive and"—Aria seemed to search for the right words—"easily impressed. Winning her over doesn't take much."

Kayla nodded, waiting for the rest of the story.

"Cammie's much easier to hang with. She gets it."

"Gets what?"

"My career. The special precautions that sometimes need to be taken. Like having you guys around." She pulled her sunglasses back down. "But Haley…" She sighed again and, this time, frowned, gazing in the direction of her cousin and best friend at the front of the boat. "My mother made me bring her." She turned to meet Kayla's gaze. "And like I said, I love her, don't get me wrong. She's family."

Kayla closed a hand over Aria's forearm. "Aria. You and I have gotten to know each other pretty well. I'm not going to judge you, okay? Haley being your family and you loving her and also being totally irritated by her can all exist at once."

Aria visibly relaxed then, her shoulders dropping, and she lay back again. "She went home with that woman. The cougar? Twice now."

Kayla squinted. "What cougar woman?"

"Miranda. Remember? She hit on me first, but I turned her down, so I guess she reset her sights, and Haley was all too happy to oblige. They've been together the past two nights, and she's floating around on a cloud now, and I'm worried. I mean, shouldn't I be? The woman's a gazillionaire from New York City, and Haley is a secretary from Ohio. It's not gonna last, and Haley's gonna get her heart broken, and I warned her, so what else can I do, right? Kay? Kayla?"

GEORGIA BEERS

Kayla gave herself a mental shake, Aria's words bouncing around her head like so many ping-pong balls. "She's spent the night there?"

"Uh-huh. Twice."

"What about…" She cleared her throat and tried again. "What about the other woman? In the suite?"

"The pretty blonde?" Aria asked without missing a beat. "I mean, I was only there once, but she said hi and then went into her own room. I didn't see her again, so I don't know."

Cammie called for Aria from the front of the boat, gestured for her to come, so Aria pushed to her feet and headed that way.

Kayla's head was spinning.

Miranda had slept with Haley? Twice?

London had her own room?

Then her brain reminded her of Miranda's possessive arm around London's shoulders, the way she'd leaned in so disturbingly close.

Okay, wow, this was messy. Or was this their thing? Did they sleep with other people? Did they have an arrangement? She thought back on her time with Miranda, short as it was, and not once did she ever mention anything about wanting a polyamorous relationship. Not once did she sleep around, not that Kayla knew of. Oh, she'd flirt mercilessly with men and women. All the time. It was literally a part of her personality that Kayla had decided she had no control over. She just did it. But while she had her issues with Miranda, infidelity hadn't been one of them. At least, she didn't think it had been.

Did London know?

That was the big question. She must, right? If they were staying in the same suite—in separate rooms? what?—she'd have to know that there was another person, wouldn't she? And then she remembered just how big Miranda's suite was—it was at the opposite end of the floor from Aria's because it was twice the size— and it made her wonder even more. Of course, the next question was, should Kayla tell her? Should Kayla tell London, a person she

• 138 •

barely knew if she was being honest, that she was concerned her girlfriend was sleeping around on her?

Jesus Christ.

She rubbed a hand across her face as the full scope of just how ridiculous her thoughts were smacked her in the head. None of this was any of her business. Yes, she'd kissed London, in a very ill-advised move. Yes, London had kissed her back, solidly and passionately, but she'd also stopped it. She'd also said they shouldn't, and she'd walked away.

Kayla needed to walk away, too.

She knew that. She knew in her heart that it was the only correct move. It didn't matter the pull she felt toward London. It didn't matter that she was sure London felt it, too. She needed to step away.

The boat slowed down then, as the crew moved around, dealing with sails and getting ready to drop anchor for snorkeling. Aria was super excited, if the giddy look on her face was any indication.

"Kay! You going in?"

Her initial plan had been to simply bask in the sun while Aria, Haley, and Cammie snorkeled, but now, she seriously needed the distraction. Crystal-blue water and colorful fish oughta do the trick.

"Absolutely." She pushed to her feet. "Let's do this."

London felt icky.

It was the best word. *Icky.* A little dirty, but mostly icky. And she couldn't get the look on Kayla's face out of her head, a combination of confusion, sadness, and horror. She was actually worried it would stay in her brain forever, like initials carved into the trunk of a tree, deep and permanent.

She'd wanted to go after her, to chase her down in the hall and apologize and tell her it was all a ruse, that she wasn't actually with Miranda, they were occasionally pretending for whatever weird reason Miranda had. And then she'd wanted to kiss her, hard and soft, giving and demanding, and tell her that she was so sorry she'd run away after their first kiss and could she please just kiss her some more.

Of course, she did none of that.

She'd stood there, riveted to the floor, until the door had closed, Miranda had grinned, and London's heart had squeezed hard in her chest.

Miranda was on her phone now, speaking firmly to whatever poor unlucky bastard happened to be on the other end, pacing the sundeck. London could see her in her peripheral vision each time she passed the open French doors.

And her brain just could not fathom it.

She tried. She did her best to put Miranda and Kayla together, to envision them dressed up and going out to dinner, Miranda's hand tucked in Kayla's elbow, but it just felt...God, it felt almost cartoonish. She just couldn't seem to make it make sense.

Nearly a year.

But how? And...just, how?

Kayla was not a person who was going to leave her mind, her heart, easily. She might not have understood that at first, but it was clear now. She didn't need to be hit over the head with it. Again.

Miranda came back inside. She was off the phone, and she just stood there for a moment. Stood looking at London and not saying anything. The clear glee she'd had on her face at Kayla's departure was gone, replaced by something London couldn't quite identify. "Would you come to the beach with me today?"

London's initial plan had been to play it by ear. And then after the whole Kayla-at-the-front-door fiasco, she'd decided she'd just hang in the suite and work. But there was something about the tone of Miranda's voice as she asked, something about what could only be called the sadness in her eyes, that had her changing her tune. "Sure, the beach sounds great." She closed her laptop. "You okay?"

A beat passed, and Miranda looked like she was about to say something but shrugged instead. "Fine," she said quietly. "I'm gonna go change."

"Okay." She watched Miranda go into her room and close the door softly behind her, and it occurred to her that it was the first time Miranda had entered or exited a room subtly.

Not long after that, they were on the beach, stretched out on lounges, umbrellas over both of them.

"I don't think it would even be possible for this day to be any more gorgeous," London said wistfully. "The temperature is perfect. Not too hot. The breeze is lovely. The water is the most amazing blue." She turned to look at Miranda. "And the company's not so bad." She wouldn't have normally said anything, but Miranda seemed…sad. That was the only word she could come up with. She seemed sad.

Miranda turned to her and gave her a weak smile. "Thank you, London. That's very kind of you. I could say the same." They were quiet for several moments, just listening to the roar of the ocean and relaxing in the breeze, and then Miranda spoke again. "I'm sorry about earlier."

London turned a questioning gaze to her.

"With Kayla. I shouldn't have done that. To either of you. It was childish and just not cool."

She'd never heard Miranda use the word *cool*, and it made her smile and made Miranda seem—again—more human somehow. "There's a story there. I can tell. I'm happy to listen. Or you can tell me to mind my own business. Either is fine."

Miranda seemed to think about that. Her head was back against her lounge, and her large, dark sunglasses kept London from seeing her eyes. Several minutes went by, and she figured Miranda had opted not to share, but then she spoke.

"Kayla is good people. Like, the best of people." Miranda spoke quietly, the breeze taking a syllable here and there and whisking it away before it made its way to London's ears. "I knew that. I knew I was lucky to have her. At first."

"How did you meet?"

"I hired her company to do security for me at a large media event. We clicked pretty quickly."

That surprised London. First, that they'd had much in common, and second, that Miranda clicked instantly with anybody. Or allowed herself to. She nodded for her to continue.

"We began spending time together. I took her out. She took me out. And before long, we were pretty much inseparable." A small chuckle. "Well, as inseparable as two very busy people with very busy jobs can be. We spent as much of our free time together as we could." Miranda's somewhat dreamy smile of reminiscence morphed a bit then, and a frown took its place. "She was always telling me how much she admired me, how impressed she was with the way I ran my family's business, how being the only woman in the Northbrooke family must be so hard. And I don't know what happened, London. I honestly don't." She swallowed hard—London could see it—and cleared her throat. "I started to think that admiration wasn't admiration at all, it was envy. Jealousy. Sarcasm. It got to the point where every time she said something nice, I'd bristle and search for what she *really* meant."

"Oh, Miranda." London grimaced, because the anguish on Miranda's face was clear. And real.

"I know. To this day, I'm not sure why it happened, but I couldn't make it stop. I questioned her constantly until she was afraid to say anything at all." She was quiet for a long time before adding, "She's the only person in my entire life who ever left me. And she was right to." A tear coursed its way out from under her sunglasses, and if she hadn't seen it, London wouldn't have known Miranda was crying. Her voice stayed steady, and the sunglasses hid her eyes.

She didn't want to ask, but the conversation sort of begged the question. "Do you think you could ever get her back?"

Miranda snort-laughed at that. "Oh God, no. Trust me, Kayla Tennyson deserves much better than me. Much better."

The waiter came by to see what they needed, and London couldn't help herself. She ordered a mai tai before she could think twice. Miranda barked a laugh. And then she ordered herself one, too. They were silent until he returned a few minutes later with their drinks, as well as a platter of things to nibble on, which was probably a good thing.

Miranda sat up on her lounge and turned so her feet were in the sand. She pushed her sunglasses up onto her head and made eye contact with London. Her eyes were slightly watery, but for the most part, she looked like she'd pulled herself together. "Thank you, London. I know it's been strange for you to pretend to be with me when you're not. Especially this morning, when I caught you off guard. I needed the confidence boost in front of Kayla, though, and having somebody like you on my arm, so to speak, was perfect. So I thank you for that." She held out her coconut shell and London touched hers to it.

London had so many questions. Well, so many more questions. But Miranda sat back on her lounge, and the sunglasses came back down over her eyes. She reached for a slice of mango from the tray and ate it while watching the ocean. She was quiet, but there was something about her that told London she was done with this part of the story, and London prided herself on her ability to read people's body language. Miranda was taking no more questions.

She sat back as well, doing her best to mentally catalog the things she'd learned. She couldn't exactly pull out her notebook and start jotting things, but there were elements of the conversation she wanted to remember, like the blurring of the distinction between admiration and envy. That would definitely need to go into the article.

But it would wait. She took a sip of her drink—which was sweet and strong—and wondered where Kayla was right then.

❖

Snorkeling had been a perfect distraction, just as Kayla'd hoped. She'd been able to put the whole Miranda–London thing out of her mind completely for a little while.

Of course, now that they were on the island of Nevis and Aria, Haley, and Cammie wanted to spend some time on the beach, Kayla had plenty of time for those thoughts to come screeching back into her brain. She grabbed herself a lounge and positioned herself off to the side and back a bit. This way, she could keep an eye on her clients, but not be close enough to, for example, eavesdrop on their conversation. If Kayla did her job right, most clients were able to ignore security. She became invisible to them. And even though Aria had invited her to sit with them, Kayla had declined, choosing to position herself to watch, but not participate. Which was perfect for now because she was all talked out from the catamaran.

Nevis was just as beautiful as St. Kitts, and as she sat and looked out over the ocean, she could see St. Kitts on the horizon. Her brain instantly reminded her that London Granger was there, on that island on that horizon, and Kayla rolled her eyes at herself. *Yes, thanks for telling me something I was already much too aware of.*

The beach was surprisingly sparsely populated, just the three of them, a small handful of women about fifty yards to the left, and various beach walkers passing by. Aria laughed at something Cammie said, and like St. Kitts, there were waitstaff taking care of their every need. On the beach. Kayla grinned, thinking how there were some things she'd never get used to, and having a waiter bring you stuff on the beach was one of them.

She pulled out her phone to see a text from her mother.

Any updates on the girl you kissed?

That was so her mom, straight to the point. No greetings. No preamble.

She typed back, *You were right. Doomed from the start.* She sent that and waited a beat before adding, *She's with Miranda.*

A long string of wide-eyed emoji came back and then a *Noooooooooooooo.* Kayla laughed. She couldn't help it.

Oh yes. Miranda was all too happy to make sure I knew it, too. She sent the text and glanced up. A couple walked on the beach holding hands. The handful of girls laughed loudly, and then a guy followed a bit behind the couple. His shoes dangled from his fingers, his feet splashing in the water. He glanced at Aria, Haley, and Cammie, who'd stopped talking, their heads back as they baked in the sun.

Her phone buzzed. *That bitch.* Kayla smiled at how her mother was always on her side, no matter what. She'd always hated Miranda, thought she was fake, inauthentic, wore masks, and nobody actually knew the real Miranda, if there even was one. Of course, she'd never said any of this until after Kayla had left Miranda.

She was about to type a text back when something tapped at her brain. She squinted and raised her head. The guy on the beach had walked past, but his pace had slowed. A lot. He was looking over his shoulder at Aria, and Kayla could see his phone, which had a red case, surreptitiously under his arm, pointed at her.

"Damn it." She pushed to her feet and began to walk toward the man. He wore a baseball hat and sunglasses, but as she got closer, she recognized him as the man in the photo she'd distributed to Bo and Jake. She got within about twenty feet of him before he realized she was following him and pulled his phone back. "Sir, Miss Keller would appreciate you not photographing or recording her without her permission."

He kept walking and picked up his pace, giving Kayla a quick glance over his shoulder. "This is a public beach. Taking photos isn't a crime," he said but kept walking.

"You're right. Still, Miss Keller would appreciate you not taking photos or videos without her permission."

"Whatever." He walked even faster, and Kayla slowed. She had no intention of chasing him. And he was right—he'd committed no crime. But part of her job was simply letting a person like that guy know that she was there, that security was watching him. And she could take him down if she had to.

Honestly, with the mood she was currently in, she'd kind of hoped he'd make a move on her so she *could* take him down. That would've been satisfying.

She stood in the sand, hands on her hips, and waited until he was well out of sight. She hoped he could feel her eyes boring into his back. Finally, she turned and walked back to where Aria was waiting.

"That was him, wasn't it?" she asked.

Kayla nodded. "Afraid so."

"How did he know I was here?" Her frustration was clear.

"Oh, for fuck's sake." Cammie held her phone out for Aria to see the post Haley had put up a few days before. It was a photo of the outside of the Bella Grande, with both Aria and Cammie in the background. The caption read *St. Kitts is gorgeous! Can't wait for an entire week of beach time!* "You gave him everything. Location, length of stay, who she's with. Jesus, Haley."

"What? I…I was just posting my own stuff! I can't even do that?" Haley pouted and folded her arms. "I'm sorry."

Aria sighed. She didn't seem angry, just resigned, like this had been totally expected. Maybe it had been. "I asked you not to post while we were here. To wait until we got home." She shaded her eyes from the sun, gave Haley a look, and glanced up at Kayla. "Now what?"

Kayla inhaled a deep breath and let it out as she looked down the beach. The guy was long gone. "We watch out for him. We do our best to keep a big distance between you and him. Unfortunately, he was right. Walking and taking photos on a public beach isn't a crime. So all we can do is stay between you and him. Don't worry. He won't get near you."

Aria looked slightly less than convinced, but this wasn't something new for her, and Kayla knew it. Being young and pretty and the It Girl of Hollywood meant people not only recognized you, but they wanted to get close. Fame was a strange thing, something Kayla worked closely with but had yet to fully understand. Even when she and Miranda had been together, they would attend functions and fundraisers, and people would want to get close to Miranda. Like, *close.* Stand near her. Touch her. Luckily for her, Miranda'd grown up in that environment, and she was able to turn on her Ice Queen persona at the flick of a switch, and people stepped back instantly. Aria didn't have that yet. Kayla smiled. *Give her ten years. She will.*

"We've got to be back at the pier in thirty," Kayla said, seeing the time.

Aria frowned, then sat up and began gathering her things. "Might as well head there now. I don't want to sit here anymore so some creep can take secret photos of me." She scratched at her neck. "I give it a week before those show up in a tabloid."

"I'm sorry, Aria," Kayla said, and she felt terrible. "I should've seen him sooner."

"I didn't see him either," Aria said and gave her arm a squeeze. "Nobody's fault."

Back on the catamaran, the mood was a bit more reserved than on the way to Nevis. Aria was quiet, and Cammie seemed not to want to disturb that. Haley stayed quiet, too, on her phone here and there, but mostly gazing at the water. She felt bad, it was clear by her expression of guilt. The three of them sat and watched the water, the breeze blowing their hair, none of them speaking.

Kayla reclaimed her seat in the back corner, as there was nothing for her to do in her professional capacity on the boat, unless Aria's stalker decided to jump out of a plane and parachute onto it. She had her doubts about that happening.

Back on the island, she walked with them up to Aria's suite and waited until Bo came up to relieve her. She took him out into the hall to bring him up to speed.

"All right, our guy is here. I saw him on the beach taking photos as he walked by. I confronted him—or tried to, as he kept walking away. Baseball hat and glasses is about all I got for him physically, but his phone case is red. That should be easy to spot."

"Jake said he was pretty sure he'd seen him yesterday. He had a Seahawks hat on."

"Well, Jake was right." She frowned. "Aria's pretty upset that he got beach pictures, so let's make sure if we see him again, we get between him and her. Fuck up any possible shots, yeah?"

"Damn straight." Bo's dark brows met in a V above his nose, an expression that said he meant business. It was something she loved about him, one of the reasons he was such a great employee—he took his job seriously. If that guy on the beach got any more photos of Aria Keller, Bo would take it personally.

She slapped him on the shoulder. "All right. It's all you now. Text if you need me or if you see him again."

With a nod, he entered the suite, and Kayla headed to her own room, feeling sad, dejected, and a bit like a failure at her job.

Oh yeah, it was gonna be a great night.

❖

Wow, today was eye-opening.

That was the thought that kept rolling through London's head on a loop. She and Miranda were back in the suite now, as it looked like an evening storm was coming through. According to the concierge, it would pass over quickly, so they'd left the beach, come back up to the suite, and dragged lounges back under the eaves so they could sit outside and watch the storm.

London had never seen anything like it. Living in New York City, she didn't get to see huge swaths of sky, thanks to all the buildings. But here, out over the ocean, she literally watched the storm clouds roll in over the water, getting closer and closer until they blocked out the sun. The wind picked up, bending the palm trees and increasing the size of the waves. Thunder rumbled. And seeing great jagged strikes of lightning cutting across the sky out over the water was something she wouldn't soon forget. She and Miranda oohed and aahed throughout the storm, which lasted less than half an hour. Then the sun was back and the sundeck was steaming as it dried, and things were as they were, like there hadn't been a storm at all.

"That was amazing," London said quietly as the sun peeked back out and the last gray cloud passed overhead. When she turned to look at Miranda, she was smiling, maybe a little sadly. "Thank you for letting me come here with you."

"To be honest," Miranda said, "I've enjoyed the company far more than I expected to. So thank *you* for that." A few minutes of silence went by before Miranda spoke again. "I'm thinking of ordering room service and having dinner here tonight. You are by no means obligated to do that, but you're certainly invited. I thought I'd eat here and then head downstairs for a nightcap later."

"Will you meet Haley?"

Miranda's smile was soft. "I think I might."

"I wanted to get some work done, so room service and eating

here actually sounds perfect, if you don't mind me joining you." It felt different now, somehow. London couldn't really put a finger on the exactness of it, but it seemed she and Miranda had turned some kind of corner. "I feel like we had some kind of breakthrough, me and you," she said after a moment. "Almost like we're friends now." Okay, that might have been a risky thing to say, but she was just being honest. It was how she felt. She wrinkled her nose at Miranda, who laughed, actually laughed, a real, honest-to-goodness laugh that came from deep in her belly.

"Oh, London, you do amuse me." She reached across the space between their chairs and, to London's surprise, held out her hand. London grasped it. "We are most definitely friends. And I don't say those words often. Or lightly." She gave London's hand a squeeze and let it drop. "All right." Miranda pushed herself up from her chair and let out a breath. "Enough sitting around. I have some calls to make and some emails to respond to, and I should give Ethan a break."

"Oh my God, I totally forgot about him," London said with a laugh. "He kinda blends into the scenery." She wrinkled her nose again, worried that maybe wasn't an okay thing to say, but Miranda barked a laugh.

"He does because that's what I pay him to do. I'm glad to see he's successful at it." She stood up and brushed her hands down her sides. "In all seriousness, Ethan is fantastic. I don't know what I'd do without him." She squeezed London's shoulder as she passed to head inside. "We'll order dinner in an hour or so."

London went inside and grabbed her laptop, along with a bottle of water, and went back outside to her lounge. Her brain had been buzzing since the beach, and she opened her notes page and jotted down everything she could remember from their conversation, which still boggled her mind.

As she typed, she realized that she'd pre-assigned Miranda a two-dimensional personality. She'd made an assumption that whatever kind of person she thought a billionaire would be, Miranda would match it. And she had, for a while. She listened as Miranda talked on the phone in the living room of the suite, and she waited until she heard her say her good-byes. When she was sure she'd hung up, she called her name.

Miranda popped her head out the door. "Hmm?"

"What would you say is the biggest drawback to being a billionaire? Like, not taxes or financially. Personally. What's hardest?"

She was surprised when Miranda only took a couple seconds before answering. "Nobody tells you the truth."

London squinted at her. "What do you mean?"

Miranda walked across the sundeck to the railing and seemed to look for her words out over the water. "People sometimes mistake being wealthy for being wise." She turned to look at London and leaned her back against the railing. "Which is not to say I'm not wise, because I am." A smile. "But I can stand up in front of a large group of people and say something completely inane, totally off-the-wall stupid. And because of who I am and how much money I have, they'll shrug and run with it. They'll think I'm brilliant. Nobody will stand up and say *But, Miranda, that's the dumbest thing we've ever heard.* Because they're afraid of me." A glance down at her feet, which were bare now. "It's hard to find genuine friends when people simply agree with everything you say." And when she looked back up, there was such a sad loneliness in her eyes, London felt her heart squeeze.

Miranda's phone rang in her hand. She glanced at it and muttered, "Gotta get this," and went back inside. And London had the unmistakable sense that she'd just seen a more honest glimpse of Miranda Northbrooke than most people ever had the chance to.

She typed.

You'd never know there'd been a storm. When she glanced back up from her screen nearly an hour later, that was her first thought. The sky was clear, the sun was setting, the breeze ruffled her hair, and her stomach rumbled. Loudly.

"Wow. I heard that from in here," came Miranda's voice. "Looks like I'm not the only one ready for dinner. What should we tell Chef Marco we'd like?"

London closed her laptop and headed inside where Miranda was on the white leather couch, her laptop in her lap, her feet on the coffee table and crossed at the ankles. "You know, I could get used to this personal chef thing." She sat down across from Miranda.

"Listen, this suite costs an arm and a leg and a half. It had *better* come with a personal chef."

"How much is an arm and a leg and a half?" The question was out before London could think about it. She'd never asked for such specificity from Miranda, but again, she felt like they'd leveled up today.

Miranda must've thought so, too, because she didn't miss a beat. "Six grand a night."

London gaped at her. "Six grand? A night?"

Miranda nodded and seemed to enjoy her reaction.

"That's...forty-two grand for the week!"

Another nod. "Just for the suite. That doesn't include drinks at the bar and the beach, food at the restaurants, excursions. Granted, I do get comped often."

"But still. My God." She thought of people she knew who barely made forty-two grand *a year*, and here Miranda just dropped that for a week of vacation. It was absurd to think about.

Miranda gave a small chuckle. "You look like your mind is boggled."

"It kind of is," London admitted with a laugh. "Wow."

"You know, it's interesting to me because I'm just used to it. I grew up this way. My father would think nothing of dropping a hundred grand for something he wanted. Didn't bat an eye, so neither do I. I sometimes forget how that computes to somebody..."

"Like me," London finished. "A regular person."

Another small chuckle. "Yes, for lack of a better phrase. A regular person."

"Can I ask you questions over dinner? For the article? I have a few."

"Of course. But we need to decide what we want first."

Forty-five minutes later, room service was delivering their own personal dinners, prepared for them, as usual, by Chef Marco.

They shared enormous filets of king salmon, sides of roasted sweet potatoes and asparagus, and London decided after the first bite she might actually kill somebody to have this meal again. Chef had sent up two different wines—a slightly chilled pinot noir and a crisp chardonnay, and they sampled both. Miranda preferred the white, London the red. They sat across from each other at the gorgeous cherrywood table in the dining room that London had completely forgotten the suite had. She had a notebook next to her, and she asked a few questions as they ate.

"When did you realize you were super-wealthy?" At Miranda's laugh, she clarified. "I mean, maybe you didn't. You probably went to school with other kids from wealthy families, right?"

"True. I went to private school with lots of other privileged kids, but I don't think I was really aware of my family's legacy until I was maybe…twelve? Thirteen? It's around then that you start to think a bit about what you want to be when you grow up. So, I started paying attention to my father and his job, and that's when I learned that our business was a family one."

London jotted notes as Miranda spoke, all of it so interesting to her. "And what about your dating life?" She looked up to find Miranda blinking at her in what seemed to be confusion. "Well, I mean, this is an article about what it's like to be a billionaire, and I assume billionaires date, so…what's dating like for you? I imagine if finding genuine friendships is hard, then finding a genuine partner is even harder."

Miranda took a bite of her salmon and chewed thoughtfully as she slowly nodded. "You're not wrong. I don't really date much. I was married for a short time, but there always needs to be a prenup and some people are very much put off by that."

It was London's turn to nod as she jotted notes. She switched from her pen to her fork and took a bite, marveling at the melt-in-your-mouth texture of the salmon. "Tell me more about the downside of your wealth. You mentioned nobody tells you the truth. What else?" She liked this new version of Miranda she was seeing.

Miranda gestured with her fork as she spoke. "Reputations

have momentum in both directions. Up and down. We rise, but we fall just as quickly, and wow, do people love to see the wealthy fail. I would blame Donald Trump for that, but I think it was true long before he was ever on the scene." She sipped her wine. "People are unfailingly nice to my face, but behind my back, they want me to crash and burn."

"Really?" London was surprised not only to hear this, but to find that Miranda was aware of it. "You think so?"

"Oh, I know so. Remember, I earned my money the old-fashioned way—I inherited it." She gave a wink, seemingly to show London that she was poking fun at herself. "People hate that. And honestly? I get it. I didn't have to work my way up any corporate ladder, and I understand completely how unfair that can seem." She leaned forward slightly. "That's not to say I didn't have to work, because I did. My grandfather didn't just hand things over to my father, and my father won't just hand things over to me. He's taught me. He's taken me under his wing. Yes. But he's also expected me to learn to fly on my own."

"And you have."

"Damn right I have. I'm the first female CEO of the company, and I take that role very, very seriously." Her eyes were steely as she held London's gaze.

London nodded and jotted some notes. She scanned what she'd written that day, and her eyes landed on the notes about dating, which made her think about Kayla. Again. How disconcerting it must have been for her to come looking for London and find her ex instead.

"All right." Miranda interrupted her thoughts by setting her fork down and tossing her napkin onto her plate. "That was lovely. I think I'm going to go shower and then head downstairs for a nightcap. Care to join me?"

"I'd love to."

"Excellent. Meet you out here in, say, ninety minutes?"

❖

She should be in her room.

The thought ran through Kayla's head as she ordered another bourbon on the rocks. Her second. Yeah, she was most definitely wallowing. Not a good look for her. She knew it, yet she sat there at the bar and sipped. Jake was on duty and Aria and Cammie had wanted to go to the club again while Haley hung back. Kayla was so glad she wasn't with them. The idea of a loud, pounding club was more than she could take. No, this bar on the resort was nice. Classy, fairly quiet, populated, but not with a rowdy bunch.

She couldn't compute that London was Miranda's newest plaything. Like, her brain just wouldn't take it in. Refused. London was beautiful, yes, but Miranda had never had trouble getting gorgeous people to sleep with her. No, London was more. She was intelligent and funny and her own person. Independent. Fierce. Had she been *that* off base in her assessment? She was usually so good at pegging a person—had she missed the mark so incredibly? She reminded herself that Miranda had also been with her, and she liked to think she was all of those things as well, so...

Still.

Didn't it just fucking figure?

She hadn't been drawn to somebody the way she was to London in a very long time. Truth be told, she hadn't even been drawn to Miranda that strongly. She sighed and took another sip. She needed this week to be over so she could go home, regroup, and get her damn shit together.

The bourbon was doing its job, warming her blood, relaxing her muscles, and she was finally starting to feel better, when she glanced up toward the entrance.

Goddamn it.

She saw Miranda first, which wasn't a surprise, given that she was tall and regal and commanded the attention of whatever room she walked into—something Kayla had always found impressive. But right behind her came London. Not quite as tall, but inarguably fucking gorgeous, even in the simple black pants and royal-blue top. She moved so gracefully, like a dancer, and again, she was reminded how London seemed to glide across the floor, rather than take individual steps. Her blond hair was down and wavy along her shoulders, and Miranda said something to her that made her throw her head back and laugh, exposing that long column of neck that Kayla really wanted to run her tongue up and down. They walked into the room and to a bistro table for two in a far corner. Good. That was good.

She resisted the urge to toss back the rest of her bourbon and leave, knowing that wouldn't help her feel any differently. She had to ride this out. She needed to stay and not be driven out of a perfectly nice bar as she drank her top shelf bourbon because her ex and her...God, what the hell was London anyway?

Didn't matter.

She turned her barstool so she was at a slight angle and could see the TV behind the bar—the joint could be classy and still have TVs—and kept her eyes on the women's tennis match. She knew little to nothing about tennis, but she made herself watch.

"Hey." A voice startled her and she turned to meet Aria's big hazel eyes. "Whatcha doin'?"

Kayla held up her nearly empty glass. "Decompressing." She took in Aria's dewy skin and the sparkle in her eyes. "How was the club?"

"Awesome. Not as busy as last time, but better music. We danced our asses off."

"And got back early."

"I know, right? We were tired and—"

"Hey." Haley had come up behind them.

"Hi," Aria said and put an arm around her cousin. "Come to hang?"

Haley nodded, and Kayla wondered if she knew Miranda was in the far corner with London. Had she seen them yet?

"We got a table over here," Aria said, pointing in the opposite direction of Miranda's table for two. "Come on."

Kayla watched as Aria led Haley to the table where Cammie was already sitting and talking to the waiter. Jake was off at a nearby table watching.

Kayla hazarded a glance in London's direction. Miranda was

speaking to the waiter, and suddenly, Kayla's gaze was snagged by London's, and the thing that surprised Kayla? She didn't look away. She held her gaze, then gave her a sort of sad smile. Well, that's what it looked like to Kayla, so she gave her one back. Except it felt all too real, the sadness in her smile. She held her glass up slightly in a silent toast to London, which seemed to make London's smile grow just a bit. The last thing she wanted was for Miranda to see her sitting there at the bar, making eyes at her girlfriend, so she tossed back the rest of her bourbon.

"Time to go," she whispered to herself and gestured to the bartender for her bill. She signed, then made her way over to Aria's table where the three of them sat happily with beers. "I will see you all in the morning, yes? Is tomorrow a beach day?"

Aria nodded. "Yeah, I think so. I've been checking excursions and might want to do one more, but there's only three days left, and I want to make sure to have a little more beach time."

"Perfect. I'll see you guys tomorrow then." She squeezed Aria's shoulder, sent a nod Jake's way, then headed toward the door, and it took every ounce of strength she had not to look back at the cozy little table for two in the corner.

But God, she wanted to.

❖

God, she didn't even look back.

London was a little surprised by how much that stung, and she watched Kayla leave until she'd turned out the door and was no longer in sight. Then she glanced over at the table with the actress and her crew, and the girl from the past couple of nights, Haley, glanced their way and her eyes went wide, clearly seeing Miranda for the first time.

"Looks like somebody's happy to see you," she said quietly, shaking her head with a smile while poking at the cherry in her old-fashioned with her swizzle stick. "What are you gonna send to the table?" She winked at Miranda.

"Whatever do you mean?" Miranda asked.

"Please, I know you're going to." She glanced back at the table to see the waiter presenting them with a bottle of wine, clearly describing it to them. Haley's smile grew, and she blew a kiss toward Miranda.

"Maybe I already did."

"You are smooth." She laughed softly. "It's impressive."

"Why, thank you. I try." Clearly pleased with herself, Miranda sipped her martini. "I noticed Kayla was at the bar. She must've left."

"She did." At Miranda's raised eyebrow, London realized what she'd let slip. She closed her mouth and gazed into her drink, the rusty-colored liquid suddenly fascinating.

"What's wrong?" Miranda asked, and her voice was gentle, a tone London hadn't heard very often in the past several days. When she glanced back up, Miranda's eyes were soft, her head tipped slightly to one side, the embodiment of friendly curiosity.

London took a deep breath. "I need to tell you something."

Miranda signaled the waiter and ordered another round of drinks. "Seems like we might need them." They waited until the drinks arrived. Then Miranda put her forearms on the table and leaned slightly forward so she could look London in the eye. "Talk to me."

Oh, where to begin, where to begin?

From the beginning, came the answer.

She cleared her throat. "I met Kayla on Saturday, the second day we were here. I was here, sitting at the bar and working on my notes, and some guy hit on me and she kind of rescued me from him."

"Sounds like Kayla." There was no sarcasm in Miranda's voice, so London went on.

"We kind of hit it off. Talked for a bit. Then I left and came back to the suite." She took a sip of her old-fashioned, strong and sweet. "And then one morning, without planning to, I watched her working out on the beach—I could see her from our sundeck." She grimaced, and Miranda barked a laugh.

"London, please. Kayla is gorgeous to look at, and I've seen her work out. I understand the draw. Stop worrying so much."

"I kissed her."

She blurted it out, and that definitely stopped Miranda short. "Oh. Um. Oh. Okay."

"I'm sorry. I stopped it. Actually, she kissed me, but I kissed her back." She swallowed and stared at the table. "I definitely kissed her back," she muttered before looking back up and meeting Miranda's gaze. "But I stopped it. I told her I couldn't. I didn't know who she was at the time, in relation to you. But I knew I was supposed to be here with you, and I didn't want to mess that up, so I stopped it and left. I did run on the beach with her the next morning and sort of touched on how what we did was a mistake. I didn't really give her a reason, and then she got called away by her job and…I haven't really talked to her since."

"And then the pen thing happened."

London nodded. "Yeah. And then the pen thing happened."

"And I made sure it looked like we were together."

Another nod.

"Oh, London." Miranda sighed loudly and gazed off into the distance. "I'm so sorry about that."

London gaped at her. "You're sorry? For what? I'm the one who risked damaging your reputation."

And then Miranda was smiling. And the smile morphed into a quiet chuckle as she shook her head.

"What?"

"London. I literally slept with another woman here. In our suite. Twice. The appearances thing was just that, so we wouldn't be harassed. It's far too easy to feel far too vulnerable when you come to a place like this alone. As for my behavior when Kayla came to the room…" She picked up her martini, and over the rim added, "I can be quite childish at times."

London let a beat pass before she, too, was smiling. "I mean, I didn't want to say."

That made Miranda laugh out loud, and London joined her. When they'd calmed a bit, Miranda studied her, really looked at her, to the point where London almost started to squirm. "You like her."

"I'm sorry?"

"Kayla. You like her."

Was there any point in denying it now? She hesitated.

"London." Miranda's voice was firm and gentle at the same time, strange as that seemed. When London met her gaze, she asked, "You do, right? I can tell by the look on your face, and I've never even seen you together." She sipped her martini and added, "I'll tell you one thing, though. The expression on her face when you opened the door…it makes a lot more sense now that I know the story."

London squinted at her. "The expression on her face? What do you mean? She didn't expect you to be there."

"No, she didn't."

"So her expression was surprise over that, don't you think?"

"Well." Miranda pulled the swizzle stick out of her drink and tugged an olive off it with her teeth. "You don't know her as well as I do, which means you don't know her face like I do."

London felt a little sizzle of jealousy that she didn't like zip through her, but she nodded her agreement.

"She wasn't as upset about seeing me as she was about seeing you *with* me."

That was a surprise. "You think?"

"I know. Kayla dumped me, remember? And well she should have. She's not upset to see me. She may not enjoy seeing me, but it doesn't upset her. I'm in her past."

"Huh."

Another laugh from Miranda. "I see how convinced you are."

London realized she'd tensed up around this entire conversation, and she made herself relax a bit, drop her shoulders. "Sorry. I'm just…surprised."

Miranda leaned in again. "Listen, Kayla's fantastic. I'm the one who fucked that up so badly. If you're interested in her, you have my blessing to make a move. You don't need it, but you have it." She sat back, sipped her martini, and watched London over the rim of the glass.

It shouldn't feel weird, right? It did, though, just a little bit. London gazed into her own glass.

"Anyway. Think about it. I'm going to use the ladies' room."

London watched for a moment as Miranda left her alone at the table. The bar was fairly busy, the stools all taken but one, most of the tables full. The din of conversation was more of a hum than a rumble, as if it was already a known fact that this place was less rowdy than some of the others. She scanned the bar and realized a guy was sitting there watching her. He looked away quickly, turned away from her so as to see the TV better, but not before she caught his eye. Wasn't he the same guy who'd sent her the drink yesterday? He'd had a baseball cap and sunglasses on, so she'd hadn't really gotten a good look, but it could've been him. Couldn't it?

Miranda returned from the ladies' room but stopped at Aria Keller's table. Haley's entire face lit up, and when she reached out for Miranda's hand, Miranda let her. Took it. Squeezed. Held.

Wow. London grinned as she watched and took a sip of her drink. Somebody had it bad. Maybe two somebodies.

CHAPTER EIGHT

B each days were easy.

Normally, Kayla loved them because, aside from keeping her eyes peeled for any nefarious characters, she could basically relax and think. Problem was, she didn't want to think at this point. She wanted occupation. Distraction. Something, anything to take her mind off not only London Granger, but London Granger with Miranda Northbrooke. Because that pairing just did her head in.

"Do you think the people that live here get bored with the perfect weather?" Aria was lounging on a chaise, sunglasses on, eyes closed, and her question didn't seem to be addressed to anybody in particular, but only Cammie and Kayla were close enough to hear her.

"What do you mean?" Cammie asked. She, too, was lying back on a lounge, but her eyes were open and she gazed out over the ocean.

"I mean, we've been here for almost a week, and aside from an occasional very quick rainstorm, the weather has been just like this—warm, sunny, and perfect—every day. I just wondered if people get tired of it being exactly the same all the time." She shrugged as if she didn't really expect an answer, was just thinking out loud.

Kayla grinned, though. "I've wondered the same thing. Maybe it's because I live in New York and the weather is all over the place much of the time. And don't get me wrong, I love this perfect weather. But maybe I love it so much because I rarely have it at home."

Aria nodded. "Truth. LA has nice weather, but it's so busy, and don't get me started on the smog." She sighed the sigh of somebody completely relaxed. "I will miss this, that's for sure. Who are you texting?" This question was directed at Cammie.

"Just making sure Haley's okay." They'd left the third member of their trio up in the suite. Apparently, she'd spent the night away. Again. Kayla had to make a conscious effort not to roll her eyes. Aria and Cammie seemed okay with it and rolled with the punches, so to speak. Cammie set her phone down on the little table between her and Aria and returned her gaze to the water.

Kayla was ready to go home. Seeing London out for drinks with Miranda last night had been hard, harder than she'd anticipated, and it was all so weird, wasn't it? She'd met many women she'd found attractive over the years, and when some had proven unavailable, she'd moved on. No harm, no foul. So why was this one driving her mad? Why couldn't she get London out of her head? Yeah, she just wanted to be back in New York, back in her Manhattan apartment, back to running in the park, back to a Starbucks on every corner, to the hustle and bustle of nameless, faceless people everywhere.

Cammie's phone pinged and she picked it up. "Did you close the door tight when we left?" she asked Aria.

Aria lifted her head. "What?"

"The door to the suite. Did you close it behind you?"

"Of course I did."

Cammie held up her phone. "Haley says she came out of her room after her shower to get some coffee, and the door was wide open."

Kayla's attention went from wandering through her own head to zeroing in on what Cammie was saying in a split second. "Can she tell if anything is missing?"

Cammie sent a text and waited. When it pinged back, she said, "She says she doesn't think so, but it's hard to tell." She glanced at Aria. "You were the last one out the door. Maybe it just didn't latch?"

"I mean, maybe?" Aria sat up and took off her shades, looking from Cammie to Kayla and back.

Kayla pulled out her phone. "Let me get Bo over there to look." When she glanced up, she saw a shadow of concern on Aria's face, and she smiled at her. "Don't worry. No big deal. Cammie's probably right. The door probably didn't latch properly." She didn't really think that—the doors in a resort this high-end were heavy and designed to close firmly, whether you tugged them closed or not. She texted Bo a brief rundown of what she'd learned and told him to check it out.

Aria was looking up and down the beach now. "What if it's that asshole again?"

"I'm sure it's not," Kayla said. "But if it is, we'll deal with him."

"Can we go up?" Aria asked, looking from Kayla to Cammie. "Do you mind? Just for a bit? I want to make sure Haley's all right."

"Absolutely," Cammie said, gathering her things.

Fifteen minutes later, they were entering the suite. Bo was already there, standing in the living area with Hayley. He met Kayla's gaze and gave a subtle shrug. Aria turned in a slow circle, her eyes stopping on things like her laptop on the couch, Cammie's Kindle on the coffee table. The doors to the sundeck were open, but they always were—there was no way to get to it unless you scaled the side of the building.

"I mean, it looks okay." It was Aria's turn to shrug. "Maybe the door *didn't* latch." She turned to Haley. "And you didn't hear anything?"

"I was in the shower, but no." Haley shook her head.

"Okay, check your rooms, just to be thorough," Kayla said, and Aria and Cammie scattered to their individual spaces. "We'll have to be more conscious of pulling the door shut behind us," she said to Haley and Bo.

"Oh my God!" Aria's voice was higher-pitched than normal, and Kayla shot a look to Bo. They both ran to her room.

"What?" Kayla asked as Aria sat on the floor in front of her dresser. A drawer was pulled out and empty.

"All my underwear is gone!" Aria's eyes were even bigger than normal, and Kayla didn't think that was possible.

"What?" Cammie asked as she entered the room.

"Every single pair." Aria made a face. "Oh, ew. Some creepy guy has my panties."

Kayla was relieved to see Aria being more angry than scared or upset—not that she wasn't the last two. The expression on her face was one Kayla hadn't seen before—angry determination. "All right, I'll go downstairs and talk to the concierge. We'll need to file a report with them and the local police."

"Ugh, do we have to get police involved?" Aria asked, pushing to her feet.

"You don't want to?" Cammie asked.

"I just…the media will get ahold of it, and then there will be a million tabloid headlines about my stolen panties all over the place and…" She lifted her arms out to the sides and let them drop.

"If you don't want to file a police report, that's your call," Kayla said. "But we definitely need to let the resort know. I'm going to give the front desk the photo I have of the guy, so they can keep an eye out. And I'll get you new keys." She frowned. "I'm really sorry, Aria."

"Please," Aria said. "This was not on you. You guys have been guarding me twenty-four seven. I told you I feel safer with you around, and I wasn't kidding. That hasn't changed."

The relief Kayla felt then surprised her. Things like this didn't happen often at all to her clients, so she was just as bothered as Aria was, and there was an element of responsibility thrown in. This had happened on her watch, and she hated that. She looked at Bo. "Can you stay here with them while I head downstairs?"

Bo nodded. "I got this."

"Thanks." She headed out into the hall, then stopped and watched as the heavy door closed firmly and latched. She pushed on it, just to be sure, and it didn't budge. "Goddamn it."

❖

London had spent several hours that day working. She wanted to say she'd been cooped up, but the reality was, she'd been on a lounge chair on the sundeck of their suite, typing on her laptop. Cooped up? Not so much. Tired of working, though? Absolutely.

She decided to take a walk.

She'd started inside, simply walking around inside the resort. The air-conditioning was nice, and the place was huge, so she did a little exploring and actually found a small rooftop bar that she hadn't known was there. She'd have to mention that to Miranda. After wandering for a while inside, she headed out to the beach. As usual, the weather was gorgeous, and once she got down to the beach, she kicked off her shoes and carried them dangling from her fingers, as she walked up to her ankles in the refreshing ocean waves.

It was beautiful here, she couldn't lie about that. It was a literal paradise, and getting a taste of what it was like to vacation at an upscale resort when money was no object? Wow. Like, unbelievable wow. She'd made a nice living when she'd been modeling, but she'd quit before she could reach the higher income ranks, and even then, she wouldn't have come close to where Miranda was. Not even on the same financial planet. She'd noticed yesterday as she'd walked past one of the housekeepers that there was a hole in her shoe. She wasn't sure what had made her look down, but she'd seen it right away, the woman's toe poking through the top of the shoe. And that made her wonder what a member of the staff here thought about servicing people like Miranda. Did she enjoy it, knowing maybe there'd be a large tip? Did she hate it, hate knowing how much one person had that maybe she didn't? Or did she just accept that this was life, this was her job, and was neutral about it all? These were questions to be explored not necessarily in the article—which was meant to be a bit lighter, it was, after all, for *TN Squared*—but definitely in the book.

She made her way back to the resort, the air-conditioning causing goose bumps to erupt across her arms when she entered the lobby. She was walking through when she noticed Kayla at the front desk, clearly waiting for somebody and looking concerned. For a moment, she considered simply walking by, pretending she didn't see her at all, but then Kayla turned her head and their eyes met—as clichéd as it was—across the crowded room.

London walked toward her.

"Hi," she said and tried to ignore the expression on Kayla's face that was a combination of what looked to be fear, irritation, and resignation.

"Hey," Kayla said, then looked away, but not before London also caught a flash of sadness.

She opened her mouth to say more, but the front desk clerk returned with another person. The concierge, if London remembered correctly, a tall, lean man with kind eyes whose accent suggested he was a local when he asked, "Ms. Tennyson. I understand there's been a problem."

"There has," Kayla said. "Somebody broke into my client's room."

"Oh my God," London said on a gasp before she could stop herself, and she reached to grasp Kayla's arm. She felt her flinch slightly, so she took her hand back.

"Oh dear," the concierge said, a split second behind London. "Are you sure?"

Kayla lowered her voice. "There were some…items taken."

"Oh dear," the concierge said again. "Have you contacted the authorities? We can do that for you."

"No, my client would rather not, but maybe you can take a look at your security footage and let me know what you see? Or I can take a look with you?"

The concierge looked like he was going to immediately decline that, but instead, he said, "Let me see what I can do. Please wait here." He disappeared through the door behind the desk, leaving the front desk agent, Kayla, and London standing there.

"Are you okay?" London asked and ventured to touch Kayla's arm again. No flinch this time.

Kayla nodded but didn't look at her. "Yeah. I'm fine. Aria's pretty freaked, though."

"I can imagine. God." She liked her hand on Kayla's arm, so

she kept it there. She felt the warmth radiate from her skin, felt the solid muscle under her hand. Kayla kept her eyes on the counter in front of her, and London's heart squeezed in her chest. "Will you not even look at me?" she asked on a whisper, very aware of the desk clerk's proximity.

Kayla shook her head slowly, but then must have changed her mind, because she finally did turn, and her dark gaze met London's. She said nothing, but her expression held so much more than words could have conveyed, and London felt a visceral reaction to it. Pain, hurt, anger, desire, confusion, trepidation, it was all there, plain as could be, written all over her face.

"Can I help?" she asked. "Do something for you?" She gave Kayla's arm a squeeze.

The concierge returned then, and London felt an irrational anger at him for the interruption. "If you come back here with me, we can look at the footage from your client's hallway." He held his arm out toward the back doorway.

Kayla gave him a nod. "Great." She moved to follow him, and London let go of her arm, but then Kayla stopped. She stared down at her shoes for a moment—sandals, and her toes were polished a deep plum, London noticed—before seeming to gather herself to look back up at London. She spoke very quietly, so only London could hear her. "Look. If things were different, maybe. Maybe I'd ask for your help. Your support. Something. But things are the way they are, so…" She shrugged, and her eyes looked sad.

London shook her head. "There's so much you don't know," she whispered.

That sadness in Kayla's eyes vanished and was replaced by something…hard. "I'll tell you what I do know. I know you're with Miranda Northbrooke, and I am *not* messing with Miranda Northbrooke. You only have to do that once in a lifetime to know never to do it again." With that, she turned away and followed the concierge back through the door to whatever lay back there, leaving London standing at the front desk feeling deflated, hurt, and like she'd just let something slip through her fingers that she should've held on to with both hands.

She stood there for a moment, not wanting to leave, but having no reason to stand there while the front desk clerk looked at her with eyebrows raised expectantly. A quick nod and she moved along, no longer feeling the pure joy she had just ten minutes ago at being in such a beautiful place. Now? She just wanted to go back to the suite.

Miranda was sitting in the living room on the couch, her phone to her ear and her laptop open on the coffee table. Her tone was firm, and whoever was on the other end of the line was getting a stern talking-to. Ethan sat at the round table in the corner, his own laptop open, and he pushed his glasses up his nose with one finger as he gave London a nod but said nothing. London could feel Miranda's eyes on her even as she spoke, following her into her room until she shut the door.

She changed into her bathing suit, grabbed a bottle of water from the mini fridge, and went out her own French doors to the sundeck. She cracked the water open, took a large slug, then left it on a table and took the steps down into the pool. The water was cool enough to be refreshing, but not cold, and she squatted so it covered her shoulders. Then she moved to the far end, put her forearms on the edge, and gazed out over the ocean, wondering what she'd been supposed to learn from everything that had happened in the past week.

The look on Kayla's face earlier was going to haunt her. She just knew it. Why did Miranda's ex have to turn out to be the one person London found so magnetic? The one person she'd totally be interested in seeing in any other setting possible? She and Miranda were friends now, and you didn't go after your friends' exes. You just didn't. Unspoken rule and all that crap.

What was the plan here? What was the point?

That's what she wanted to ask the Universe. What had been the damn point? Why show her something amazing, only to snatch it away and say *Sorry, not for you?* Why? What was she supposed to learn? She inhaled deeply and blew it out forcefully.

"Well, that is quite a sigh coming from somebody looking at such a view." Miranda waded into the pool and walked through the water, arms held up in the air, a rocks glass in each hand. When she reached London, she handed her a glass and held the other aloft. "First, we toast to this view with some of the best old-fashioneds I've ever tasted, while we understand that very few people ever get to see it. Then we sip. And then you tell me what's on your mind." Miranda's voice was so gentle and the small gesture was so kind, London felt her eyes well up. "PS—I don't do well around crying women. Just so you know." But there was a hint of a smile on Miranda's face as she said it.

"I don't believe that for a second." London touched her glass to Miranda's and sipped dutifully. Miranda hadn't been kidding—the drink was delicious, both citrusy and a little smoky. "Wow."

"Told you." They were quiet for several moments as they both took in the view before them. "It never gets old, does it?"

"I think probably not." She turned and met Miranda's gaze. "Thank you. For letting me tag along, for giving me a peek into your world."

Miranda touched her glass to London's again. "And I'd like to thank you as well. I said it before, but I feel I've made a new friend." She glanced away and there was a flash of emotion on her face that surprised London. "That doesn't happen to me very often."

"That makes me sad," London said, taking another sip.

"Eh." Miranda lifted one shoulder in a half shrug, clearly done with that. "Par for the course." They watched the ocean, listened to its roar, gazed at the people on the beach. London breathed in a deep lungful of the fresh salt air just as Miranda spoke. "So, tell me what has you sighing like the sad main character in a country song. Is it Kayla?"

London looked at her in surprise, and that made Miranda bark out a laugh.

"Please. First of all, you clearly underestimate me if you think I couldn't figure that out. And second—your underestimation is likely accurate. I'm not that in tune to others, unfortunately. Kayla would tell you the same thing. But honey, it's written all over your face every time her name is mentioned. And the times I've actually seen you occupy the same space, it's been clear that it's mutual." She lowered her voice and leaned closer to London. "Don't forget how well I know Kayla."

Talking to Miranda Northbrooke about not only her ex, but about how much London wanted her ex, was not on London's bingo card. Not today. Not this week. Not this year. Not ever. And yet here they were, standing in a pool that was the perfect temperature, looking out over a perfect view, while they sipped perfect cocktails. "This is so surreal," she whispered.

"Life often is, I've found." They were quiet for a moment. "Why don't you talk to her?" Miranda finally asked. "Tell her the truth. I'm fine with that."

London made a face, knowing she should feel relief, but also hesitant. Very, very hesitant. "I don't know. I've been sort of shady from the beginning. I let her kiss me, and then she learned I was with you, and that makes me look like a cheater. I had plenty of opportunity to tell her the truth, and I just didn't. She probably doesn't trust me, and I wouldn't blame her. Maybe it just wasn't meant to be."

"Wow," Miranda said, then sipped her drink and kept her gaze out over the water. "I know you were talking, but all I heard was *poor me, poor me, poor me.*"

London blinked at her in shock. "I'm sorry?"

"First of all, *meant to be*?" She made air quotes using the one hand that wasn't holding her glass. "Ridiculous. Doesn't exist. Things aren't meant to be, things are made to happen. *You* make them happen. How do you think I got where I am today?" Miranda met her eyes. When London quirked an eyebrow at her, she grinned. "Aside from inheriting. Yes, I inherited, but I also work my ass off."

"I know." London nodded. "Sorry. I just thought that was funny. You do work like crazy, I've seen it."

"That's right. And one of the most important things I've learned from all that work is that there isn't time in life to beat around the bush, to tiptoe. Say what you mean. Mean what you say. You don't wait for things that are meant to happen. You go after the things you want. Sometimes you get them, sometimes you don't, but you have to *make the effort.*"

London tipped her head. "You really think it's that simple?"

"I know it is."

She shook her head, unconvinced.

"All right, let me put it another way. What have you got to lose?"

That made her stop. Think. Wonder.

"Right?" Miranda said after a beat went by.

"I mean, it could turn out terrible. She could call me a liar and a phony."

"She could. *Or* you could end up with something really, really terrific. So, that's what you need to ponder: What do you have to lose, and what might you possibly gain?" Miranda held out both hands and alternately lifted them like scales. "Pros and cons." She glanced at her watch, then drained her glass. "All right, I need to go check on a presentation Ethan's working on for me." She put a hand on London's forearm and gave it a squeeze. "Think about it."

London was pretty sure she was going to think about nothing else.

Miranda wandered back toward the steps and climbed out. Over her shoulder, she tossed, "And stop sighing."

London couldn't help her grin. It was something she hadn't expected, to actually become friends with Miranda Northbrooke. Like, actual friends. She sipped her drink.

Life was so weird.

"I hate that this happened on my watch, Bo. Hate it." Kayla had a headache now, probably from how tightly she'd been clenching her jaw since the moment she found out Aria's underwear was missing.

"Our watch," Bo corrected, his voice low, his brow furrowed. "Ours."

She let that go. She knew Bo felt the same level of responsibility she did when something went wrong, but when it came down to it, it was Tennyson Security, not Bo Rheinhart Security. It was her reputation, not his. And the fact that she now considered Aria a friend as well as a client didn't help matters. Now it just felt like she'd let down a friend as well as a business acquaintance, and that felt so much worse.

The guy they'd been doing such a good job—or so she'd thought—of looking out for was right there on the security camera recording, as clear as if he'd stopped in front of the camera and smiled for it, somehow opening the door to Aria's suite with zero issue. The concierge had mentioned that it looked like he had a key and said he'd check with his housekeeping staff to see if anybody had lost one. He was clearly as upset as Kayla, if not more so, and she realized that his reputation was also on the line here, if not his job.

The concierge told her that whether or not Aria filed a report, the resort needed to contact the authorities, but that he'd keep her name out of things. Kayla was relieved to hear that. All she needed was to have Aria find out the media would know all about her missing underwear. On top of the stress and trauma of the actual theft itself, she would be horrifically embarrassed.

"We need to find this guy," she said as she and Bo headed back to the suite where Jake was stationed. She tapped on the door and he let them in.

"Agreed," Bo said.

"And?" Aria asked, getting up from the couch. She crossed to Kayla and grabbed her arm. "Was it him?"

Kayla nodded. "Plain as day on the security footage." She squeezed Aria's hand. "Listen, the resort has to call the authorities." Aria blanched and Kayla squeezed harder. "No, it's okay. They're going to keep your name out of it. Guests are anonymous, so no worries there."

Aria didn't look a hundred percent convinced, but she gave a nod. "Okay. I trust you."

Those words stung because, at the moment, Kayla didn't feel worthy of that trust. "They've also reprogrammed the lock on the door, and I have new keys for you." She looked past her into the room where both Haley and Cammie sat. "Do you all want to order dinner in? Hang here?"

"No," Aria said immediately. "I need to get the hell out of here. Knowing he was here"—she grimaced—"rummaging through my underpants..." A full body shudder followed. "No. I need to get out of here for a while. I might even sleep on the couch tonight."

Cammie crossed to her and wrapped her in a hug. "You can bunk with one of us. No problem. Right, Haley?"

Haley was crossing to them and she nodded. "Absolutely. I was gonna go see Miranda tonight, but maybe I'll stay here instead." And then the three of them were in a group hug, and Kayla admired their loyalty to each other.

The mention of Miranda had her thoughts zipping back to seeing London in the lobby. God, she hated how much her simple presence affected her, how she could *feel* her, even when she wasn't looking at her. What the hell was that about?

"Let's get dressed," Cammie said. "I think dinner out sounds fabulous." The three women broke and headed off to their respective rooms, leaving the three security guards standing in a group.

"How do you want to do this now?" Bo asked, looking from her to Jake and back.

"I think we need to have two on from now on," she said. "You guys okay with that?"

Both men agreed without hesitation, and not for the first time, she was so grateful for the dedication of her employees. She knew Jake was, like Bo, taking this development as a blight on his record. He was likely just as pissed off as Kayla, but his face would never give that away. His eyes were steely, though, as were Bo's.

"Okay, Jake, you've been here awhile. Why don't you take a break. Get a shower, order some dinner, grab a nap. I'll text you when we're back up here and getting ready to bed down. Then you guys can switch out."

Bo looked like he was going to argue with her, but he clearly knew better. Yeah, she'd be staying with Aria for the remainder of this trip. She'd get a shower or a nap where she could, but Aria was not going to be out of her sight until her assignment was over—Saturday, back in the States.

Half an hour later, they were filing out of the suite and down the hall to the elevator, five of them—Aria, Cammie, Haley, Bo, and Kayla. The three had opted for the sports bar type restaurant. Aria wanted casual and busy, wanted to be surrounded by a lot of people, and Kayla understood that. It was interesting, too, because most people would think, after somebody suffered some sort of violation like Aria had, that she'd want to be alone, or at least be around fewer people, a number easier to keep track of. Not Aria. She wanted other humans. She wanted the hum of conversation and the heat of other bodies nearby and the lights of a busy place, and Kayla totally understood that.

She'd picked the right one, too. The sports bar was hopping. Like most of them in the resort, it had an indoor seating area and bar, and it also opened to its own patio, which also had seating and a bar. Aria's trio was led directly to a corner table, and Bo and Kayla took seats close by, but inconspicuous. Kayla sat at the corner of the bar and ordered a club soda. Bo sat at a two-top table on the other side of the girls and got himself a nonalcoholic beer. They settled in.

Kayla was hyperalert, not a feeling she enjoyed. She was nervous and felt a little twitchy. This guy…goddamn it. This guy. He'd made her feel incompetent, and she did not take kindly to that. She scrutinized every single male that walked into the place, especially ones wearing hats or sunglasses or anything to obscure their identities. Older men, men with women on their arms, sharply dressed men, more casually dressed men. She studied them all. This asshole was not getting anywhere near her client or her client's things again.

Aria was also hyperalert. Kayla watched her as she conversed with her cousin and best friend but also glanced around the restaurant every few minutes. Her scoping was very much like Kayla's, and their eyes met over the dinner crowd several times. Aria would give her a tentative smile, and Kayla would smile back at her, but inside, Kayla was screaming. Aria wasn't supposed to be worried about her surroundings. That was literally what she was paying Kayla to do, and Kayla hated that Aria didn't feel a hundred percent safe now. It was going to take her a while to deal with this.

As the evening went on, however, the trio seemed to relax a bit. Laughter became more frequent and a bit louder. Aria looked around less, while Kayla looked around more. She knew the guy would be stupid to show his face this close to Aria, likely knowing what he'd done had been discovered at this point. Hell, maybe he'd already left the island. A girl could dream, right?

By the time the girls' crème brûlée had been delivered, Kayla's bladder had had more than enough of the club soda. She met Bo's gaze across the room and they had a silent conversation wherein she told him she needed to use the facilities. He gave a nod and she held up three fingers. *Back in three minutes.* He nodded again and she slid off her stool.

The restaurant itself was the only one in the resort without its own restrooms, but there was a set just outside the entrance, down a short white marble hallway to the right. Kayla headed that way, used the ladies' room, and was headed back down the hall when a man came out of the men's room ahead of her and turned so he was walking away from her, looking down at his phone.

His red phone.

The hairs on the back of her neck stood up.

It was him.

"Excuse me," she said loudly. "Sir. Excuse me."

He glanced back at her, and in a split second, he knew who she was.

"Sir, can I speak to you for a moment?"

He picked up his pace, hurrying down the hallway just this side of running.

"Sir." Kayla picked up her own pace as well. "Wait. *Wait.*" She jogged close enough to touch his arm, her phone out and in her other hand so she could call Bo, and when she made contact with him, he spun on her so fast, she never saw his hand, didn't even know he was preparing to hit her until his fist sank into her gut with alarming strength, forcing all the air from her lungs as she doubled over and struggled for breath. Her phone flew from her hand, clattering on the hard floor somewhere behind her.

"Kayla!"

She heard the screaming of her name—was that London's voice? She tried to look up, tried to see, but the guy gave her a hard shove, and because of her position, she was completely off balance. She slammed backward into the solid marble wall, absently wondering if she'd cracked her skull open or possibly shattered some vertebrae, as she crumpled to the floor in a heap. She heard the scrambling of footsteps on the floor, various shouts, and suddenly there were hands on her. Warm, gentle hands.

"Kayla. *Kayla*." It *was* London. Oh, it was London. That made her so happy.

"Hey you," she said, and did her voice sound kind of wistfully dreamy? Dreamily wistful? That was the last thought she had just before everything went black.

❖

"Kayla!"

London saw it happening. She saw it all happening. She was on her way to the sports bar to decompress a bit, maybe order some fries because she suddenly had a craving for salt and grease. She turned the corner and saw the guy leaving the restroom, followed by Kayla. Kayla asking him to wait, the guy speeding up, Kayla chasing him.

And then he'd spun around and punched Kayla hard in the stomach. London heard the air rush out of her from down the hall, saw her phone fly, and that's when she'd screamed. She must've scared the guy because he shoved Kayla hard into the wall and took off running.

Kayla's eyes had been weirdly glassy when she'd said hi to London—just before she lost consciousness. "Oh God," London had muttered and was ready to scream for help when several of the resort staff, one of whom seemed to be a medic, suddenly surrounded them. London held Kayla's hand as they looked her over, lifting her eyelids one at a time and flashing a light, checking her pupils. She stirred slightly, mumbled something London couldn't make out, and then two EMTs with a stretcher appeared, impressing her with how quickly they'd arrived. She didn't want to let go of Kayla's hand, but she was in the way, and she reluctantly let go and stood aside.

London took a wild guess that Kayla had been in the sports bar, and she hurried in, scanned the crowd, and made eye contact with Bo at the corner table. Whether it was her expression or the sudden flurry of activity visible through the entrance, she wasn't sure, but he'd known instantly that something was wrong, and he'd made his way to a table where Aria Keller and her friends sat, leaned to say something in Aria's ear, and hurried to London, who'd simply pointed down the hall, where there was clear commotion, people crowded around Kayla on the floor, staff members running.

Bo swore and ran past her, already dialing his phone. London moved out of the way as people rushed to Kayla's aid, a pit of worry and dread sitting solidly in her stomach. Kayla was on the stretcher now.

"Oh my God, what happened?" She turned to see Aria Keller standing next to her, enormous eyes even wider, fingertips at her lips.

"Some guy punched her and shoved her," London said softly, not even sure if she was actually speaking. "She lost consciousness."

"God, it was him, wasn't it?" That came from Haley, who now stood behind Aria.

"Who?" London asked, but then the stretcher was being wheeled by, and the girls all followed it until Bo stopped them. London had to force herself to stay where she was, to not follow as well. None of these people knew her, and she had no right to try to comfort Kayla now, not after their last conversation. Kayla had made it clear they were not going to happen, and hard as it had been to hear, much as she'd wanted to fight it, to argue, especially given what Miranda had said in the pool, she knew she should respect Kayla's wishes. For now, anyway. She sighed but made no move to leave. Instead, she continued to watch and noticed the other guy that worked for Kayla skid into the lobby, his hair at all angles, as if he'd just gotten out of bed and run right down there without so much as glancing in a mirror. He and Bo conversed briefly, and then the guy with the crazy hair led Aria and her friends out of the lobby and, London assumed, back to their suite. Little by little, the lobby cleared and quieted, and in a matter of fifteen minutes, it was as if nothing at all had happened.

And still, London stood there.

Feet rooted to the floor. Eyes still wide. She could still hear Kayla's *Hey you* in an almost playfully goofy tone that said she was happy to see her, even if she had been just about to black out.

"Ma'am? Are you okay?"

London blinked rapidly, as if coming out of a trance, and made herself smile at the young man in a resort uniform who looked at her with concern in his brown eyes. "Yes." She forced a nod and made herself move so she was no longer standing alone in an empty hallway like some lost child. "I'm good. Thank you."

Forcing her feet to move, she left the hallway, passed the front desk, went through the lobby, and walked out the front door. And for a moment, she thought about how interesting it was that she'd only used that set of doors when they'd arrived and when they left to go into town. Every other time she'd gone outside, it had been through other doors in the resort. Such a weird, inconsequential fact to suddenly take up space in her brain. She let her eyes wander down the access road that led to the main road, the path the ambulance took once Kayla was safely ensconced inside. London wanted to go to the hospital so badly, she had to make a conscious effort to stay where she was, to not move, to not pull out her phone and try for an Uber, to not find the doorman and ask him for a taxi. Kayla wouldn't want her there.

Would she?

She replayed Kayla's *Hey you* over and over again in her mind. The goofy half grin. The clear happiness to see her.

Yeah, 'cause she'd had her head bashed against the wall.

Whatever she'd said and however she'd said it, Kayla probably had zero control then and zero idea now.

"You have to try to let it go," she whispered into the night air. She inhaled deeply, tasted the salt on the breeze. God, it was beautiful here…and she couldn't wait to go home. She'd had enough of beautiful here. "You have to try."

A walk on the beach was tempting, especially given how warm and delicious the night air was, but she knew if she did that, she'd be stuck in her head the whole time. No, she needed a distraction.

Back in the suite, Miranda and Ethan were seated at the table close together, both of them looking intently at an open laptop, and she could hear a man's voice coming from it. It crossed London's mind to tell Miranda what had happened, but first of all, she didn't want to interrupt what was clearly an important meeting—a video chat, she realized when Miranda spoke to the screen—and second, she was afraid if she told the story of what she'd seen, she'd break down into tears. She gave a wave to Miranda, who met her gaze and smiled, then went into her room and shut the door.

Where she broke down into tears.

It took a few minutes. She let herself cry silently, just to release the emotions she hadn't quite realized she'd been carrying around.

She grabbed her laptop and her phone and moved them to the bed. A quick change into her pajamas that consisted of lightweight joggers and an old worn T-shirt, and she was ready to distract herself with a movie. Preferably something scary.

"No love stories tonight, thank you," she mumbled as she called up Netflix. That's when her phone pinged a text from Claire. *Been a while. Update me.* And an emoji making a stern face. Because Claire was not wrong. It had been a while. She started typing, and before she even knew she was going to do it, she'd typed out a synopsis of everything that had happened that night and sent it. She was typing a second text when her phone rang in her hand, and she smiled as she answered the FaceTime call and saw Claire's face on her screen.

"What in the actual fuck happened?" Claire said, her eyes wide. "I mean, lemme grab a drink 'cause I think I'm gonna need one." She'd propped her phone on the coffee table in their living room, and now she disappeared from view. She returned with a can of beer and popped it open, then took a swig. Then she opened a bag of barbecue potato chips, put one in her mouth, and made a show of getting comfortable. "Okay. Go."

London laughed. She couldn't help it. Just the familiarity of Claire alone made her feel the tiniest bit better. She reiterated what she'd said in her text, ending with, "It was so surreal, Claire. Like, she was happy to see me, but she was also on her way to passing out, so..."

"So, you're not sure if she even knew what she was saying."

"Exactly. And after telling me to basically get lost..." She sighed. "I have never been more confused by a woman before. Like, in my life. Ever."

"Okay, but"—Claire tipped her head and gave her the narrow-eyed face that warned London shit was about to get real—"didn't Miranda tell you to tell Kayla the truth? Isn't she okay with that?"

"*Yeah.*" London drew the word out. "I guess I'm just thinking I've likely destroyed any trust I may have started with by lying in the first place. And I know she was really hurt by the end of things with Miranda, so..." She sighed and shook her head. "Maybe it's just all too close for her. You know?"

Claire popped a chip into her mouth and crunched while she stared at the phone, then arched an eyebrow and ate another. And another, her gaze never leaving the screen.

"Oh my God, what?" She was half annoyed and half amused.

"You know what. I can't believe you're even asking me."

"Clearly I'm lacking in both brain cells and an ability to read your mind. Tell me."

Claire sighed loudly. Very loudly. Dramatically loudly. "Girl, it's a good thing I'm not there because I'd have to slap you."

"Listen, I could probably use it right about now." She suddenly felt deflated. Beaten. Hopeless. "What do I do?"

"Jesus, Mary, and Joseph," Claire muttered as she rubbed her forehead like she was trying to stave off a headache. Then she added loudly, "You go to her. You go there, and you tell her. *You tell her.* All of it. The truth about you and Miranda. The truth about how she makes you feel." At London's quick look back at her, Claire laughed. "Yeah, it's apparently clear to everybody but you." Claire waited a moment. "And then, if she turns you away, at least you'll know. At least you can say you gave it a shot. God, London, this is, like, basic love story advice. You watch Hallmark movies all the time! What is wrong with you?" Her tone had gentled, but her expression was one of concern.

London shook her head. "I don't know. I'm all discombobulated. She does that to me."

Claire laughed then, a loud, musical sound, and she pointed at the screen. "And that's another basic love story clue. The person who has you all messed up is usually the person who's meant for you. Even I know this. Again, for somebody who watches beaucoup Hallmark movies, you don't really pay attention to them, do you?"

They talked for a little while longer, until Claire started to get sleepy, and they said their good nights. London got out of bed and went out onto the sundeck. The moon was full, and it reflected on the water, the ripples sending a gorgeously ethereal blue off over the horizon. It was late now, but she could hear Miranda and Ethan both talking, along with another male voice, and she figured they must be talking to somebody in a different time zone. She was glad of that—she wasn't in the mood to socialize, and she knew Miranda might have wanted to if she'd been free. No, she needed to sleep, to end this day.

Once she was in bed, lights off, her mind kept replaying the scene of Kayla getting punched. God, that had been horrifying. And then to see her crumple to the ground? London's heart had leapt into her throat, and it did so now as she flashed back, seeing her fall to the ground over and over again. The stress of the flashback would ease, though, when she replayed Kayla's goofy *Hey you.* It was a whirlwind in her head, and she fell into a fitful sleep in the midst of it, blowing her around in a combination of confusion, desire, and worry.

❖

"Hi there. I'm hoping you can help me." London stood at the front desk bright and early on Friday morning. She'd slept fitfully, tossing and turning and seeing Kayla get hurt over and over. When her brain had become overtired, it had thrown little edits into the replays. One time, there was a talking opossum sitting near Kayla's head. Another time, she was blond. A third time, she sat up and asked London if she wanted fries with that. That's the one that did it. She sat up in bed and sleep was no more.

She'd waited until the sun came up, at least, before she'd taken her freshly showered self down to the front desk. She needed to see Kayla. She needed to talk to her. She needed to tell her the truth. That's what her brain—and her best friend—had been trying to tell her for the better part of twelve hours. Hell, even Miranda had given her the go-ahead.

"I can certainly try, ma'am," said the woman behind the desk. Her voice was soft and pleasant, and she looked a little bit tired, making London wonder if she'd been on all night. "What can I do for you?"

London leaned her forearms on the desk. "The woman that was hurt last night, she's a friend of mine." The woman gave a slight nod. "I'm not asking for any personal information, but could you just tell me what hospital the ambulance took her to? I'd like to visit, make sure she's okay."

The woman frowned, and her tired face took on an expression of apology. "Oh, I'm so sorry, ma'am. That whole party checked out overnight."

London blinked at her. "I'm sorry?"

"Yes, unfortunately, they left a day early." She tapped on her keyboard, then added, "At two thirty-five this morning. Checked them out myself." London stood there and stared at the woman in utter disbelief for several moments until she shifted from one foot to the other. "I'm very sorry," she offered, as if it was her fault.

"No. No, that's okay." London's voice was barely a whisper. "Thanks."

She was gone. Kayla was gone, and London had no way of contacting her. Well, okay, that wasn't exactly true, but...

Maybe this was how it was meant to be. Maybe Miranda and Claire were both wrong, and the Universe was trying to tell her something. She walked slowly out the side door that led down to the beach, kicked off her shoes, and simply started walking. It didn't take long for her to realize she didn't want to walk. She wanted to stand there in front of the water, to watch the waves roll, to listen to them crash, and to feel sorry for herself.

"Oh, I blew it," she said softly into the fresh morning breeze. She recalled what it had felt like to kiss Kayla. To be kissed by her and to kiss her back, and all the emotions and feelings that had welled up to the surface of her mind so quickly, just from that one kiss from that one person. She should've told her the fucking truth right then. "Goddamn it."

She wasn't sure how long she stood there in front of the ocean, but eventually, she had to force herself to let go and move her feet. "All right, Granger, that's it. Enough wallowing. Get your shit together," she muttered to herself. The sun was bright and warm on her face, but inside, she just felt dark and chilly, and when her eyes welled with tears, she knew she needed to get back to work, to focus on something other than the way her heart ached from missing a woman she barely knew. Was she officially ridiculous? Probably. But that didn't stop the tears.

With a resigned sigh, she turned in the sand and headed back to the resort.

CHAPTER NINE

Kayla had never bailed out of a job early. Never. Not once in her nearly ten years of owning her own security firm. Even if the client had been a giant pain in the ass—and she'd had more than one of those, absolutely—she always stuck it out and fulfilled the duties outlined in her contract.

She'd also never been given a concussion before.

She was not proud of that. The guy had gotten the drop on her, and she hadn't been prepared for it, which she should have been. Maybe it had been the resort, how warm and happy and friendly everything and everybody was, but it had never occurred to her for a moment that the guy would get violent. And that was on her. He was a *fucking stalker*. Of course he was prone to violence. God, she had really messed things up.

Aria Keller didn't think so, though, and that was Kayla's only saving grace here. It was Aria who insisted they leave St. Kitts early, and she chartered a private jet to get them out of there in the middle of the night. And it was Aria who would hear no arguments from Kayla and who insisted on paying her for the full week, no matter how much Kayla protested.

"This was *not* your fault," was all she kept saying to Kayla.

That's not how Kayla felt.

The stalker had gotten too close to Aria. Three times on her watch. The only thing that made it any better was that the authorities on St. Kitts had caught him in the airport trying to leave the island.

He likely wouldn't be detained for long, but he'd have a record of some sort.

It was now Saturday, and she had to admit, she was thrilled to be home. She'd dozed a bit on the plane, but neither Bo nor Aria would let her sleep much. The doctors hadn't even wanted her to fly, given she'd had a mild concussion, but the second Aria had mentioned leaving early, she'd been ready to get home. She'd slept a little bit once she'd arrived at her apartment—by then, it had been more than twenty-four hours since she'd gotten bashed on the head, and sleep was therefore allowed, so she'd curled up on her couch, covered up with the blanket her mother had knitted for her when she was a kid that she usually kept in her bedroom but, for whatever reason, wanted with her on the couch, and conked out for six solid hours. She probably would've slept longer if Bo hadn't called to check on her, followed closely by a text from Aria.

Checkin' in on my pal. How's the noggin? That's what my mom calls it.

She was pals with a movie star now, and that was pretty cool.

She sent a text back to Aria, telling her she was fine, that she'd slept and was just going to take it easy for the rest of the weekend. Aria was off to Egypt on Monday to start shooting a movie but promised she was going to check on her from there.

A storm was rolling in. She could see the dark clouds out the living room windows of her penthouse apartment, which was on the thirty-seventh floor. It was dusk, but the dull nickel gray had taken over the sky, which was likely going to open up on them momentarily. It was one of the things she loved about this apartment, the view. There had been two available, one on each side of the building. One had a view of a slice of Central Park, and from the other, you could see some of the East River. She'd chosen the river side for exactly this reason—she could see storms rolling in off the water.

She considered ordering something for dinner but realized she wasn't terribly hungry. Knowing she had to eat something, regardless, she decided to scramble some eggs. She'd been gone a week, and the eggs were still good, but her cherry tomatoes were on their last legs, so she cut them up and tossed them into the frying pan and soon was back on the couch, simply watching the sky.

Her head ached.

And if she was being honest, so did her heart.

She could still remember London screaming her name, could still hear her voice echoing through her skull. She could still remember London's face, etched with worry, looking down at her. She could still remember London's warm hands on her face, on her body, checking her for wounds she couldn't see, maybe blood. And all Kayla could do was wheeze—God, when was the last time she got punched in the stomach? grade school?—and blink and look at London's beautiful face.

Then she sort of faded back into the crowd of people that was suddenly all around her, and Kayla hadn't seen her again.

If she'd known that would be the last time…

"What?" she asked out loud. "What would you have done? She's with fucking Miranda, screwy as that whole thing is." She shook her head and ate a bite of eggs, which felt like they dropped into her stomach and sat there, as if she'd eaten gravel. Heavy and hard. Just like the idea of London and Miranda together.

She set the plate of eggs aside, unfinished, and drank some water, as a zigzag of lightning cut across the sky. It was followed by a rumble of thunder, and Kayla hunkered back down on the couch, turned so she could watch. It was her favorite, watching a storm, and for the first time in a long time, she wished she had someone under the blanket with her. Someone snuggled up and warm and holding her close. Someone whose grip would tighten each time the thunder rolled.

She thought about London, told herself she'd allow herself to do that for the rest of the night. Through the storm. *Only for tonight.* And starting tomorrow, she'd have to move on. She'd have to let go. The reality was that London was with somebody—it didn't even matter that it was her ex or that it was unconventional, considering the whole Haley angle—she was with somebody. And Kayla didn't get involved in that kind of a mess. No way. Yes, they'd clicked instantly. Yes, they had a lot in common, and talking with London had been easier and more comfortable and more *fun* than talking to any other woman had been in months and months. Yes, they kissed like they were meant to be kissing. God...she took a few minutes and closed her eyes, just remembered what it was like to feel those lips, to taste her tongue, to feel London kissing her back, her hands gripping Kayla's arms, her shirt...

"*Fuck*," she whispered, drawing the word out into four syllables. How could she miss somebody she never had? How was that even possible? And why couldn't she reconcile that London was with Miranda? She seemed better than that, far too good for the billionaire bitch, as Kayla had dubbed her, only in her head, of course. She seemed grounded and independent and solid—not Miranda's usual type.

"Present company excluded," she said quietly. She had not been Miranda's usual type either, and she knew that because Miranda had told her. More than once.

Now, Aria's cousin? Yeah, she was Miranda's type. And again, she wondered what London thought about that little tryst, and did she even care? Maybe they had an agreement. An arrangement. Maybe it happened all the time. It wasn't any of her business.

"Oh my God, just stop," she said, this time loudly. Her voice echoed through the empty room, bounced off the glass of the windows, and her head started to throb again.

The thunder rolled and then cracked loudly, as if punctuating her directive.

"Just stop," she said again, but this time, it was quiet. Barely a whisper. Her eyes welled up, and she allowed herself to cry silently and miss a person who was never hers in the first place.

The storm rumbled on.

❖

London had been home for a week.

A whole week, and she missed the beach, the sun, the warmth, the pool, and Kayla.

Yeah. She missed a woman she'd spent a total of about two hours with. What kind of sense did that make?

"None," she whispered to her laptop. "Zero." She said it even as she typed in the URL for the Tennyson Security website for the sole purpose of staring at the headshot Kayla had posted on the Our Team page. She was the only one who had a photo up—London figured maybe she didn't want the public to know what her security guys looked like. But as the CEO, she needed to be the face of the company.

So London stared.

"Hey, how's it going?" Claire's voice startled her so much that she jumped and quickly slammed her laptop shut. "Nope. That didn't make you look guilty at all." Claire laughed as she came up behind her and lifted the top of the laptop, opening it up again. "Not at all. Are you still leering at this girl's headshot?"

"I'm not *leering*," London said in a weak attempt to defend herself.

"You are so leering." Claire made an exaggerated face with her eyes crossed and her tongue hanging out, then added a groan to complete the picture of a creeper.

"Stop it." London swiped playfully at her.

"I don't know why you don't just call her. It's clear you can't let it go."

Claire's cell rang then, and London sent up a prayer of thanks as Claire had to take the call and stepped into her own room.

Claire was only partially right. London hadn't fully let go of Kayla—as evidenced by being caught staring at her photo—but she had done her best to move on. She wasn't on the Tennyson Security website often. She had her article almost finished, so that had taken her focus, and she'd already begun mapping out the book she was going to write. She had a meeting with Silas next week about the project, and Claire was all over it, fully intending to pitch it to her contacts. She even texted with Miranda on a regular basis. That had maybe been the biggest surprise of all, their friendship.

Her phone pinged an incoming text, and as if London had conjured her, it was from Miranda.

Join me for a drink. Bergman's in half an hour…

London laughed softly and shook her head, now used to the fact that Miranda never asked. She told. Her invitations came across more like commands, not because she was being a dick, but because it's how she'd always done it, and that method had always been responded to.

London couldn't afford more than half a cocktail at Bergman's if she went on a regular basis the way Miranda did. It was upper scale. Fancy. Exclusive. But Miranda would never let her pay, and London knew it, so she could set that hesitation aside. She typed back, *Gonna take me an hour.*

There was no way she could get dressed—in something appropriate enough for Bergman's—catch a cab, and get uptown in thirty minutes.

Dirty martini will be waiting…

God, a dirty martini sounded divine right about then. She saved what she'd been working on, took one last look at Kayla's headshot, then closed out of that tab as well.

One hour and four minutes later, she walked into Bergman's dimly lit lounge and was led to Miranda's table for two, where an icy-looking, very dirty martini sat waiting for her. She gave Miranda a kiss on her cheek and sat.

"You are the best," she said as she picked up her drink and held it so Miranda could touch hers to it. "Good to see you."

"Same. I have a conference call at nine with my China office but was craving a martini." She glanced over her shoulder at the bar. "Nikita there makes the best one I've ever had." She waited, clearly wanting London to take a sip, so she did.

"Oh God, that's good." And it was the truth. Salty and tangy with a bit of a first-sip burn down her throat. Delicious. "What's new?" she asked as she set her glass down. "Last time I saw you was on a plane." She grinned, referring to their return trip from St. Kitts. They hadn't seen each other in a week, and it was weird how that fact felt weird.

"Oh, you know, same ol' same ol'. Making calls, ordering

people around, spending money." There was something odd in her tone, and London squinted at her.

"You okay?"

With a nod, Miranda made an attempt at changing topics. "How's the article coming along?"

London took a beat to just study her face before answering, "It's almost done."

"That's fantastic."

"All right." London sipped again and then leveled Miranda with a gaze. "What's going on?"

Miranda sighed. Then she gave her head a slight shake and her eyes darted around the room. Uncomfortable was the only word London could come up with to describe her behavior, and she wanted to push but thought better of it. So, she just waited.

Finally, Miranda sighed again and met her gaze. "I'm worried."

"About?"

"Your article."

London tipped her head. "What do you mean?"

"I'm worried I will come off like a mean, entitled bitch." She blinked several times, and London couldn't help it—she burst out laughing. Which only made Miranda seem more nervous and look away, so she reached across the table and closed a hand over her forearm to get her attention.

"Miranda." She waited until their eyes met again. "I do not think you're a mean, entitled bitch. And just the fact that you're worried about that says that you're not. You get that, right?"

"I mean, I can be." Miranda lifted one shoulder.

London laughed softly. "You can be demanding, yes. But I don't think that's so much related to your wealth as it is to your job. Am I wrong?"

Miranda seemed to ponder that "I guess not." She drained her glass and signaled the waiter for a refill, then visibly cringed. "See? I just did it. I just ordered that guy to get me a refill." Her eyes were wide with what seemed to be horror.

"He's the *waiter*. It's his *job*."

Miranda seemed to relax slightly. "Okay. Okay. You're right. I just..." She swallowed and seemed to search for the words. "I feel a bit discombobulated lately." She moved her hands around to demonstrate confusion. "Since the trip. Since the resort. Since Haley. Since making you lie to Kayla." She looked to London, clearly needing something.

"All right." London drained her glass, because this was going to call for some fortification, and signaled for a refill. "See? I did it, too." She cleared her throat and looked steadily at Miranda. "Are you ready for some straight talk?"

"I don't know. Am I?"

"You started this conversation, so..." London waited her out. A fresh martini was set in front of her. Damn, Nikita was fast.

Miranda took a sip of hers, then set the glass down, her eyes steely. "Okay. I'm ready. Hit me."

One nod. "I think Haley did something to you."

"What do you mean?"

London nibbled on her bottom lip as she looked for the right words. "Correct me if I'm wrong, but I got the impression that you intended her to be a one-night stand. Maybe two nights. And that you do that fairly often."

"Valid."

"But she lasted the whole week."

Miranda nodded.

"Are you still talking with her?"

"We text."

"I think that's great." London smiled at her. "I mean, it's a big age difference, but you two seemed to connect."

"She makes me feel young."

"That's awesome. I mean, you're not old. You know that, right?"

Miranda tipped her head from one side to the other, agreeing but not, and it made London chuckle. "Can I be frank with you?"

"Of course."

"Wealth can be isolating. Very, very isolating. People think they know you. Or they don't care to know you, they just want to get close to your money." She scratched at the tabletop with a thumbnail. "And I know how weak that sounds. Oh, the poor rich lady feels lonely. But there is some validity to it."

London didn't want to interrupt. She knew not many people got the real and genuine Miranda Northbrooke, and she wanted to hear more, so she stayed quiet but kept her eyes on Miranda's face.

"It's easy to take somebody to bed when they look at you like you're the golden ticket, you know? And then the morning rolls around, and I see them with fresh eyes—just like they see me with fresh eyes—and then it's awkward and uncomfortable and nobody can get away fast enough." She glanced down at her drink. "Haley didn't look at me that way. Did I tell you that?"

London blinked in surprise. "You didn't."

Miranda nodded. "I usually cut that cord right away the next morning." She made a slashing motion. "Keeps them from getting too clingy."

"But Haley's different."

Miranda inhaled a deep breath and let it out slowly. Her voice was wistful. "She was funny. Self-deprecating. Sarcastic." Another sip. "And very sexy."

London grinned. "I bet if you'd tried to cut the cord with her, she wouldn't have taken it well."

"That's because she's *fiery*. Another thing I liked about her."

"I know you've texted. Have you called her? FaceTimed her?"

Miranda looked at her like she'd grown a third eye on her forehead as they sat there. "Oh God, no."

"Why not?" A beat went by. Two. "What? Miranda Northbrooke, at a loss for words? Has hell frozen over?" She softened the words with a grin.

"I don't really know how to do that."

"How to FaceTime?"

"How to date. I don't really know how to date."

"You dated Kayla." The words were out before she thought about it, as bringing Kayla up wasn't part of the plan today.

"True, but she did most of the heavy lifting, I'm slightly ashamed to say." A moment of quiet passed. "Have you talked to her?"

"Who?"

It was Miranda's turn to give her a look. "Mrs. Claus. You *know* who."

"No. I haven't." She felt Miranda's eyes on her, studying her, and she had to work hard to keep from squirming.

But Miranda said nothing aside from making a small *hmm* sound.

They sat in silence for a few minutes, sipping their drinks and shooting covert looks across the table at each other, until their martini glasses were empty, and Miranda glanced at her phone.

"Much as I'd like to sit here and get blotto with you, I have to go." She signaled for the check and waved away London's attempts to pay for her own cocktails—which they both knew was a little dance they'd play because Miranda would never let anybody buy anything. It was a very generous quality of hers.

Once they were outside waiting for the doorman to hail them each a cab, London said, "For what it's worth, I think you should call Haley. Make a move. A real one."

Miranda didn't look at her but responded, "I may do that. And I think you should call Kayla." She turned to face her. "Make a move. A real one."

London gave her a sad smile. "Yeah, maybe."

"Liar," Miranda said as a cab pulled up and the doorman opened the door for her. She gave London a quick kiss on the cheek. "Bye."

London laughed softly at this new reality of hers where she was good friends with a billionaire media mogul who sought advice on her love life from London.

Kinda surreal.

She headed home.

❖

Kayla closed her laptop and pushed to her feet, then moved to the windows to gaze out onto the late-April afternoon. The sun was shining on the East River, making it sparkle almost as if it wasn't brown and polluted. Almost. Across the street on the roof, the Plant Woman, as Kayla referred to her in her mind, was working on her beds, likely preparing them for planting in the next few weeks. She knew from experience that the woman would grow peppers, tomatoes, eggplant, and a whole bunch of herbs right there on the roof. It made Kayla happy, for some reason, seeing all that lush green right across from her window. Maybe because the woman signified the beginning of the summer, and summer was Kayla's favorite season.

"All right," she said softly to her empty loft apartment. "Invoicing is done. Assignments are sent out. I guess packing is all that's left."

She and Bo were booked on a flight to Toronto later that evening to run a job for an IT conference. The keynote speaker was Bryan Joseph, the inventor of some new AI technology that was going to be huge in several marketplaces. Unfortunately, not everybody was thrilled about the far-reaching implications of AI, and Mr. Joseph had received several threats of varying degrees, from bodily harm to death, so his team had reached out to Tennyson Security.

She packed quickly and carried her bag to the entryway near the front door.

Her phone pinged in her hand. A text from Bo.

Good 2 go

A man of few words was Bo Rheinhart, but Kayla was okay with that. She knew him well. Even better, he knew her well. He was like the brother she'd never had. She texted him back that she'd meet him at JFK, ordered herself a car, then slid her phone back into her pocket and headed into her bedroom to get her bag packed.

A knock on the door stopped her in her tracks, and she spun on her heel to answer it. It must've been a neighbor because normally either Frankie or Vince, the doormen of her building, would buzz her and let her know who was there. Since it was Friday, it should be Frankie on duty. The knock came again. It was probably Mr. Smithson from down the hall, locking himself out again. She checked her watch. Two forty-five. Yup, Frankie was on his smoke break, she knew, as he was every day from two forty-five to three, so Mr. Smithson probably couldn't reach him.

She pulled the knob as she said, "Did you lock yourself out again, Mr.—" Her voice died in her throat as she stood there looking at what was still the most gorgeous face she'd ever seen. "London."

"Oh. Um." London looked just as flabbergasted as Kayla felt, her expression colored with confusion, her light brows forming a V above her nose. She blinked rapidly, her big blue eyes darting to look down the hall, then back to Kayla. She opened her mouth to speak when both their phones pinged. London reached for hers at the same time Kayla pulled hers out.

London's face relaxed somewhat, and she held her phone up for Kayla to see it. A text from Miranda.

Tell her the truth. Followed by a heart emoji.

Kayla held her phone up so London could see the text on the screen, also from Miranda.

Hear her out. Followed by a heart emoji.

They stood there, the two of them, just looking at each other, across the threshold to Kayla's apartment. Seconds ticked by. Finally, Kayla spoke. "Well, far be it from me to disobey an order from the great Miranda Northbrooke." She stepped aside. "Come on in."

London hesitated for a split second before stepping into the apartment, where she looked around, eyes wide. "Wow," was all she said.

"So," Kayla ventured. "Um, hi."

London's eyes finally settled on Kayla's face, and her expression seemed...relieved? It was all Kayla could think to describe it. "Hi. God, it's good to see you."

That was a surprise. "It is?"

"It really, really is." London seemed as if she hadn't expected it to be good, and she took half a step toward Kayla like she wanted to hug her, but then stopped as if she'd thought better of it, and Kayla was so confused right now.

"Um, can I get you something to drink?" When in doubt, fall back on manners.

"Some water would be great if you have it."

"Sure. Have a seat." Getting water was good. Getting water gave her time to right herself because her world felt like it had tipped just enough to make her feel off balance. What the hell was going on? She filled a glass and really wanted to brace herself on her hands against the counter and just take a minute, but her apartment was open-concept, and London could see everything she was doing. So instead, she took a deep but quiet breath, blew it out slowly, and took the glass back into the living room. London was seated on the chocolate-brown couch and thanked Kayla as she took the glass. Kayla sat down slowly on the big square ottoman that matched her ivory overstuffed chair. "So." She held out her arms, at a loss. "What brings you here? How did you even know where I live?" There was no accusation in her tone, simply curiosity. She stayed as unlisted as possible, just as a matter of principle, due to her job.

London gave a sarcastic chuckle. "I didn't. I thought I was meeting Miranda. She sent me the address. I thought this was her place."

Kayla frowned. "I am so confused right now." And then she gave a soft laugh because, despite everything, London Granger was sitting in her living room, and hard as she tried to be, she wasn't mad about that. At all.

"I'm not with Miranda," London said suddenly. Blurted, really, like the words had shot from her mouth without her permission.

Kayla blinked. "I'm sorry, what?" What was she saying? Did they break up?

"I'm not with Miranda. I never was." London's swallow was audible.

"I—I don't understand."

London sighed and gazed out the large windows. "I know."

"I mean, I *saw* you. She was in your suite. She had her arm around you. She seemed to be *with* you."

"You did. But it was *her* suite. And she did that. Made it seem like that." London's smile was soft and seemed a little uncertain.

"I'm so confused. You're *not* with her?"

"No."

"And you were never with her?"

"No."

"Was *anything* from that week the truth?"

London looked down at her feet—Kayla noticed her cute wedges, open-toed, her toenails polished a soft blue. She seemed to gather herself, and Kayla waited, let her do what she needed. London wet her lips—something that sent a flutter through Kayla's lower body—and then met Kayla's gaze. "I *am* a writer. I work for *The New and The Now*. And I was a model. All true."

"You work for *TN Squared*, huh?"

"I do. And in St. Kitts, I was on assignment."

"And that was?"

London sighed and turned toward the windows again. Her hands were clasped on her lap and had been the whole time she spoke. But now, she separated them, stretched her fingers out, then balled both hands into fists. "I was writing an article on what it's like to live like a billionaire."

Kayla snort-laughed before she could catch it, and a flash of pain shot across London's face. "I'm sorry," she said immediately. "That wasn't cool of me."

London shook her head, and Kayla thought she felt a tiny bit of London shut down. "No, it's fine. It's a fluff piece, so it's not *not* funny." She shrugged and Kayla could tell she was slightly embarrassed, and that made her feel terrible. But then London sat up a little straighter as she went on. "But I went into it with more in mind, touching on our class systems in this country, the pressures of not having money, as well as the pressures of having it, the socioeconomics of today. I'm writing a book. Actually."

"You are?" At London's nod, she went on. "That's amazing. Good for you."

There was a beat of silence before London spoke again, and she cleared her throat first. "So, my boss set me up with Miranda, whose company owns ours. As I'm sure you know. And she agreed to take me on vacation with her." London cleared her throat again and was clearly uncomfortable about her next words. "We had an incident at one of the bars early in the week where a guy tried to pick us up, and we decided after that, we'd present as a couple if we needed to. Just to fend off guys like that." Her voice dropped to a whisper, and a look of anguish parked on her face. "I had no idea you guys had been a thing until the moment you showed up at our suite. I swear. And then Miranda started playing that role, which she apologized for later and said she was being childish." London cleared her throat. "Not that that makes it okay."

"I..." Kayla blinked. She felt like that was all she could do in the moment. Just blink at London while she tried to absorb what she'd told her. "So, she was..." She shook her head.

"Faking it? Yes."

"I..." It was crazy. The whole thing was so crazy. The emotions she'd hit in the week in St. Kitts and the subsequent weeks that had followed were all over the board. They ran the gamut from excitement to arousal to sexual desire—harder and deeper than she'd felt in longer than she could remember—to more excitement to utter collapse to pain to anguish to anger to guilt to recovery... she'd been through them all. Sometimes, she'd backtracked. But she'd hit every single one just over this one girl. This. One. Girl.

"I know," London said, and it really seemed like she did. Her expression was soft, her eyes kind, but also a little sad. "I'm so sorry."

"I...wow." More blinking, because Kayla didn't know what to do or what to think. So she sat there until it became almost uncomfortable, and then her intercom near the door buzzed, causing both of them to flinch. "Shit." She knew what it was, even as she answered and held the button for Frankie to speak.

"Ms. Tennyson, your car is here."

She nodded, her eyes never leaving London. "Okay, thanks, Frankie. I'll be right down."

London stood, looking slightly flustered, her cheeks blooming pink, and headed toward the door. "Oh my God, I'm so sorry to have interrupted. You're clearly busy."

"No!" Kayla said, holding out a hand that somehow ended up on London's shoulder, and her voice was much louder than she'd intended. She lowered it. "Sorry. I mean, you weren't interrupting.

You…" She swallowed and consciously lowered her voice again. "You're not an interruption."

They stood there, Kayla's hand on London's shoulder, and held eye contact. It should've been strange, should've felt uncomfortable or weird, but it didn't. At all. Kayla was pretty sure she could look into those big blue eyes for the rest of her life and be perfectly happy.

London cleared her throat again, but didn't move. "So, where are you off to? Protecting the celebrities of the world?"

Kayla grinned and tipped her head one way, then the other. "Something like that. Toronto."

"Great city. I love it."

"Same."

London looked torn. It was the only way Kayla could describe the expression on her face, like she wanted to say something but was thinking better of it.

"What?" Kayla asked softly. "Say it."

That seemed to be all London needed. "Do you think…Can we continue this conversation when you get back?"

And just like that, light flooded back into her world again. Like blackout curtains being shoved open. Like the proverbial sun coming out from behind a big gray cloud.

"I'd love that."

CHAPTER TEN

L ondon had only been home from her visit to what she'd thought was Miranda's place and had actually been Kayla's place for a little over two hours when the first text from her came.

Are you interested in Miranda?

London gave a little laugh through her nose and whispered to herself, "Okay, so no preamble or anything. Straight to the point. I kinda like it." She thought for a moment, felt a little mischievous tug, then she typed back, *As a friend? Source? Mentor?*

The little dots bounced, disappeared, bounced some more, disappeared again. Finally, her message came back and London laughed out loud.

Girlfriend.

"All that thinking for one word." London shook her head and kept grinning. She couldn't help herself. Kayla was pretty clear in where she was headed. London typed, *No. Not my type.*

More bouncing dots, but this time, they didn't stop, and Kayla's message popped up. *What is your type?*

London considered messing with her a bit, sending her something that said her type was super short with red hair and an Irish accent—something the polar opposite of tall, dark Kayla Tennyson—but she couldn't do it. Somehow, this felt serious, and she made herself give it some thought.

My type, huh? Let's see, I like a woman who is kind and funny and independent. A woman who knows who she is and isn't threatened by my success. A woman who lifts me up rather than holding me down. A woman who loves me for me and who doesn't try to change me to fit some mold of who she thinks I should be...

It was the most honest she'd been with anybody in a very long time. Including herself. She hit *Send* before she could change her mind and held her breath.

Kayla's response came right away. *Wow. That's a great description and remarkably similar to my type as well.*

London's smile grew. *What a coincidence.*

Kayla sent, *Right?* Then, *I have to board. Can I text you?*

A chuckle. *Kinda already are.*

You're funny, came Kayla's response.

London typed, *Good thing that's part of your type.*

Kayla sent a laughing emoji and then went quiet so, London assumed, was off on her flight.

She didn't want to get into things like *fly safely* or *let me know when you land*, but they both crossed her mind, and she gave herself a pat on the back for resisting the urge to type either. And when her phone pinged about two hours later, her heart skipped a beat, and she wasn't proud of how quickly she ran to the living room to grab her phone off the coffee table.

How'd it go?

London sighed, and it felt like her entire body deflated, which she did not like. She typed back to Miranda, *You tricked me.*

Miranda's response was to send a line of laughing emoji. Of course. London waited her out, and a few minutes later, she clearly got serious and sent another text. *No really. How'd it go?*

London gave it some thought. What exactly was *it*? She knew but also didn't, and so she was as honest as she could be. *Well, we talked a bit and she headed off on a job. But we're texting, so...* She added a shrugging emoji and left it at that.

Good.

Apparently, either that was all Miranda had to say or she got harangued by somebody else because she disappeared. And London was okay with that. She wasn't ready to give words to any of this. Whatever *this* was.

Claire was out of town for the weekend, so London had the

apartment to herself and decided to indulge in a Friday night of relaxing. She made a big bowl of popcorn and found herself something scary to watch on Netflix. She turned off the living room light, curled up on the couch under a blanket that Claire's grandmother had made, and settled in. The first victim in the film had already been sliced and diced when her phone pinged.

Kayla was back.

Hi. Whatcha doin'?

London was very aware of the smile that broke out across her face. It wasn't something she did often, feel her own facial expressions. But this one? She absolutely did. She paused her movie. *Hey you. I'm watching dumb college kids get picked off by a serial killer. You? How's Toronto?*

Kayla's response came right back. *Canadian.*

London laughed. *Not sure what that means, but okay.*

A laughing emoji came, followed by, *It means that everybody is super nice and the hotel is super tidy and this job should be super easy.*

London nodded. *Sounds like the best kind of job.*

It truly is. Hey...

A squint. *Hey yourself.*

The dots bounced, then stopped. A minute or two went by. London squinted some more, unsure if Kayla was struggling with her words or if she'd gotten called away—something she suspected came with the job. She was about to restart her movie, had the remote in her hand, when her phone finally pinged.

When I get back, could I take you out?

There it was. London's goofy grin was back. She'd had a feeling—hoped?—this was coming. Hell, she'd toyed with asking Kayla out herself, but had hesitated, given the whole Miranda thing. But Kayla asking her out seemed to say she was moving past that.

You absolutely could. I'd love that.

Kayla sent a line of smiling emoji, which made London laugh. Then she said, *Okay, gotta work.*

Go. Be a bodyguard. Then she searched until she found a GIF of a sexy woman in a suit and sunglasses, an earpiece in her ear, dark hair slicked back, and sent it. Then she made herself put the phone down, turn the movie back on, and do her best to focus.

It worked, for the most part. Kayla didn't text back, and London imagined she needed to be present and paying attention in her line of work, not scrolling on her phone.

She hunkered down under the blanket, watched the movie, and ate her popcorn, the whole time thinking about Kayla. What she was doing, when she would get home, where they would go on their very first date.

Oh my God.

They were going on a date.

❖

I'm sending a car to pick you up at 3.

It was a cryptic text, and it gave London butterflies, little flutters low in her body. She and Kayla had texted a bit over the weekend while Kayla was in Toronto, but she hadn't had a ton of time. Apparently, somebody named Bryan Joseph had kept her on her toes for forty-eight solid hours, and by the time she returned home Sunday night, Kayla had been wiped out.

Which didn't mean she wasn't up with the sun and texting London bright and early Monday morning. Her first text had asked if Monday was a dumb day for a date, because she didn't want to wait any longer. London had lain in her bed, having been woken up by Kayla's text, and smiled at her phone as she typed, *I don't think any day is a bad date day.*

The dots had bounced and Kayla's text popped up. *Great! I'm sending a car to pick you up at 3.*

She was sending a car?

Oh, one more thing, you said you're not afraid of heights, right?

London barked a laugh at the random question. *I'm not, no.*

Great! Dress comfortably and I'll see you then.

She laughed some more, which brought a light tapping on her door, and then it opened and Claire stuck her head in. "What are you laughing at? TikTok? Send it to me."

London held up her phone, and Claire came into the room. She wore boxer shorts and a tank top, her hair wrapped in a silk scarf. She took a seat on the edge of the bed and read the texts, her eyes getting wider and wider as she went on.

"Where do you think she's taking you?"

"I have no idea. Someplace high?"

Claire tapped her chin with a forefinger. "Empire State Building?" Then immediately shook her head. "No. Too common. She seems classier than that."

"You've never even met her. How do you know she's classy."

Claire leveled a gaze at her. "She's *sending a car* for you."

London blinked. "Valid."

The squeal Claire let loose was high-pitched and piercing, but London laughed anyway. "This is so cool! I love a good mystery date. What are you gonna wear? We should figure it out before I have to go to work. I assume you're WFH today?"

"Yeah, Silas has me writing an article on that chef that won on *Kitchen Champs* a couple months ago. She opened a fusion restaurant in Chelsea, so I've gotta research her and then set up an interview. And I want to work on the book some more."

"How's that coming? Don't forget about your Penguin meeting next week. That guy loved your article. Loved it."

A nod. London still couldn't believe the guy from Penguin had reached out to Claire after he'd read her article. It was a little bit mind-blowing and she still hadn't completely absorbed that yet. She did wonder if Miranda had poked anybody, given her some help, but she wasn't sure she wanted to know.

Claire slapped London's thigh under her comforter. "Girl, let's find you something to wear. Casual but hot, right?"

London laughed as she sat up and threw off the covers. "I mean, she didn't specify hot…"

"It's a given. Trust me."

The spent the next hour going through London's clothes, picking one thing, tossing aside another, until they came up with what they both deemed casual yet sexy. Tight jeans, a white T-shirt—a *clingy* white T-shirt—and a black blazer with black ankle boots.

"I wish it was summer," Claire had commented at one point. "Then you could show some *skin*." She pointed a finger at London's chest and moved it in a circle to encompass her boobs. "But those will do nicely."

London gave her hands a playful slap. "You stop that."

Claire laughed. "All right, I have to get ready and head into the office. You'll be gone before I get home, so *please* remember to text me where you are." She was out the bedroom door but turned back and met London's eyes. "And if you get nervous, if she turns out to be crazy and you think she's about to throw you off a roof or something, text me then, too!"

"I am reasonably sure I'm not getting thrown off a roof."

"Listen, reasonably sure isn't the same as super-duper sure, so…" Claire gave her a wink and headed off to get ready for her day.

Okay, so working from home when you were stupidly excited for midafternoon to roll around made the day stretch out for way more than six hours. Every time she looked at the clock, she swore it had gone backward ten minutes.

And writing? London scoffed. Yeah. Not happening. Her creativity was completely overshadowed by her excited anticipation to see Kayla. She did manage to do a little research and made a couple calls and got an interview with the chef lined up for the following week. So the day wasn't a total loss. But it was pretty damn close.

At one o'clock, she gave up completely, closed her laptop, and turned off the light at her desk. She tried to eat some leftover pizza for lunch, but her stomach was churning with excitement and said *No, thank you* to the slice, which ended up in the trash.

It was too early to get ready, but she did so anyway, taking a shower and shaving thoroughly, per Claire's instructions. She applied her makeup carefully, subtly, the way her makeup artist friend Ernesto had taught her when she was modeling. She could hear his heavily accented voice in her head. *For everyday, less is more. Subtle is best.* So she focused on that and then slipped her arms into her blazer sleeves, stepped into her boots, and looked at her reflection in the full-length mirror in the corner of her room. The outfit worked. She'd been undecided about her hair but decided to twist it up and clip it to the back of her head. She could let it down later if she wanted to.

And then her brain hit her with an image of Kayla reaching around and unclipping her hair, watching it fall around her shoulders in a blond cascade of waves, her dark eyes going even darker—

Her phone pinged, jerking her out of her fantasy as harshly as if she'd been slapped.

Ready? It was Kayla, and it made her smile.

She typed back, *Ma'am, I have another hour.*

Wasn't my question.

She sighed, and that little flutter hit her stomach again. *Fine. Yes, I'm ready.*

The dots bounced. Then, *Thought you might be. Car's outside.*

Outside her building sat a black town car, the uniformed driver leaning against it clearly waiting for London.

"Ms. Granger?" he asked as she exited the lobby. At her nod, he opened the back door and waved her inside, then closed it behind her and went around to the driver's side.

The interior was comfortable, with soft leather seats and the scent of cherries and almonds in the air. She looked around for an air freshener but couldn't find one.

The driver met her eyes in his rearview mirror. "Ms. Tennyson left some water for you. Make yourself comfortable. We'll be there soon." The car was shifted into gear, and they pulled into traffic.

"Where are we headed?" she asked, watching the streets of Manhattan pass her window as they drove.

"I'm not at liberty to say," the driver said, and the corners of his eyes crinkled with his slight grin, as he glanced in the mirror again.

London thought about pressing him, but why? They'd arrive at their destination soon, and then she'd know. And it took over an hour—driving through Manhattan was rarely quick—but they made it. She read the sign as they drove past it.

McArdle Private Airfield.

Private airfield? She didn't understand, was racking her brain to try to figure out Kayla's plan, but then they pulled into a hangar, and there she was, standing there in all her dark-haired, nearly-six-foot tall, absolutely stunning glory. Her hair was pulled back. On her face were mirrored Ray-Bans and a huge smile, and honestly, London couldn't remember the last time she was so fucking happy to see somebody. The car slowed to a stop, and Kayla was at London's door before the driver even shifted into Park.

"Hi," Kayla said, holding a hand out as she beamed at London. "I'm so glad to see you."

London took her hand and let herself be pulled from the car and directly into a warm, firm hug. Kayla knew how to hug a person—none of that light arms, gentle tapping on the back crap—no, she *hugged* her, and London felt herself melting into her body. She counted to three, then pulled back enough to see Kayla's face. "I'm happy to see you, too. Like, really happy." She looked around the hangar. "What are we doing?"

"You haven't figured it out yet?" Kayla asked, but the last part of the question was drowned out by the sound of a helicopter that suddenly appeared over the building and landed not far from them. Kayla looked at it, looked at London, then back at the helicopter, and it finally dawned on her.

"*No*," she said in utter surprise, drawing the word out, and couldn't keep the smile from blossoming across her face.

"Oh yes." Kayla still held her hand and now gave her a tug. "Come on." She led her into the hangar where two men were waiting for them, all kinds of gear made of straps and clasps and buckles spread out around them. "London, this is Lucas and Bart. They're going to get us all hooked up for safety and then take us up in their chopper and fly us over Manhattan."

"Seriously?" London knew she sounded like a teenager, her voice high-pitched and incredulous, but she couldn't help it.

"Seriously." Kayla's expression shifted, and she looked London in the eye. "That okay?"

"Are you kidding? I've seen the ads for this ever since I moved to New York. I was hoping to be able to afford it someday."

"Well, now you don't have to. This one's on me."

And before London could stop herself or second-guess or wonder what kind of signals she was sending, she threw her arms around Kayla and hugged her close a second time. "Thank you," she whispered, her mouth close to Kayla's ear. And God, she smelled good, like cinnamon and warmth. Inviting, like home. London let go but stayed close, let her gaze float in those rich dark eyes for a beat before turning to the men and spreading her arms out to her sides. "Gentlemen, hook me up!"

What London hadn't realized was that this was no ordinary helicopter ride. This was a doors open helicopter ride. A hang your feet out helicopter ride. A type of ride she hadn't even known existed until they got into the bird and were clipped in. She and Kayla had headsets and harnesses, and they were clipped to the helicopter in several places. There was no worry they'd fall out, and the freedom she felt, the utter bliss from sitting there with her feet dangling, thousands of feet up in the air, with the whole of Manhattan stretched out below her...there were no words. Not a single one. And she was a writer. Words were her life.

Kayla sat next to her, their thighs pressed together, and for the first few moments, they were both silent. In awe. The view was like nothing London had ever seen, and when she turned to Kayla, she knew instantly by the look on her face that she felt the same way.

"Have you done this before?" London asked, and her voice had that tinny radio sound to it when she heard it through her own headset.

Kayla shook her head. "My first time."

London grabbed her hand. She couldn't stop herself. She linked their fingers. "Thank you for sharing it with me."

Kayla's response was to squeeze her hand, and then they returned their attention to the view.

Stunning didn't begin to describe it. The things they saw that were boring and regular to New Yorkers who'd lived there for years—the Empire State Building, Central Park, the Statue of Liberty—took on a whole new element of excitement and wonder when seeing them from up above. London felt like a little kid, her eyes wide in wonder, her mouth open in astonishment for much of the ride. They spent the whole ride pointing out things to each other, arms and pointer fingers moving all over the place. London had her phone out for a short time and took several photographs but then looked at Kayla. "I really want to take a bunch more pictures, but I also just want to sit here and *look*. With my eyes. You know?"

Kayla's eyes held understanding. "I totally get it."

"Plus, it would be just my luck to drop it."

Lucas, the pilot, chimed in then. "That has happened more times than I can count," he said with a chuckle. He narrated the ride in their headsets, pointing out different sights and interesting things to look for. He bantered a bit with Kayla, joked, and there was a familiarity there. London figured they must know each other beyond this arrangement. She'd ask later. For now, all she wanted to do was gaze in awe while absorbing the heat and feeling of safety from having Kayla's hand in her own.

They flew for nearly an hour before Lucas turned them back toward the airfield, and she did her best to hide her disappointment. Part of her had wanted the ride to go on forever.

As if reading her mind, Kayla gave her hand a squeeze and said, "Next time, we take the night ride."

London gasped. "There's a *night ride*?"

"Sure is. The skyline is all lit up. I've only seen pictures, though. Wanna go?"

"Damn right, I wanna go."

"We'll set it up when we land."

Just like that. Like it was no big deal. London would have to tell her she'd like to be the one to pay for the next ride, though she was also pretty sure it was out of her price range.

Once they landed and were unbuckled, unstrapped, and unclipped, London leaned into Kayla and whispered, "Thank you, Kayla. That was spectacular. The most exciting thing I've ever done."

"Ever?" Kayla's brows rose up to her hairline.

"Ever."

"Well. Points for me, then."

"All the points." And there it was, that chemistry, that sizzle of arousal she'd felt the first time they'd met. The way Kayla held her gaze, she knew she felt it, too.

"Hungry?" Kayla asked, and London toyed with answering truthfully that yes, yes, she was starving, but not for food. But the guys were still only steps away, so she simply chose to nod.

"I am."

"Then let's eat." Kayla held out a hand and London grasped it. "Guys, thank you so much." She pointed at Lucas. "I'll call you next week." And then she tugged London out of the hangar where the black town car sat waiting. The driver opened the door for them, and they slid in. When the door slammed shut, all the sound from the hangar disappeared, as if the car was nearly soundproof. Kayla turned to her. "So, I wanted to take you someplace really fancy for dinner, but"—she looked down at her jeans and casual jacket—"not really dressed for it, and I didn't want us to have to go back and change. Next time, okay?"

London tipped her head. "While I do love how you keep saying next time, you don't have to impress me with fancy dates and expensive dinners, you know. I'm easy." Kayla's mouth quirked, and London rolled her lips in and bit down on them as soon as she realized what she'd said.

And then they were both laughing.

London shoved at Kayla playfully, and her hand was grabbed, held. "You know what I meant. I'm casual. I like burgers and fries! McDonald's. Taco Bell. A doughnut. That kind of easy." Right then, her eyes met Kayla's, and it felt like they'd been snagged. Captured. And she knew, without a tiny shade of doubt, that with Kayla, she'd be easy the other way, too. The sexy way.

"This is actually good news," Kayla said. "I kind of suspected, but this solidifies it."

"Solidifies what?"

"That I made the right dinner plans."

"Cryptic."

Kayla lifted one shoulder in a half shrug, and her grin was playful, mischievous, and London decided she liked this version of her. Very much.

When the car rolled to a stop, they were still holding hands—amusing how much they'd done that today—and London looked out the window.

"We're back to your place?"

Kayla nodded but suddenly looked worried. "Yes, is that okay?" She nibbled her bottom lip as they got out of the car. "I didn't think about how presumptuous that might seem. It's just...I had a plan." She met London's gaze. "Trust me?"

It wasn't even a question. She wasn't afraid of Kayla. She gave her hand a squeeze. "I have no issues being back at your place, and the fact that you just got worried about how it might look says a lot about you."

"Yeah? Does it say I'm an idiot who didn't think?"

"No. It says you're a person who cares about what *I* think." At Kayla's look of relief, she added, "Is there food in there?"

"There is."

"Excellent. Lead the way."

❖

Kayla wasn't a person who got nervous. In her job, she couldn't afford that. Nerves equaled mistakes. She was steady and calm—but nervous? Never. No way.

Tonight, however?

Yeah, *so* fucking nervous.

She'd been nervous all day, headed into the date, and the excitement of finally seeing London—looking nothing short of ridiculously sexy in her jeans and jacket—shot her nerves up into whatever was beyond overdrive. She had to literally talk herself down, mentally counting down from ten. She was pretty certain she'd played the role well, acting calm and not like a complete weirdo, but it had been close.

And now? Now, she had a special dinner planned. A special evening, really. A small part of her worried that she'd gone overboard with the planning, that London would see it and be alarmed or overwhelmed or both, but this was her. This was Kayla. This was who she was. She planned things. She planned big things, often. And it made her stupidly happy to do it. If they had any shot of being together, London needed to know.

Any shot of being together.

Yeah. That's where Kayla's brain had been recently. Being together with London.

She nodded to Frankie as they walked through the lobby hand in hand.

"Ms. Tennyson." He tipped his hat. "Have a great night." He was a New York City Italian boy, born and raised in Brooklyn, and he sounded like it.

Once they were alone in the elevator, London grinned and said, "That guy ever been on *The Sopranos*?"

"Doubtful. If he had been, I'd have heard all about it by now."

Kayla's apartment was on the top floor, and they were the only ones in the elevator as it went up, up, up. There was a moment of silence or two, and when she glanced at London, her entire body went hot. London was looking at her, eyes hooded, the blue of them gone dark, lips shiny, and before Kayla even had time to register what was happening, London pushed up on her toes, circled her hand around the back of Kayla's neck, and pulled Kayla's mouth down to hers.

It wasn't a gentle kiss. It wasn't tentative or hesitant. No, London Granger knew exactly what she wanted—clearly, to kiss Kayla's face right off—and she took it. Holy shit.

Kayla, of course, gave as good as she got, once she pushed past the surprise of London's move. She was taller and stronger, and she used that, walking London backward until her back hit the side wall of the elevator and a quiet *oof* escaped her. Kayla ran her thumb across London's bottom lip before crushing their mouths together once again.

The same rush of pleasure and wonder and utter perfection that had hit her when she'd kissed London in St. Kitts washed over her again, and again, she marveled at how kissing somebody could feel so exactly *right*. There was no explanation other than this was who she was meant to be kissing. Obviously. Undoubtedly.

The elevator slowed to a stop, and the bell dinged, and the doors slid open, and still they went on kissing. It wasn't until the doors began to slide closed again that Kayla was able to come up for air long enough to reach out an arm and stop them.

A clear of her throat. A deep breath. A swipe of a fingertip at the corner of her mouth. Then, "Still hungry?"

London's face was flushed. Her lips were swollen. Her eyes were still a super-dark blue. Jesus God, she looked impossibly sexy, her voice husky as she said, "A different kind of hungry now."

Kayla quirked an eyebrow at her, trying to look sexy and sure of herself, rather than like somebody whose underwear was suddenly uncomfortably damp.

"But yes, I also need food." There was an honest-to-God twinkle in London's eye as she brushed her fingers down Kayla's cheek, then pushed past her and out the elevator doors, leaving Kayla standing there like a person who'd just been erotically ambushed. Because that's exactly who she was.

She cleared her throat, gave herself a full body shake, and followed London to her front door. When she let them inside, London stopped just a few steps in, her surprise clear. The kitchen was bustling, brightly lit, and a man in a white chef's coat was working. He glanced up and gave Kayla a nod and a soft smile just as a second white-clad person—a woman with a brilliant smile— came from down the hall.

"Ms. Tennyson," she said. "You're all set up there. Chef is finishing dessert. I'll bring it up to you, and we'll be out of your hair."

"Thank you so much, Carla." Kayla shook the woman's hand, very aware of London's eyes on them.

"Anytime." The woman met London's gaze. "Enjoy your evening." Then she headed into the kitchen.

"What in the world?" was all London seemed able to say. She looked up at Kayla, her expression curious.

"Come on." She took London's hand and led her down the hall, past the powder room on the right to a door on the left that stood open, stairs leading up. She held out an arm, gesturing for London to go first. "After you."

London squinted at her, suspicious, clearly, but also much too curious to even consider not climbing the stairs. All of that was as obvious on her face as it would've been if it had been written on her forehead. She tipped her head to the side, grinned at Kayla, and headed up the stairs. Kayla followed close behind.

In the dim lighting of the stairwell, Kayla grinned when she heard London's gasp.

"Oh my God." London's voice was barely a whisper.

She emerged onto the rooftop behind London and moved to stand next to her so she could see what London was seeing, but also watch her reaction.

"This," London said, her eyes wide, like a child on Christmas morning. "This is…" She turned to look at Kayla. "You did this?"

Kayla nodded. "I wanted tonight to be special." She watched as London looked around, at the twinkle lights strung around the table for two set up in the middle of the space. Two portable heaters were running, warming things up. A bottle of red wine was breathing, ready to be poured into the crystal glasses that sparkled in the light from the flickering candles in the center of the table.

"Kayla, this…" London was clearly at a loss for words, but the smile on her face was wide.

"Let's sit." She gave London's hand a tug, then held her chair out for her. Just as she sat down herself, Carla appeared with two salads, which she placed in front of each of them. Then she filled their glasses with the wine and headed back downstairs.

The rooftop had been one of the reasons Kayla had bought this place to begin with. You had a three hundred sixty degree view of the city. There were a few buildings in the way, but for the most part, it was stunning, and London clearly thought so.

"This is incredible. I can't believe this is yours." She held her wine but kept turning in her chair, craning her neck to see different sights, everything lighting up in the growing dark. When she faced forward again and her eyes met Kayla's, her smile softened. "Tell me why you wanted tonight to be special."

"Look at you, putting me on the spot." She probably shouldn't have said that about wanting the night to be special, but now she was stuck, and for whatever reason, she felt the only path with London—ever—was total honesty. She cleared her throat. "Okay. Well." She wet her lips and gazed down at her salad. "Our time in St. Kitts was…" She looked back up at London, who watched her steadily. "It was like nothing I've ever felt. For anybody. I don't know why, and I don't understand how. And when I thought you were with Miranda"—she shook her head and gazed off at the lights of Manhattan—"it crushed me, to be honest." She chuckled, but it was sad, and London tipped her head. "When you told me you hadn't actually been with her at all, it felt like I'd come out of a deep, dark cave and into the light again. Dramatic, I know, but…" She shrugged. "And I wanted our first official date to be the most special, most memorable night, so that years from now, when people ask us about our first date, you have a fun story to tell them." She swallowed hard and glanced back down at her plate, feeling more exposed and vulnerable than she ever had in her life. She grabbed her fork and stabbed a cherry tomato, just as she heard London's chair scrape on the floor.

And then London was next to her, looking down at her, her eyes shimmering with what looked like unshed tears. She took Kayla's face in her warm hands, stared into her eyes for a moment, and then kissed her softly on the mouth. Softly, but skillfully, and when she broke the kiss, it left Kayla's head spinning and her grasping for words.

"Sorry to interrupt," said Carla, appearing again with plates, an amused grin on her face.

Kayla made some sort of grunting noise, still searching for her own voice, but she managed to nod and smile and gesture at the table. Across from her, London looked very pleased with herself, and that made Kayla's smile grow.

Carla set plates in front of them. Cheeseburgers and french fries.

"*What?*" London said, injecting that one word with utter delight and disbelief and stretching it to three syllables.

"I mean, it's not McDonald's, but I hope it'll do," Kayla said wryly, happy to have located her voice.

"This is"—London blew out a breath and met Kayla's gaze over the table—"amazing. This is amazing. *You* are amazing. Thank you."

Her words and her expression and the softness of her eyes all worked together to turn Kayla into a giant pile of mush. Warm and happy mush, which only grew as she watched London pick up her burger and take a huge bite. She looked happy. Delighted. And that's all Kayla wanted. It was everything. It was what she wanted to do for the rest of her life, make London happy.

And *that* realization hit hard.

"Oh my God." London's voice, paired with the dreamy look on her face, made Kayla laugh and pulled her back to the here and now.

"Good?"

London dropped her head backward as she chewed. "Oh my God," she said again, and Kayla laughed some more. She swallowed the bite and met Kayla's gaze. "Seriously. Best burger I've ever had in my life."

"Wow. That's quite an endorsement. I'll be sure to tell Chef."

London took another bite, and she seemed to study Kayla as she chewed.

"What?" Kayla asked.

London smiled but shook her head. She took a sip of her wine, looked at Kayla for another moment, then went back to her burger. She took a bite, chewed some more, and swallowed, and only then did she speak. "This might be the best day of my life." She said it quietly, and Kayla knew by her serious expression that she meant it.

"Of your whole life?"

"The whole thing. Yes. This has been…" London shook her head. "I don't even have words."

Kayla could not have been happier. "I'll take that."

❖

The burgers and fries were gone. The wine bottle was empty. Carla had shown up with crème brûlée that London had been sure she had no room for, which turned out to be so decadently delicious that she ate her entire ramekin.

It had gotten chilly, despite the heaters, and after they'd sipped nightcaps as Carla had whisked away their place settings, they'd agreed to head back down into the apartment. London wandered into the huge living room to the giant windows that looked out over Manhattan. It was fully dark now, the glittering lights making the city look downright magical. She could hear Kayla speaking with the chef as they walked toward the door.

"I appreciate it so much," Kayla said, and when London glanced over her shoulder, she was signing a computer pad. "Please thank Carla again for me. I'll see you at the restaurant for dinner soon."

London had been shocked when they'd come down to see that the kitchen was spotless. Any clues that there had been anything at all happening in there had been scrubbed, wiped down, or removed, and the counters gleamed.

Now, Kayla closed the door behind the chef, and the apartment was quiet. She heard Kayla breathe a sigh. Of relief, maybe? Kayla crossed the room and stood close to London as they gazed out the window together.

"I will never get tired of this view," she said quietly, and London leaned her head against her shoulder.

"I can see why. It's beautiful."

"You should see it when it snows. It looks like a movie."

"I bet."

They stood quietly next to each other, and London could feel the heat radiating from Kayla's body. When she turned her head,

Kayla was looking down at her, and that body heat translated to her expression. Everything about her in that moment was *hot.*

London lifted her chin and met Kayla's mouth with her own. Again, it wasn't a gentle kiss, but it was less frantic than in the elevator or on St. Kitts. London wanted to take her time, to explore Kayla's mouth—and the rest of her—but she also felt like she wanted to climb right inside her, to curl up and be safe, warm, and protected. Loved.

Wait, what?

She broke the kiss gently and didn't move away. She simply looked into Kayla's eyes. What she saw there surprised her and also didn't, and she wasn't sure how that was possible. But she saw kindness. Sexiness. She saw a person who didn't play games, someone who was genuine, someone who would give her whole heart if you asked her to. London placed her palm on Kayla's chest and felt that heart beating strong against her skin.

"Are you okay?" Kayla asked, a look of concern crossing her face. She swallowed, clearly trying to shift from being kissed senseless to having a normal conversation. "Should I call you a cab?"

Keeping her hand on Kayla's chest, she looked up and met her gaze before she spoke. "No, but I'd like you to take me to your bedroom."

Kayla blinked at her as if she'd misheard.

"I mean, if that's okay."

"That's more than okay," Kayla said. She cupped London's face in her hand and kissed her once more, softly and tenderly, then slid her hand down London's arm until she reached her hand and interlaced their fingers. "I want you to know," she said as they walked through the apartment and down the hall, "that this isn't what I was expecting. It wasn't my goal." They stopped in the doorway of what London assumed was Kayla's bedroom. "But I couldn't be happier that you're here." She reached around and flipped a switch, and the lights on the nightstands turned on, offering enough light to see, but not so much as to be shocking. It was dim and comfortable. Mood lighting. Kayla held out an arm. "This is my room."

London walked around slowly. The furniture was classy, elegant, a reddish-brown wood of some sort—oak? The bed was large and far more feminine than London had expected, with a lavender bedspread and ivory and purple throw pillows. A thick, plushly piled ivory rug circled out from under the bed, somehow accenting the hardwood floor rather than covering it. She hadn't really noticed the details of much of Kayla's art throughout the rest of the apartment, but the piece over the bed struck her, and she stood at the foot and just stared. It was the simple silhouette of a naked woman from the back. She was sitting on a step with a blanket draped around her hips, and she was gazing to her left. There were few details—it was little more than a line drawing—but something about it made London *feel*.

To her left were large windows, the drapes drawn partially across them, but through the part that wasn't covered, the view was the same as the living room. As if reading her mind, Kayla turned the lights back off, then crossed the room and pushed the drapes all the way open, bathing the room in the light from the city and the moon.

London smiled. "Come here."

Kayla obeyed, and then they were kissing again, standing at the foot of Kayla's bed, and London was pretty sure she could become utterly lost, in the best of ways. Easily. Just from kissing Kayla. What was more, she wanted to. How was it possible? She pulled back far enough to look into Kayla's hooded eyes. "I don't understand it," she whispered into the dark of the room.

"What don't you understand?"

"How I can feel so connected to you after just one date."

"Well," Kayla said, her voice soft and her smile softer, "it's more than one date, really. We actually kind of had two on the island. I mean, we did make out there for a second or two. We also just hung out of a helicopter and ate dinner on the roof, so it's been a bit more than one date." She toyed with the lapels of London's blazer.

"Those are valid points," London said, nodding. And then, she shouldn't ask this, but she was going to. She could almost hear

Claire's voice in her head, shouting for her to shut her mouth, that it was too soon. But she pushed that voice back and used her own, however small and quiet it came out. "Do you feel it, too?"

Kayla's soft laugh was gentle and almost musical, and she tipped her head to one side. "Oh, London, I felt it the second I saw you at the bar on St. Kitts. The literal second." She reached around London's head, grasped the clip in her hair, and released it. London's hair fell in waves around her shoulders. "I thought you were the most beautiful thing I'd ever seen. And then I talked with you, and I discovered that you were beautiful inside, too. Smart. Funny. Kind. All of which was...unexpected." She toyed with the ends of London's hair, twirling it around her finger. "And then I found out you were with Miranda." She laughed and gave the hair a teasing tug. "Oh, that was a cruel, cruel twist of fate."

"I'm so sorry I didn't tell you." London couldn't remember the last time somebody played with her hair, and she was reminded how much she loved it.

"I get it now. You were doing your job and honoring an agreement. However dumb it was."

"It was kind of high school."

"That's Miranda for you."

"Now, hang on. She's the one who got us together, let's not forget."

"Are we?" Kayla's voice was small. Soft. Hopeful.

"Are we what?"

"Together."

"Certainly feels like it to me." She pulled Kayla's head down and her mouth to her own, and suddenly, she felt like they'd blown past questioning the speed and validity of this whole thing. It would drive her crazy if she let it, so she decided not to. Whatever forces decided to introduce her to Kayla, she wanted to thank them. Shake their hands, bump their fists, hug the crap out of them. Because this was it.

This was it.

She could feel it in her bones, and how that was possible, she had no idea. But she knew. This was it. Kayla was her destiny. It was cheesy and corny, yes, but also, she'd never been more sure of anything in her life.

This was it.

Sex with Kayla was a surprise, and also everything London dreamed it would be. They kissed for a long time, standing in Kayla's bedroom at first, then moving to the bed, London on her back and Kayla settled next to her, one leg thrown over hers. And in the very minute she started to squirm, started to want more than a heavy make-out session, Kayla pulled up the hem of her T-shirt and laid her palm flat against London's stomach. It was the first time they'd experienced skin on skin that wasn't kissing or holding hands, and London thought her entire body might burst into flame.

Kayla must have felt something similar because all of a sudden, she picked up the pace. All of a sudden, she was tugging London's clothes. The blazer came off, followed by the T-shirt and then her bra, and then she was lying there under Kayla, both of them breathing raggedly. Their eye contact not only held, it sizzled, like an electric current ran between their bodies.

"You're gorgeous," Kayla whispered as she raked her eyes over London's bare torso. She'd taken off her jacket in the living room, but now she pushed to her knees and peeled her shirt off, sending it to the floor with London's. Her black bra followed, as if she didn't want London to feel more vulnerable than she was, and London loved that, the consideration. She lowered herself back down slowly, until their breasts touched, and again, the skin on skin was volcanic. Intense. London gasped softly.

Kayla kissed her again, gently at first, just small, tender kisses, until she moved one hand up her stomach and closed it over her breast, toyed with a nipple. London groaned into her mouth and tightened the hold she had on the back of Kayla's neck, pulling her down and in, deepening the kiss until tongues were battling for control.

Things went blurry after that. London did her best to stay in the moment, to pay close attention to every sensation, but it wasn't long before they all merged into one big feeling of pleasure. It wasn't long before she couldn't differentiate between Kayla's hands, her lips, her tongue. Her jeans came off, and then Kayla was kneeling between her legs, and there was a beat, a moment of simple and sheer connection when their gazes met. Kayla's brown eyes were so full of emotion, too much for London to comprehend fully, but she knew it was there, and she felt the same.

As if she couldn't stop herself, Kayla almost fell forward, caught herself on her hands, and kissed London so deeply and thoroughly that if she'd had an orgasm just from that, she wouldn't have been at all surprised. But then Kayla pushed herself back up to her knees and, without any kind of preamble, lowered herself to London's center and stroked the flat of her tongue from bottom to top.

London thought she would explode.

"Oh my God," she whispered, reaching over her head for the headboard, something to grasp, as Kayla repeated the maneuver. "Oh my God," she whispered again, her hips rocking like she had no control over them.

Third time's the charm.

One more stroke of Kayla's tongue sent London off the cliff and into oblivion. Colors exploded behind her eyelids. A guttural cry issued from her throat, one she didn't recognize as her own. Her back arched and her hips came up off the mattress, and she could vaguely feel Kayla's hands on her hips as she worked to stay with her. One hand still grasped the headboard, and with the other, she dug her fingers into Kayla's hair as she rode out the orgasm, until her body finally started to relax.

Kayla's tongue was still pressed against her center, but she'd stopped moving it, just held still and followed London's hips back down to the bed. Her breathing was ragged, her lungs heaving a bit still.

"Holy shit," she whispered as she gently pressed Kayla's face away, her legs twitching as she did.

"Wow," Kayla said, her voice soft and filled with a tone of reverence. "That was fast."

London laughed softly. "My God, it so was. I don't think I've ever come that quickly."

"I'll take that as a compliment."

"You should."

"I'm bummed, though."

London lifted her head and looked down her body at Kayla. "Why?"

Kayla arched an eyebrow as she said, "I didn't even get to go inside." And then she pressed her fingers into London, stealing her breath and any ability to think that she might have regained.

"*Oh...*" London drew the word out as Kayla's fingers moved in and out, slowly at first. She was on her knees still, between London's legs, and she inched forward a bit, forcing London's legs open wider. She picked up the pace a bit and added another finger until London felt completely full. And suddenly, Kayla was crouched over her again, above her, balanced on one hand and rocking her body into her hand, moving them both to a rhythm that was so fucking erotic, it sent waves of sensuality rolling through London's body. Kayla's face was close, her eyes intently looking into London's, and London grabbed her head and kissed her. Hard and demandingly, shoving her tongue into Kayla's mouth, satisfied when it was Kayla who groaned this time, and then...

"God, Kayla." London wrenched her mouth away and slammed her head back into the pillow as a second wave of unbridled pleasure tore through her, just as intense as the first one, maybe more so.

Kayla waited until London's breathing had returned to almost normal before she slid her fingers out, and again, London's legs twitched, which made her laugh.

"Come up here," London said, holding her hand down by her hip and wiggling her fingers.

Kayla obliged and crawled up her body, dropping gentle kisses on her overheated skin as she did, first on her thigh, then her hip, then her stomach, her breast, her collarbone, her chin, and her mouth, where she took her time.

Finally, she lay down on her side, her head propped in her hand, and pulled a blanket up over their lower bodies. "I don't want to cover all of you, 'cause I want to look." She dragged a fingertip across London's stomach. "That okay?"

London nodded with a smile. "Don't get too comfortable, though. We're not done. I just need to wait for feeling to come back to my legs."

"I will take that as a compliment," Kayla said for the second time.

"You should," London said, for the second time as well.

They lay there quietly for what felt like a long while, Kayla drawing random designs on London's skin, as they looked out the window at the city outside.

"This is amazing," London said, whispering because she didn't want to disturb the beauty of the moment.

"Yeah?"

"Being here. With you. Like this. I feel..." She shook her head. She felt so much. So much. It was frightening. Perfect and wonderful and amazing. And terrifying.

"I know," Kayla said. "I feel it, too."

London looked into those deep, dark eyes, eyes filled with such tenderness and intelligence and love. Yes, love. It was there. She could see it just as plain as if it had been written in Sharpie across Kayla's forehead. She didn't point it out—it was way too soon for that. But seeing it, knowing it was there? That was all she needed, because it was within her as well. They'd get to the words. They'd say them, sooner rather than later, she was sure.

She pushed herself up and rolled, tipping Kayla onto her back so she could look down at her. "Guess what."

Kayla's eyes were hooded and dark, her lips swollen as she asked softly, "What?"

"My turn."

EPILOGUE

Two years later

London took a deep breath and blew it out slowly as she studied her reflection in the full-length mirror. She'd wanted to look attractive and approachable, but also serious. Intelligent. Like somebody who knew her shit. And she did. The pantsuit was new, and Kayla had insisted on it and had sent her to her tailor. Yes, she had a tailor, how weird was that? Black and literally made for her, the suit looked damn good. The blazer was tapered at the waist just slightly enough so it didn't look boxy. The pants fit her so perfectly, she wondered how much it would cost her to have all her pants custom made. She gave a little snort. A lot. A lot was the answer, she thought, as she turned her back to the mirror to check out her ass.

"It looks amazing," came Kayla's voice from the doorway. "Always has. First thing I noticed about you."

"My ass?" London laughed. "Liar."

"Okay, fine." Kayla crossed the room and wrapped London up in her arms from behind. Kayla's chin on London's shoulder, they looked at their reflection together. "It was the third thing I noticed, after your smile and your boobs."

London grinned and shook her head.

"You were incredible tonight," Kayla said, meeting her gaze in the mirror.

"You have to say that. You're the girlfriend."

"True. But I mean it. You were amazing. Your reading was

smooth, and your pacing was perfect. You were approachable, you sounded smart, and you were nice to everybody, even the creepy guy that got a little too handsy with the photo…"

London laughed. The poor guy had been flustered but had managed to ask for a picture of him with London. She'd obliged, of course she had. He was so nervous, he was shaking, and one of his shaking hands had shaken itself a little too close to her behind. Kayla had almost stepped in. "Spoken like a true bodyguard."

"Occupational hazard." They were quiet for a moment. "I'm so proud of you."

"Thank you, babe."

They stood like that for a moment, and then Kayla's phone pinged. "Gonna let the caterer in." She kissed London's cheek, then headed out into the apartment to get the door, tossing, "People will be here soon, don't take too long," over her shoulder.

London returned to her reflection, but she wasn't looking at her outfit any longer. She was looking at her face, at how relaxed and happy she had become. She stood in Kayla's bedroom—now their bedroom. She'd lived there for nearly a year now. It was the first time she'd ever lived with a partner, and she'd been worried. But Claire had talked her through it, and she'd finally told Kayla she'd very much like to move in.

Kayla had been amazing. She'd purged her enormous walk-in closet to make room for London's ample amount of clothing. "Holy shit, you've got a lot of clothes," Kayla had said, only half joking. London had waved her hand in the air and said simply, "Hello, ex-model." London's bedroom furniture had furnished their guest bedroom where Claire had spent more than one night after their dinners and wine on the roof had gone into the wee hours. The third bedroom had been Kayla's office, until one day when London had come home from *TN Squared* to find Kayla'd had a second desk delivered and the whole room rearranged so it was now an office for two, with desks on opposite walls. Kayla traveled often enough that it was rare they were working in there at the same time anyway.

Kayla had done everything for her. It was astonishing when

London looked back on it all. She glanced at their bed, at the nightstand next to Kayla's side, at the framed photo of the two of them holding wineglasses from a tasting they'd gone to last summer, and looking in each other's eyes. Anybody who looked at that picture would know those were two happy people, two people in love. London remembered that exact moment because she'd already been in love with Kayla, way in love by then. But that moment was the one when she'd realized this was her person, that she wasn't going anywhere, that this was forever.

And she'd started making plans.

Today was the day for those plans. And it was perfect. Today had been her first book signing. The day was all about her, and Kayla would never expect things to take the turn they were going to.

The woman in the mirror smiled back, a wide, clearly joyous smile, and she fluffed her hair, patted her pocket, and headed out into the huge apartment to help.

Two hours later, the evening was in full swing, an endless flow of friends and colleagues dropping by to congratulate London on her book, *Can't Buy Me Love: What it's* really *like to be a billionaire.* While she wouldn't go so far as to say the book was flying off the shelves, it actually was doing quite well. She was proud of it, and that was all that really mattered. She'd gotten a modest advance from her publisher, who seemed pleased with the book's performance so far.

"So?" Claire sidled up next to her, glass of wine in one hand, and as if reading her thoughts, commented, "Your publisher looks happy." They both watched the woman in the ivory dress with red heels and her dark hair slicked into a bun. She threw her head back and laughed at something Silas said.

"That's because my agent is the best." London sipped her own wine, trying to hide the smile.

"Very true," Claire said. "And I'm setting you up a meeting to talk about your next book. There have been some ideas mentioned…"

"Like I said, my agent's the best."

Claire snaked an arm around London's waist and squeezed her close. "I'm so proud of you, you know that?"

When London turned to meet her gaze, her best friend had tears in her eyes. "I do know that. I love you, you know."

"Me, too." They took a moment to bask in the strength of their friendship. Then Claire gave her head a little shake and said, "I think it's time. Don't you?"

It was. She looked around—all the important people in her life were there. Her parents had flown in. All her colleagues from *TN Squared* were mingling. Kayla's mom was in the corner talking with Bo. Jake was on the balcony. And of course, Kayla was actually talking to Miranda, who actually stood with Haley—God, life was nuts. London gave a nod, and just like that, her heart rate sped up somewhere into overdrive territory. She met Kayla's gaze across the crowd of people, and Kayla excused herself from her conversation and crossed to London.

"Ready to give a little speech?" she asked as she got to her.

London nodded. "Yes. It's the perfect time."

"You got it." Kayla took London's hand and led her toward the front door. It was the spot where you could see the most of the apartment, making it a perfect spot to address all the guests. Kayla grabbed a spoon and a glass and tapped. The sound of the crystal tinging got everybody's attention, and in a matter of seconds, the entire apartment had fallen silent, all eyes turned to them. "Thank you all for being here," Kayla said, voice raised a bit. "My lovely girlfriend, the reason we're all here, would like to say a few words." With a flourish of her arm, she stepped away a few feet. "All you, babe."

London let her eyes wander over all the people in the apartment as she took in a deep breath. "Look at all of you." She shook her head with a smile. "I'm so grateful. So very grateful. I need to start there. So many people contributed to me being able to write this book. Silas, for assigning me what I was pretty sure was a fluff piece."

A rumble of laughter ran through the crowd as Silas said loudly, "It was!"

"Miranda, the living, breathing billionaire who let me into her life and took me on vacation with her and really held nothing back. And somebody I'm happy to say is now my dear friend."

Over by the dining room table, Miranda blew her a kiss and held up her glass.

"My best friend and agent, Claire, who convinced me I could do this at all. If I'm honest, the book was as much her idea as it was mine."

"I take cash or checks, sweetie," Claire said to more laughter. "I'm not picky."

"And that brings me to this person right here." London held out her hand to Kayla, who stepped back toward her and took it. "This book will always hold a special place in my heart because it led me to the love of my life. Even though we started off like a bad rom-com, with misunderstandings and obstacles in our way, we still made it to each other." She glanced toward the dining room table again. "Thanks in no small way to my new bestie, the billionaire over there." She raised her glass. "I owe you, Miranda."

"I'll be sure to collect," Miranda called back. The crowd chuckled as Miranda lifted Haley's hand and kissed her knuckles.

"Anyway." She took a deep breath. "So, I want to say thank you, to all of you. For being people I care about, for being there for me throughout the writing of this book, but most of all for supporting what has turned out to be the greatest gift of my life." She held up Kayla's hand. "This woman." Another deep breath. "So. I guess there's only one thing left to do." She met Claire's eyes just behind Kayla. Claire was grinning like a fool and nodded at her. London reached into her pocket and at the same time, lowered herself to one knee. She held up the diamond and emerald ring she'd had custom made, thanks to the jeweler Miranda had hooked her up with. "Kayla Marie Tennyson, will you marry me?"

The look on Kayla's face was slightly confusing to London— surprise, yes, but also what seemed to be concern—and she had a moment of panic because, God, she'd never considered what she'd do if Kayla said no. Here, on her knees, in front of everybody they knew.

But instead of saying no, Kayla did something completely different.

She dropped to one knee as well and held out a ring toward London. "I will marry you, yes, absolutely, but only if you'll marry me."

"Yes," London said without a second's hesitation. "I will marry you every day for the rest of my life. Yes!"

The entire crowd erupted into laughter and applause. Whistling. Hooting. The sound was deafening as Kayla stood and held out a hand to pull London to her feet. They stood close together as they slid rings onto each other's fingers.

"I love you more than you'll ever know," Kayla said near London's ear, so she could be heard over the crowd.

"Right back atcha," London said with a grin, then reached up and laid her palm against Kayla's cheek. Kayla pushed her head against it, and those deep, dark eyes were so filled with love and hope and want that London felt her own eyes well up, and she wrapped her arms around Kayla, pulling her into a hug.

And as they stood there, holding each other in the midst of the thunderous applause of their loved ones, London knew just how lucky she was. Some people never found their perfect match. Some people never knew unconditional, undying love. Some people said money can't buy you love.

But in London's case?

It very much had.

About the Author

Georgia Beers lives in Upstate New York and has written more than thirty-five novels of sapphic romance. In her off-hours, she can usually be found searching for a scary movie, sipping a good Pinot, or trying to keep up with little big man Archie, her mix of many little dogs. Find out more at georgiabeers.com.

Books Available From Bold Strokes Books

Can't Buy Me Love by Georgia Beers. London and Kayla are perfect for one another, but if London reveals she's in a fake relationship with Kayla's ex, she risks not only the opportunity of her career, but Kayla's trust as well. (978-1-63679-665-9)

Chance Encounter by Renee Roman. Little did Sky Roberts know when she bought the raffle ticket for charity that she would also be taking a chance on love with the egotistical Drew Mitchell. (978-1-63679-619-2)

Comes in Waves by Ana Hartnett. For Tanya Brees, love in small-town Coral Bay comes in waves, but can she make it stay for good this time? (978-1-63679-597-3)

The Curse by Alexandra Riley. Can Diana Dillon and her daughter, Ryder, survive the cursed farm with the help of Deputy Mel Defoe? Or will the land choose them to be to the next victims? (978-1-63679-611-6)

Dancing With Dahlia by Julia Underwood. How is Piper Fernley supposed to survive six weeks with the most controlling, uptight boss on earth? Because sometimes when you stop looking, your heart finds exactly what it needs. (978-1-63679-663-5)

The Heart Wants by Krystina Rivers. Fifteen years after they first meet, Army Major Reagan Jennings realizes she has one last chance to win the heart of the woman she's always loved. If only she can make Sydney see she's worth risking everything for. (978-1-63679-595-9)

Skyscraper by Gun Brooke. Attempting to save the life of an injured boy brings Rayne and Kaelyn together. As they strive for justice against corrupt Celestial authorities, they're unable to foresee how intertwined their fates will become. (978-1-63679-657-4)

Untethered by Shelley Thrasher. Helen Rogers, in her eighties, meets much younger Grace on a lengthy cruise to Bali, and their intense relationship yields surprising insights and unexpected growth. (978-1-63679-636-9)

You Can't Go Home Again by Jeanette Bears. After their military career ends abruptly, Raegan Holcolm is forced back to their hometown to confront their past and discover where the road to recovery will lead them, or if it already led them home. (978-1-636790644-4)

A Wolf in Stone by Jane Fletcher. Though Cassilania is an experienced player in the dirty, dangerous game of imperial Kavillian politics, even she is caught out when a murderer raises the stakes. (978-1-63679-640-6)

The Devil You Know by Ali Vali. As threats come at the Casey family from both the feds and enemies set to destroy them, Cain Casey does whatever is necessary with Emma at her side to bury every single one. (978-1-63679-471-6)

The Meaning of Liberty by Sage Donnell. When TJ and Bailey get caught in the political crossfire of the ultraconservative Crusade of the Redeemer Church, escape is the only plan. On the run and fighting for their lives is not the time to be falling for each other. (978-1-63679-624-6)

One Last Summer by Kristin Keppler. Emerson Fields didn't think anything could keep her from her dream of interning at Bardot Design Studio in Paris, until an unexpected choice at a North Carolina beach has her questioning what it is she really wants. (978-1-63679-638-3)

StreamLine by Lauren Melissa Ellzey. When Lune crosses paths with the legendary girl gamer Nocht, she may have found the key that will boost her to the upper echelon of streamers and unravel all Lune thought she knew about gaming, friendship, and love. (978-1-63679-655-0)

Undercurrent by Patricia Evans. Can Tala and Wilder catch a serial killer in Salem before another body washes up on the shore? (978-1-636790669-7)

And Then There Was One by Michele Castleman. Plagued by strange memories and drowning in the guilt she tried to leave behind, Lyla Smith escapes her small Ohio town to work as a nanny and becomes trapped with an unknown killer. (978-1-63679-688-8)

Digging for Destiny by Jenna Jarvis. The war between nations forces Litz to make a choice. Her country, career, and family, or the chance of making a better world with the woman she can't forget. (978-1-63679-575-1)

Hot Hires by Nan Campbell, Alaina Erdell, and Jesse J. Thoma. In these three romance novellas, when business turns to pleasure, romance ignites. (978-1-63679-651-2)

The Land of Death and Devil's Club by Bailey Bridgewater. Special Liaison to the FBI Louisa Linebach may have defied all odds by identifying the bodies of three missing men in the Kenai Peninsula, but she won't be satisfied until the man she's sure is responsible for their murders is behind bars. (978-1-63679-659-8)

McCall by Patricia Evans. Sam and Sara found love on the water, but can they build a future amid the ghosts of the past that surround them on dry land? (978-1-63679-769-4)

Promises to Protect by Jo Hemmingwood. Park ranger Maxine Ward's commitment to protect Tree City is put to the test when social worker Skylar Austen takes a special interest in the commune and in Max. (978-1-63679-626-0)

Sacred Ground by Missouri Vaun. Jordan Price, a conflicted demon hunter, falls for Grace Jameson, who has no idea she's been bitten by a vampire. (978-1-63679-485-3)

When You Smile by Melissa Brayden. Taryn Ross never thought the babysitter she once crushed on would show up as a grad student at the same university she attends. (978-1-63679-671-0)

A Heart Divided by Angie Williams. Emmaline is the most beautiful woman Jack has ever seen, but being a veteran of the Confederate army that killed her husband isn't the only thing keeping them apart. (978-1-63679-537-9)

Adrift by Sam Ledel. Two women whose lives are anchored by guilt and obligation find romance amidst the tumultuous Prohibition movement in 1920s California. (978-1-63679-577-5)

Cabin Fever by Tagan Shepard. The longer Morgan and Shelby are stranded together, the more their feelings grow, but is it real, or just cabin fever? (978-1-63679-632-1)

Clean Kill by Anne Laughlin. When someone starts killing people she knows in the recovery world, former detective Nicky Sullivan must race to stop the killer and keep herself from being arrested for the crimes. (978-1-63679-634-5)

Only a Bridesmaid by Haley Donnell. A fake bridesmaid, a socially anxious bride, and an unexpected love—what could go wrong? (978-1-63679-642-0)

Primal Hunt by L.L. Raand. Anya, a young wolf warrior, finds herself paired with Rafe, one of the most powerful Vampires in the Americas, in an erotic union of blood and sex.(978-1-63679-561-4)

Snake Charming by Genevieve McCluer. Playgirl vampire Freddie is on the run and a chance encounter with lamia Phoebe makes them both realize that they may have found the love they'd given up on. (978-1-63679-628-4)

Spirits and Sirens by Kelly and Tana Fireside. When rumored ghost whisperer Elena Murphy and very skeptical assistant fire chief Allison Jones have to work together to solve a 70-year old mystery, sparks fly—will it be enough to melt the ice between them and let love ignite? (978-1-63679-607-9)

Aubrey McFadden Is Never Getting Married by Georgia Beers. Aubrey McFadden is never getting married, but she does have five weddings to attend, and she'll be avoiding Monica Wallace, the woman who ruined her happily ever after, at every single one. (978-1-63679-613-0)

Flowers for Dead Girls by Abigail Collins. Isla might be just the right kind of girl to bring Astra out of her shell—and maybe more. The only problem? She's dead. (978-1-63679-584-3)

Rainbow Overalls by Maggie Fortuna. Arriving in Vermont for her first year of college, an introverted bookworm forms a friendship with an outgoing artist and finds what comes after the classic coming out story: a being out story. (978-1-63679-606-2)